Georgia Paton

(1965 - 2011)

Originally from Fife, Scotland, Georgia Paton was a global no-mad for several years, living in Australia, Chile, and Germany with her husband, three boys, two dogs and an adopted cat. The Witching Stone draws heavily on her childhood experiences in her hometown on the Firth of Forth, where the Buckie House's shell walls still stand and Scabinory, with its mysterious and some say bottomless pool, continues to enchant local children.

A donation from book sales will be gifted to
Leukaemia and Lymphoma Research.

THE
WITCHING STONE

GEORGIA PATON

Lumphanan Press

Self-published in 2013 with the aid of Lumphanan Press
Roddenbrae, Lumphanan, Aberdeenshire, AB31 4RN

www.lumphananpress.co.uk

British Library Cataloguing in Publication Data.
A catalogue record for this book is available from the British Library

ISBN: 978-0-9566149-7-1

For Andy, Ruairidh, Sean and Andrew – my dream makers

Acknowledgements

From Georgia

Many wonderful people supported this novel on its path to publication. First thanks go to my patient and optimistic husband, my beautiful boys and my mum and dad. Next, I am eternally grateful to my Australian, Chilean and German friends and readers who assumed without question that I would publish. Special mention must go to James, and to Declan who loved *The Witching Stone* enough to carry it around in his school bag, so he could read it at every chance. Finally, thanks to my agent, Keelane Lake, for her guidance and support.

From the family

Our thanks go to our many friends whose encouragement and support has sustained us. A very special thank you to Duncan Lockerbie and Talis Archdeacon for their diligence in helping us to publish this fine story.

A labour of love, a legacy to cherish.

Contents

1

SCOTLAND

'Sorry Ruairidh couldn't meet you at the airport,' Mrs McBride said, smiling over her shoulder at Rossi and her two younger brothers. 'There wasn't enough room in the car, I'm afraid.'

'He spells his name funny,' Drew said.

Rossi glared at her youngest brother. 'It's not funny, stupid. It's the Gaelic spelling of *Rory*, but it's still pronounced the same way, isn't it Mrs McBride?'

The elderly woman chuckled. 'Yes dear, and please, call me Bridie, everyone else does. Oh, it'll be so good for Ruairidh to have friends his own age this summer holidays. He's such a serious wee boy. Having you three around will be just the ticket.'

The children's grandad glanced over at his housekeeper, frowning slightly. 'Now Bridie, they'll work out their friendships for themselves, I'm sure.'

'All I'm saying is a boy his age shouldn't spend so much time alone. Besides, I'm sure they're looking forward to meeting him too. Isn't that right children?'

'Yes,' Rossi said, although in truth she knew very little about her Scottish cousin except that his mother, her Aunt Kate, had left him with Bridie and her grandad when he was just a baby and hadn't been heard of since.

It was strange thinking of him as part of her family, or the elderly couple in the car, for that matter. In Australia she had no relatives outside her parents and brothers and had never missed them. They were an odd couple, she decided. Mrs McBride, *Bridie,* as she'd insisted they call her, was much more than just her grandad's housekeeper. She'd taken on that role when his wife died, but she was also the only mother Rossi's dad, and Ruairidh too, she supposed, had ever known. She was sprightly and immaculately dressed and looked like she wouldn't miss much, unlike Grandad, whose rather absentminded appearance marked him as every bit, the retired professor of history that he was.

'There's a castle over there,' Drew said, straining against his centre seatbelt for a better view.

Rossi peered out through the rain-spattered window over the grey, bleak, Firth. On the opposite shore, high on a craggy hill, sat a huge castle, austere and gloomy beneath gathering storm clouds.

'That's Edinburgh Castle,' the professor said, 'and the mountain to its left is Arthur's seat.'

'I've read about Arthur's Seat,' Rossi said, eagerly. 'It's an extinct volcano, supposed to be shaped like a sleeping lion, isn't it?'

Sean pushed the peak of his cap up just high enough to catch a glimpse of the curiously shaped hill, then tugged it back down and sank lower in his seat. 'Doesn't look like a lion to me,' he said. He hadn't wanted to come to Scotland in the first place and wasn't about to be interested now.

'Me neither,' Drew said.

Rossi sighed, wondering why she bothered. Sean found everything boring these days. Mum reckoned if he got any cooler, he'd freeze over. And whatever Sean thought, Drew did too. Brothers were so stupid!

'What do you think, Grandad?'

'It's one legend, certainly… one of many about Arthur's seat, and most good stories have a grain of truth in them somewhere…'

'How old is the castle, Grandad?' Drew asked, already forgetting he was supposed to be bored.

'That one was built about six hundred years ago,' Rossi said quickly, keen to show off what she'd read on the plane, 'but it's not the first castle built up on that crag. There's been a fortress of some sort there for thousands of years.'

'You know your Scottish history,' the professor said, grinning in the rear-view mirror.

Sean raised the peak of his cap just high enough to roll his eyes at his brother.

'My mum calls it the family affliction,' Drew said, grimacing back. 'Rossi and Dad are mad about history, just like you Grandad.'

The professor's youthful blue eyes twinkled behind his heavy black-rimmed glasses. 'Well, if it's old stuff and legends you children are interested in, you'll find plenty of it in Scotland.'

'We'll soon be there now,' Bridie said as they caught sight of a little seaside town curving neatly around a sandy bay below the road.

Despite trying not to be interested in the passing countryside, Sean's eyes fixed on a small group of trees on the crest of a nearby hill. They seemed out of place somehow behind a row of industrial warehouses, and amongst the trees tall, odd-looking stones stood in a circle, like sentinels standing guard. He felt curiously drawn to the sight.

'What's that place over there, Grandad?'

The professor seemed not to need to look away from the road to know what Sean was talking about. 'That's Scabinory,' he said, and for a second the strange word hung in the air between them.

'Oh, that old place,' Bridie said. 'Should have been filled in years ago if you ask me. It's a danger to children, an open pond in the middle of a field, like that.'

'Is it a billabong?' Rossi asked, thinking of the watering holes that dotted the fields at home.

'No,' Drew and the professor said together.

Rossi and Sean stared at their younger brother.

'How on earth would you know?' Sean asked, screwing up his nose.

Drew shrugged, just as surprised by his response as the others.

'He's right, though,' the professor said, glancing at him thoughtfully. 'There is a pond up there, but by no means is it manmade. The pond at Scabinory is an old volcanic vent, part of a vast field of volcanoes that covered this region long ago. It's said to be very deep, bottomless some say. And the stones you see up there are ancient too. We call them *Standing Stanes*. There's five in total, some of the best examples of their kind in all of Scotland.'

Sean sat up a little straighter, intrigued despite himself. 'But who would bother to put them there, and why?'

'The ancient people of this land, many thousands of years ago, but as to why, well, there are a number of theories. Some say the stones commemorate a great battle fought on the slopes of that hill, while others believe people were sacrificed up there in homage to some pagan god.'

Human sacrifices! Rossi shuddered at the thought, and the little circle of trees and stones in the field seemed suddenly menacing to her.

'And what do you think, Grandad?' Sean asked, fascinated by anything scary or macabre.

'I think all the theories may well be equally correct or none at all,' he said, smiling at Sean's newfound enthusiasm for Scottish history. 'We just don't really know. That's what's so interesting, don't you think? But there is a stone up there, not one of the five, but another whose name has survived through all the ages. *Carlin Meg* sits on the water's edge at the very heart of Scabinory, which suggests our ancestors believed it to be a very magical place indeed.'

'*Carlin Meg*,' Sean said. 'That's the name of a stone? Why would anyone name a stone?'

The professor smiled seeing his dubious expression in the mirror. 'There are many named stones in Scotland, Sean. *The Dwarfie Stone* for one, and the *Stone of Destiny,* on which the kings and queens of Scotland were crowned, for another. The stone at Scabinory was named for the witch who practiced her craft there,' he said matter-of-factly. '*Carlin Meg* is a Witching Stone.'

'Random!' Drew and Sean said together and the professor laughed.

Sean knocked his cap away from his eyes and leaned forward,

excited for the first time since being told about their move to Scotland. 'I'd love to see the stones up close, especially the Witching Stone. I've never seen anything to do with a real witch before. Can we go up there?'

'Me too,' Drew said.

Bridie scowled. 'Now look what you've done professor, telling the children fairy tales and encouraging them to go to that wicked, dangerous place. They'll like as not fall in the water and drown... or worse, and their parents not even arrived from Australia yet.' She turned in her seat, her warm brown eyes suddenly serious. 'No one would be able to help you away out there if something bad happened to you children. Best you stay well away from Scabinory!'

'You can't make the whole world safe for children, Bridie,' the professor said, and his expression in the rear view mirror was curiously intense as his eyes touched on Rossi and the boys, 'nor should you. They're capable of much more than they're given credit for, and some places... well, it's in their nature to be dangerous, and that is as it should be.'

Rossi and her brothers turned to stare out the window at Scabinory; their curiosity piqued even more by the adults' strange exchange. It was with great reluctance that they pulled their eyes away when the little circle of trees and stones disappeared from view behind shops and houses, and they entered their father's childhood home.

2

THE BUCKIE HOUSE

Daylight had faded to dusk and the rain had stopped by the time they drove along the promenade to their grandfather's house.

'Gosh, it's old,' Drew said when they pulled up in front of the big, grey whinstone building. He clambered over Sean in his rush to get out of the car, ignoring his protests, and peered through the gateway, with its trailing honeysuckle, at the pretty garden within. A white pebble path wound its way through the lawn to the front door where, to his delight, two magnificent stone dragons crouched as if ready to pounce, on either side of some wide steps.

He cocked his head to one side. There was something odd-looking about the house, he decided, but for a second he couldn't work out what it was. 'There should be four,' he murmured, counting two rows of five windows across the front of the house and five more garret windows on the roof.

'What's that, son?' the professor asked.

'Oh, nothing. It's just, well, very old buildings like this are usually symmetrical.' He shrugged at his grandad's quizzical expression. 'It's something I'm interested in, that's all. Not that we have any really ancient houses in Australia, but all the grand old ones I've seen in pictures have windows evenly spaced on either side of a central door, in rows of two or four and so on, not five.'

'We have a budding architect in our midst,' the professor said, winking at Bridie. 'Fours and sixes are boring, Drew, but fives, fives hold much more promise.'

Sean screwed up his nose. 'Promise of what?' he asked, coming to stand beside them.

'Oh, of just about everything, son,' the professor said, reaching out to turn Sean's cap the right way round.

Sean ducked. 'Hey, don't touch the hair,' he said, taking off his cap and flicking his long brown locks artfully to one side before replacing it, just so.

Rossi rolled her eyes, knowing he was only half kidding – she'd never known any boy so vain about his hair – but Grandad and Bridie just laughed.

'So like his father,' Bridie said, fondly.

'Oh, I'm much better looking,' quipped Sean.

The professor drew him in for a quick hug. 'Indeed he is like his father, and not just in looks. That's just the type of thing your dad would have said at your age.'

He opened the car boot and handed them each a bag.

'And yes, the house is very old,' he said, responding to Drew's original comment while leading the way through the gate. 'The front part here is the old school house, which dates back to the late fifteen hundreds, but the rear and foundations of the house are older still. Indeed, as far as we can tell, a house of some sort has stood continuously on this spot for at least a thousand years – probably much longer.'

'Did you go to school here?' Sean asked, only half listening as usual.

Drew rolled his vivid blue eyes in disgust. 'No, stupid!' he said, as the professor and Bridie roared with laughter.

'I'm glad to say I'm not quite that old,' the professor said. 'It's always just been a family home in my time. I was born in this house, as were my father before me and his father before him.'

'And our dad,' Drew said. 'He was born here too, wasn't he?

'He was, dear.' Bridie pointed to the third window on the first floor. 'In that very room up there.'

Rossi and the boys stared up at the house. They'd never thought about belonging to it or to Scotland in such a way, but the old school house looked and felt curiously familiar and well, *right* somehow. They followed the professor along the path toward the door and were amazed to see that the garden walls were covered in a collage of broken china, coloured glass, and seashells, creating an elaborate seaside mosaic.

Rossi ran to it, delighted. 'Who did this?' she gasped, touching the giant conches framing the mosaic's upper border.

'Oh, I think everyone who's ever lived here had a hand in it at some time, dear,' Bridie said. 'The house is known locally as the Buckie House, *Buckie* being Scots for a type of shell. You'll see shell walls like this all along this part of the east coast, but none as fine as ours,' she added proudly. 'Some of the china dates back centuries, which means the school children most probably did a

lot of it. We did some ourselves when we were kids and so did
your dad. Over here, look.'

They followed her across the lawn to a picture of a dragon fash-
ioned from mismatched pieces of gold, green and blue china and
curling its head around the figure of a boy with a sword clutched
in his outstretched hand.

'Wow! Our dad did that?' Rossi had never thought of him as
artistic before. She suddenly felt homesick, knowing her parents
were very far away. They'd all hated it when the sale of their house
in Australia had fallen through and their parents had decided
they'd have to join them in Scotland in a few weeks.

'They were married here in the garden, weren't they?' she said,
softly.

Bridie pulled her in for a hug. 'Yes dear, and it won't be too
long before they're here again,' she added brightly, looking round
at the boys' glum faces, 'only this time you three will be right here
with them. I spoke to your mum this morning and she thinks the
house will be sold within the month.'

'I don't know why we couldn't just wait for them,' Drew said.
'It's so unfair.'

Bridie chuckled and ruffled his dark brown hair. 'And what
would you have done for a month in an empty house with your
television and furniture already on its way by sea? No, your parents
were quite right to send you on ahead. This way your grandad,
Ruairidh and I have the whole summer to get to know you before
you start your new life in Edinburgh.'

Beyond the garden wall, an unusually shaped hill drew Rossi's
attention. Its twin peaks formed a large and distinct 'M'.

'That must be Largo Law,' she said, remembering her parent's wedding photographs and what her mother had told her about that day.

'The volcano?' Sean asked, suddenly interested.

'Random!' Drew said. He looked up at the professor with a mixture of excitement and concern in his eyes. 'It won't erupt while we're here, will it?'

The professor laughed. 'Oh, I should hope not. Largo Law's been extinct for a very long time. We can climb it one day if you'd like to.'

'Come on, dears,' Bridie said, 'let's go in and get you settled. It'll be dark soon and Ruairidh will be waiting to welcome you.'

But Ruairidh wasn't waiting for them and, although Bridie fretted and complained bitterly about it, he didn't arrive for supper, nor was he back when, weary from their long journey, the children climbed the stairs to bed.

'Shouldn't you call the police or something?' Rossi asked when, still muttering about him, Bridie tucked her in. 'My mum and dad would freak if one of us was out this late.'

'Oh I'm not so much worried about Ruairidh's safety as I am disgusted by his rudeness, dear. His sleeping bag is gone so he's camped out somewhere, and he has his dog with him. Believe me, that big beastie is enough to deter anyone who might mean him harm. But I'll "freak" all right when he gets back, and that'll no doubt be when whatever food he has runs out. He'll do without himself if it pleases him, but there's no way he'll deprive that dog of his, and the other animals of course will need tending to. I expect he'll put in an appearance tomorrow.'

'What other animals?' Rossi asked, thoroughly intrigued by her strange-sounding cousin.

Bridie smiled ruefully. 'Oh, our Ruairidh loves his animals. You'll see if you go down to the back garden tomorrow, dear. He has all sorts of creatures in the shed down there. There's rabbits and birds and a hamster, and I think he has a hedgehog at the moment. People bring all manner of injured wildlife for him to look after, and pets they don't want. He has a talent with animals just like his mother.'

A cloud passed over Bridie's eyes at mention of Rossi's Aunt Kate and she shook her head sadly. 'Pity she didn't apply the same talent to people.'

Bridie seemed to forget Rossi for a moment; lost in her thoughts, and feeling a little awkward, Rossi looked around the room at the sweet rosebud wallpaper and pink satin quilt. A thought suddenly came to her.

'This was Aunt Kate's room, wasn't it?'

Bridie cast her eyes around. 'Yes, just as she left it all those years ago.'

'What was she like?' Rossi asked, unsure how much she could ask without upsetting the older woman, but Bridie seemed to brighten at the question.

'I'll show you if you like, dear.'

She reached into a drawer next to the bed and took out an old photo in a simple wooden frame. 'I don't always keep this put away,' she said as though feeling guilty about it. 'Sometimes I like to look at it when I come in here to do my cleaning, but other times it just makes me too sad.'

Four teenagers, with their arms draped around one another's shoulders, smiled back at Rossi. She recognised two of them immediately.

'That's my mum and dad!'

'Yes it is, dear and next to them your Auntie Kate and Philip Crane, her boyfriend at the time. They were inseparable that summer, the four of them. This photo was the last taken of Kate and Phil. They disappeared not long after.'

Rossi stared at the two young faces. 'But they don't look much older than me, and I didn't realise her boyfriend was missing too!'

Bridie nodded sadly. 'They were fourteen when they went, so young, so very, very young.'

'And you've no idea what happened to them? They just disappeared?'

Pain was all too evident on the elderly woman's face as she shook her head. 'No trace was ever found of them, nothing at all until some years later when we found Ruairidh waiting for us on the doorstep. There was no note, just his name embroidered on a blanket, but at least we knew that Kate was alive somewhere.'

'But how did you know he was Aunt Kate's child?'

Bridie smiled. 'Oh, that was easy. The baby was the image of Kate right down to the flash of blonde in his hair. Look at the photo and you'll see.'

Rossi looked closely at her aunt's pretty, heart-shaped face. Warm hazel eyes stared back and, sure enough, running across the front of her wavy brown hair was a distinctive blonde streak.

Loud banging and raised voices sounded in the corridor outside

Rossi's bedroom, and the spell was broken. Bridie rose, placing the old photo carefully on the dressing table.

'I should go and settle the boys down,' she said, smoothing the spot on the quilt where she'd sat, 'and who knows, that naughty boy Ruairidh might even be back by now. Ha, fat chance!' She turned off the light. 'Sweet dreams, Rossetta.'

'Good night Bridie… and Bridie?'

'Yes, dear?'

'Would you mind calling me Rossi? I know Rossetta was my great grandmother's name, but I really hate it.'

Bridie laughed. 'I'll let you into a little secret. I knew your great granny, and she hated it too. Sweet dreams, Rossi.'

Rossi felt sure she'd never get to sleep, not with so much to think about – her aunt's mysterious disappearance, her strange cousin, this old house – but the thought was fleeting as she drifted off, lulled by the low growl of the sea outside her bedroom window.

3

THE STRANGE COUSIN

Warm sunshine falling on her face woke Rossi the next morning, and for a second she wasn't quite sure where she was. She looked around the pretty attic room at yellow curtains framing a quaint little window, and a vase of blue cornflowers sitting cheerily next to the photo of her parents and aunt on an old whitewashed dressing table.

Scotland!

She threw back the quilt and, mindful of her head on the coved ceiling, crossed to the window to look out at the day. The sea opposite the Buckie House danced and sparkled in the sunlight, lapping softly against the shore with a gentle *shhh*. Only seagulls' cries punctuated the stillness as they stalked fishermen digging for worms at the water's edge. The air was so fresh and clear after the rain that she could see Edinburgh Castle glistening on the distant shore. She dressed quickly, then crossed the corridor to her brothers' room and threw open the door.

Sean was still in bed but Drew was leaning through the window, checking out the day.

'Come on guys, it's really nice outside,' she said. 'Let's have breakfast and go to the beach.'

Sean groaned beneath the covers. 'Go away,' he said, 'it's too early.'

'No, actually it's almost nine o'clock,' Rossi said, tugging on his quilt without success. 'We've slept late, jet lag, I expect. Come on, the beach looks gorgeous.'

'Look Rossi,' Drew said, beckoning her over to the window, 'you can see it from here. Look, way over there.'

Rossi looked out over the rooftops and church spires that was the view from the rear of the house. 'See what?'

'Scabinory,' Drew said, pointing.

Rossi followed the line of his finger until her eyes fixed on the distant circle of trees in the field above the town. In the warmth of the summer morning it shimmered on the landscape like a mirage, seeming closer than she knew it really was. She shivered involuntarily at the sight, just as she had in the car. *Wicked*, Bridie had called it. Just the thought of it gave her the creeps.

'Why don't we go there today?' Drew asked. 'It doesn't look that far, maybe two or three kilometres.'

Sean poked his head out from beneath the quilt. 'I'd be into that, ' he said, eagerly.

'I don't think so, Drewbie,' Rossi said, using her superior-older-sister tone. 'You heard Bridie. It sounds horrible and dangerous, and anyway I suspect it's much farther than it looks. Now come on you two, I'm starving.' And she ripped Sean's quilt off on her way out, dashing down the steps before he could retaliate.

'I'll get you for that!' he yelled after her. He stretched, yawning, and sat up on the edge of his bed. 'My life is a nightmare that starts at the crack of dawn,' he grumbled.

But Drew wasn't listening. His eyes fixed again on the curious cluster of trees and stones in the field above the town, and as he stared he felt as though the distance to Scabinory collapsed in on itself and, in a rush, he was there. He heard the wind howling through the trees, the buzz of insects in the air, and he could smell it – long summer grass overlaid with the sweet pungent odour of rotting flesh. He wrinkled his nose in disgust and, as if by that very action, zoomed back. He gripped the window ledge feeling dizzy and nauseous – sure he was going to fall – then scanned the garden below seeking some reasonable explanation for what had just happened.

Only one large tree stood in the Buckie House's rear garden – an old laburnum sheltering the gate that led to the footpath beyond. Only the slightest breeze rustled its cascade of yellow blossoms and the sweet scent of roses from the climber that almost topped his windowsill was all that he could smell, nothing like the horrid stench of only moments before. Spooked, he pulled the window shut and locked it securely.

'What's up, Drew?' Sean asked, seeing the strange look on his face. 'Someone walk over your grave?'

Drew recoiled at his brother's choice of words. He opened his mouth to tell him what had happened but suddenly felt stupid for letting his imagination get the better of him. Instead he headed for the door. 'It's nothing,' he said. 'Come on, I'm starving too.'

They'd all been too tired the previous night to pay much attention to the Buckie House's interior, but now they looked around the kitchen with interest. The walls in this part of the house were built of thick, whitewashed stone which was hung with an assortment of kitchen equipment, much of it very old. Gloss-painted shelves stacked with mismatched crockery completely covered one wall, while an old painter's ladder, heavy with pots, hung above the kitchen table and large bunches of lavender dangled from bare beams in the roof. There were only two small windows set deep in the metre thick walls, their old distorted glass criss-crossed with timber. To let in more light, Bridie had thrown open the back door, framing a colourful kitchen garden bursting with summer fruits and sweet pea blossoms. Rossi was already at the worn kitchen table, tucking into a big bowl of steaming oatmeal, but there was still no sign of Ruairidh.

'Oh, there you are, sleepy heads,' Bridie said, turning from the stove with a wooden spoon in her hand. 'We thought you'd never get here, didn't we Rossi?'

Rossi nodded, her mouth too full to speak.

Bridie lifted the pot she'd been stirring and propped it expectantly on the table. 'Would you two like some porridge?' she asked.

Sean and Drew looked at it doubtfully. Oatmeal wasn't exactly their favourite cereal – in fact, they never ate it in Australia.

'Have you got Coco Pops?' Sean asked hopefully.

Bridie laughed. 'I'm afraid not, dear. Why don't you try some porridge today and if you don't like it, I'll see what I can do for tomorrow. Go on, it'll put hairs on your chest!'

With that she ladled a generous helping into two bowls followed by a large spoonful of honey and a dollop of fresh cream. 'There,' she said, finishing off her creation with a mound of fresh berries.

'I picked these myself from the garden just this morning.'

'It's delicious,' Rossi said through a big mouthful, 'honest!'

And it was. They finished everything in their bowls and, at Bridie's insistence, followed it up with eggs and some dubious-sounding but equally delicious fried potato scones, washing the whole lot down with sweet milky tea.

'Your dad's favourite breakfast when he was a boy,' Bridie said, pleased with their willingness to try everything on their plates. 'There now, *if yer no foo, yer no fastin'!* Now out you go into the sunshine. We don't waste beautiful summer days like this in Scotland. Goodness knows they're few and far between.'

The children could hardly believe the difference a day had made to the weather. The sky was blue and the vibrant cottage garden awash with colour. Butterflies and ladybirds flitted across the rose beds, and bumblebees hummed over the thick carpet of clovers and daisies on the lawn.

'Come on,' Rossi said, 'let's go and see the animals Ruairidh keeps out the back. Bridie says he has a hamster and something else, a hedgehog I think she called it.'

'I know what that is,' Drew said, excited at the thought of seeing one. 'It's some kind of spiny insect eater, a bit like an echidna, 'c'ept not so big and not a marsupial.'

'So nothing like an echidna at all, idiot!' Sean teased.

Drew punched his brother on the arm. 'Last one there!' he yelled, charging off.

The others raced down the side of the house and across the long back garden after him. Sean excelled at all sports and as usual he beat the others by a comfortable margin, arriving first at a small,

neat garden shed. A small aviary attached to it contained a number
of dull brown birds and a one-legged pigeon, but there was nothing like the kookaburras and fantastically coloured parrots they
were used to seeing wild in their yard at home. The shed itself
was locked and the windows hung with net curtains to prevent
prying eyes.

Disappointed, Drew repeatedly tried the door handle. 'Bridie
probably has a key,' he said at last. 'Let's go and see if we can get it.'

As they turned back towards the house, they heard Bridie's voice
spilling into the garden through the open kitchen door.

'Really, Ruairidh,' she said crossly, 'was it too much to ask you
to be here to welcome your cousins when they've come all the way
from Australia, and without their parents too? Out you go into
that garden right now and show some manners. And get that big
smelly dog out of my kitchen.'

'He's not smelly,' was all the children heard before a very large,
lolloping dog bounded out of the kitchen and across the garden
towards them, his tongue cheerfully hanging out of his wide, grinning mouth and his tail wagging sixteen to the dozen. He reached
Sean first, knocking him to the ground with one bound, then
licked his face lavishly before turning on Rossi. Squealing with
laughter, she turned her back to deflect the blow but not before
he caught her ear with a big wet lick. He was just about to turn his
licking attack on Drew when a firm voice shouted, 'Ted, down!'

The dog dropped immediately and looked up at his master, or
at least he seemed like he might be looking. It was hard to tell because his eyes were completely hidden by a fringe of the same thick,
shaggy golden curls that covered his entire body. The children fol-

lowed his gaze to where a boy stood a few metres away, but despite Bridie's instructions, his expression was less than welcoming.

Rossi stepped forward, undaunted. 'You must be Ruairidh,' she said. 'I'm Rossi and these are my brothers Drew and Sean.'

'Hi,' Drew said.

'G'day,' Sean said, offering his hand.

Ruairidh sullenly ignored the gesture. 'Hello,' was all he said.

Rossi and her brothers looked awkwardly at each other, unsure what to say next, while Ruairidh continued to scowl and said nothing. It was Ted who broke the uncomfortable silence, crawling across the grass commando-style in a bid to get the attention he so badly wanted, without directly disobeying his master. He rolled onto his back at Drew's feet and, laughing, the three Australian children crouched down to scratch his chest.

'He's a beauty,' Drew said. 'I've never seen such a big dog. What breed is he?'

'He's a Labradoodle,' Ruairidh replied, his expression softening as he spoke about his dog, 'a cross between a Labrador and a large Poodle.'

Rossi brushed the hair from Ted's face and melted at the sight of his big, brown, teddy-bear eyes. 'He's much bigger than any Lab or Poodle I've ever seen.'

'When you cross two large breeds you sometimes get an even larger result,' Ruairidh explained, solemnly. 'That's how I got him. He grew too big for his first owner. Here, Ted.'

Ted obediently moved to Ruairidh's side. He licked his hand and looked up at him adoringly as the boy rested his hand on his huge, curly head.

The others regarded their cousin with keen interest. He was tall and athletic-looking with brown wavy hair and hazel eyes. *Handsome,* thought Rossi, strikingly so, if it wasn't for the sullen set of his mouth and his perpetual frown. But most striking of all was the flash of blonde running through his hair. *Just like his mother,* she thought, remembering the photo.

Ruairidh seemed to know exactly where her eyes rested and his scowl deepened. He moved off towards the shed, taking a key from his pocket, and the others followed, eager to see what was inside. Drew made to step in behind him but Rossi put her arm out, signalling for him to wait. She sensed their cousin wouldn't take kindly to their being too pushy. They watched from the doorway while Ruairidh went from cage to cage checking on rabbits and mice and filling their food and water bowls. At one cage a little golden rodent came sleepily out of its house to greet him and he crooned gently to it.

'Is that a hamster?' Drew asked, desperate to examine the cages. 'Can I see it? I've only ever seen pictures. We can't have them as pets in Australia.'

Although he didn't go so far as to say the words, the children knew from the slight relaxation of Ruairidh's brow that it was okay to enter. They crowded around the hamster's cage with Ted as Ruairidh opened the door and reached inside, laying his hand palm up on the sawdust near the hamster.

'Come on Hammy,' he said softly.

To the children's surprise the little creature climbed willingly on to Ruairidh's hand, not seeming at all frightened even when Ted whined and wagged his tail.

'You can't just grab her, it frightens her too much,' he said, lifting her from the cage. 'When I got Hammy she'd been frightened half to death. Every time her stupid owner put his hand in her cage he got bitten, but at least he brought her to me instead of just letting her go. They can't survive in the wild in Scotland, it's too cold, but now she's great aren't you?' He held her out to Drew. 'You can hold her if you like,' he said gruffly.

Drew flattened his palm and was rewarded when the little creature moved voluntarily from Ruairidh's hand to his. 'Wow, she's so soft,' he said, lightly stroking her back. The others crowded around him and stroked her too before Ruairidh slipped her into the breast pocket of his T-shirt.

He opened a second cage and rummaged around in some straw, this time removing a small brown spiky creature tightly curled to about the size of a tennis ball. 'Have you seen one of these?' he asked. The little animal relaxed in his hand and its tiny brown snout and two dark, bright little eyes peeked out at them. 'It's a baby hedgehog.'

'No, never,' Rossi said, captivated by the little creature. 'We were just wondering if it's related to the Australian echidna. It seems kind of similar.'

Ruairidh was suddenly animated. 'No, no relation at all, it's a completely different species. Have you seen an echidna?'

'Oh, yes, often,' Sean said, 'at the farm where we stay for the weekends and kangaroos too. We've even seen a platypus in the wild and that's pretty rare.'

'I'd love to see a platypus,' Ruairidh said, wistfully. 'I reckon Australia has the best wildlife in the whole world.'

The others smiled, thinking how agreeable their strange cousin was after all. They filed out of the shed and waited while he locked the door.

'We're heading to the beach in a minute if you'd like to come,' Drew ventured.

'Or perhaps there's something else we could do?' Rossi offered generously.

But when Ruairidh turned to face them again, his frown was back in place. 'Let's get one thing straight,' he said, signalling for his dog. 'I didn't ask you to come here, and I'm not interested in hanging out with you this summer, no matter what Bridie says. You stay out of my way and I'll stay out of yours.'

Ted looked over his shoulder at the children with what they were sure was regret as he followed his master out the back gate and into the lane beyond. The others looked at each other, amazed at how quickly their cousin's mood had changed.

'Nice dog,' was Sean's deadpan comment, and the other two burst out laughing.

'Come on,' Rossi said, 'let's go to the beach.'

4

THE SHELL WALL

They had such a wonderful time at the beach that they soon forgot about Ruairidh. The sea was surprisingly warm, especially in the sandy shallows, and they were amazed how far they could wade without getting out of their depth. It was mid-afternoon when, ravenous, they returned to the Buckie House.

Bridie spread a blanket on the front lawn, laying out thick-cut sandwiches which they washed down with tall tumblers of cool lemonade. 'There you go,' she said, never happier than when feeding visitors, 'fresh air and exercise always did give children an appetite. I'm off to the shops now, but there's plenty more in the fridge if you get hungry again. Your grandad is in his study if you have any problems but best not disturb him unless you really have to.'

'This is bliss,' Rossi sighed, gazing up at the fluffy white clouds that dotted the sky.

'Do you think it's going to Australia?' Drew asked idly as a plane passed overhead, leaving white tracks in its wake.

Sean scoffed. 'Don't be stupid. It's going in completely the wrong direction and anyway, you can tell it's just a small plane.'

Drew launched himself on top of Sean's full stomach in retaliation but he just laughed, easily throwing him off, and it was on for one and all.

'Honestly,' Rossi grumbled, 'it's like living with bear cubs, living with you two. Do you have to wrestle constantly?'

The boys ignored her as usual, rolling over and over together in her direction. She got to her feet, knowing better than to get in the way of their rough and tumble, and wandered over to the shell wall, eager to examine it more closely. Following it around the garden she realized how varied and intricate the mosaic really was. Some sections were simple patterns, spirals in particular seeming to repeat frequently. Others were pictures, some real and some mythical like the dragon her father had made. In fact, that image was one in a series framed in circles and squares made from clamshells and periwinkles and following on from one another like the pages of a book. One image in particular caught her attention. In it, a hideous creature poked its head above the waves while a little sail boat bobbed nearby. There was something oddly chilling about the scene, she thought, quickly moving on.

The most fascinating patterns in the mosaic seemed abstract at first glance but, to Rossi's amazement, she found that if she stared at them for long enough recognizable shapes emerged, rather like looking at a magic eye picture. The mosaic was quite remarkable, she decided, and like nothing she'd ever seen before.

As she got closer to the house, the glass and china used in combination with the shells became noticeably older. She came to a section made from blue and white porcelain, spanning an area as tall as her, and as wide as she could stretch from fingertip to fingertip. The colour combination was so pretty that she stepped back to admire the design, waiting to see whether, by staring, she could pick out a recognisable shape. It took a few seconds, but rather than pictures, this time she recognised rows of letters roughly set in a grid and, just like the word puzzles they did at school, some of the letters formed words. She stared at the wall, her heart racing, hardly able to believe what she was seeing.

'That's impossible,' she heard herself say.

This was surely one of the older parts of the shell wall. It must have been completed years – perhaps hundreds of years – before they were born, but there, as plain as day on the wall, were their names, ROSSETTA, ANDREW and SEAN.

'Sean, Drew!' she yelled, 'Come here! Quick!'

The boys appeared, running down the side of the house, still pulling and shoving one another. 'What's wrong Rossi?' Sean asked, aiming one last punch at Drew, 'have you been stung or something?'

Rossi pointed at the wall. 'No, look!' she said, bursting with excitement.

The boys stared at the pattern on the wall for a few seconds trying to make sense of it.

Sean shrugged. 'What?'

'What do you mean what? It's our names, idiot!' But when she turned back to the wall the letters had disappeared and no matter how hard she stared, the jumble of blue and white china now took no recognisable shape.

'It's gone,' she gasped, searching further along the wall in case she had the wrong spot, 'but I swear I saw it!'

'Saw what?' Drew asked, unsure whether she was pulling his leg or not. Rossi was always telling him not to be so gullible, but usually about something outrageous Sean had told him.

'Our names amongst lots of other letters,' insisted Rossi, searching frantically.

Sean folded his arms. 'But there aren't any letters, so either you're imagining it or you're having a go.'

Rossi turned bright red. 'I did not imagine it.' She looked at Drew for help but he just shrugged.

'I can't see any letters, and anyway, what on earth would our names be doing on the shell wall?'

'I don't know, but I did see them. Honest, they were right here just a minute ago.'

Sean raised a brow. 'You're usually weird, Sis, but today you win the weirdness award. Come on, let's go back down to the beach.'

Rossi stared at the wall, blinking away tears of frustration. Always first to feel bad about teasing her, Drew put his arm around her shoulder. 'Come on Rossco, give it up, it's a great story but we're not falling for it.'

Rossi shook him off. 'It's not a joke, idiot! Why won't you believe me? I really did see it and what's more I'm going to tell Grandad.' And with that, she flounced off towards the front of the house.

The boys watched her go.

'This should be good,' Sean said, running after her.

'Too right,' Drew said, right behind him.

Rossi let herself in through the Buckie House's large front door.

The hall was, as she remembered from the day before, more like a museum than the entrance to a house. Every inch of space surrounding the main staircase was filled with glass display cases, holding an eclectic mix of old artefacts. There were fossils and bits of driftwood collected from the beach, teeth and bones, arrowheads and broken daggers, bits of ancient jewellery and lots of stones, many glittering with minerals. But Rossi wasn't interested in any of it. She already regretted saying she was going to tell Grandad. The boys would love it if he thought her as silly as they did – she'd never hear the end of it, but there was no turning back now.

She wasn't exactly sure where Grandad's study was, since they'd followed Bridie straight through to the kitchen the night before, and then up the back stairs to the attic bedrooms. By the time the boys burst in she'd already tried all the wood panelled doors on the ground floor.

'Upstairs,' Sean yelled, gripping the rosewood banister and taking the steps two at a time.

'Me first!' Rossi yelled, tearing after him.

Sean banged on the first door he came to on the landing.

'Come in, come in,' called a muffled voice.

Sean twisted the handle and opened the door, revealing a large sunny room with fantastic views out to sea and over the golf course to Largo Law. Rossi pushed past him, desperate for the professor to hear her version of events first, and Drew crowded close behind.

'Children? Well, well,' the professor said, 'and I was sure I heard a whole herd of elephants coming up the stairs.'

Rossi and the boys gazed around his study, forgetting for a moment what had brought them there. Books and rolled up maps stacked in high precarious towers completely covered the professor's desk and most of the floor, leaving only the narrowest pathway for the children to reach him, but it wasn't the mess that caught their attention, it was the spectacular dragons that graced the walls and all the remaining surfaces. A golden dragon glowed upon his reading lamp while green and red dragons were embroidered on curtains and chairs, and books about dragons lay open everywhere.

Drew picked up a small skull he recognised as belonging to the lizard family. 'Random!' he said, impressed. 'What's with all the dragon stuff, Grandad?'

The professor put his well-worn book to one side. 'Dragons are a passion of mine. Have been since I was a lad just like you two.' He winked at Sean and Drew. 'Not the stuff of serious study at the university you understand, more's the pity. But now that I'm retired, I can indulge my little hobby as much as I like.'

Sean looked at him dubiously. 'But dragons aren't real. I mean they don't really exist.'

The professor rested his elbows on the arms of his chair and touched his fingertips together thoughtfully. 'Well, that rather depends on your point of view. Dragons have featured in the folklore of many different cultures all over the world, so it seems to me more useful to ask, why *wouldn't* they have existed? But I suspect there are none now, sadly.'

His eyes fixed on Rossi's distressed face. 'But you didn't come to talk about dragons. So tell me my dears, what can I do for you?'

They all spoke at once, Rossi shouting over her brothers.

'One at a time, please. I can't understand a word you're saying.'

When all three shouted again he picked up a large fossil and banged it sharply on his desk. 'You first, Rossetta,' he said firmly.

Rossi's words tumbled out in a rush. 'On the wall outside, Grandad, down the side of the house, there's a word pattern in the mosaic and our names are on it.'

'There's nothing there,' Sean said, 'she's lying. We looked and we couldn't see anything and she won't admit she's wrong.'

Drew nodded furiously. 'That's right.'

The professor looked sternly over his reading glasses, first at Sean and then at Drew. 'Calling someone a liar is a serious matter. You'd want to be very sure of yourselves before doing so.' He considered Rossi for a moment before rising stiffly. 'Show me.'

Rossi disappeared down the side of the house with the boys. 'This way,' she called as the professor followed behind at a surprising speed. 'Over here, Grandad.' She pointed to the section of wall, willing it to spell out their names again, but the blue and white patterned china remained abstract and meaningless, just as it had before.

She fought back tears. 'I don't understand. I really did see our names in a jumble of letters right here not five minutes ago, and then by the time the boys came to look they were gone.' She looked up at the professor, pleading with him to believe her.

The professor regarded the wall, and then Rossi, thoughtfully. 'There were three names?' he said at last. 'Just three, you're sure?'

'Yes,' replied Rossi, surprised by the question, 'mine, Sean's and Drew's.'

'Just three,' he muttered to himself, examining the wall closely, 'not five, interesting.'

Drew stared at him. 'You believe her, Grandad? You really think she saw our names in the mosaic?'

The professor removed his glasses and polished them thoughtfully on a corner of his jacket. 'Well now, as an historian, I have to allow that an eyewitness holds a lot of weight when establishing the truth of a story. Your sister seems to be a sensible child and this house…' He held his glasses aloft and checked them in the sunlight before replacing them on the bridge of his nose. He stared at the children, his blue eyes owlish behind the thick lenses. 'This house is most unusual, most unusual indeed. So much history, so much experience in these old walls. This house is a bit like dragons, my dears,' he said, wryly. 'Who's to say what's real and what's not?'

He stooped, resting his hands on his knees, bringing his face level with the children's, and when he spoke his tone was strangely tense. 'But if there were five names, you'd come and tell me then, wouldn't you? Five, you see, would be a different matter, oh yes, a very different matter indeed.'

Rossi's stomach tightened, her satisfaction at his not dismissing her claims out of hand suddenly replaced by a horrible feeling of foreboding.

'Why would five names be different?' Sean asked, staring at him as though he were completely mad. 'Isn't three disappearing names on a shell wall bizarre enough?'

The professor laughed. 'Yes! Quite bizarre enough for one day, at any rate.' He straightened and waved his hand dismissively at the boys. 'Now why don't you two go and find something to do. Rossetta,' he said firmly, 'come with me. I have something to show you.'

With that he turned back towards the front door.

5

AN EXTRAORDINARY HOUSE

This, as you know, is the new part of the Buckie House,' the professor said, waving his hand around the entrance hall. 'Of course by new I still mean hundreds of years old, from when the schoolhouse was added on to the original cottage.' Reaching down to the skirting board he pressed one of the many oak panels furnishing the walls. To Rossi's amazement the panel slid open, revealing a small crawl space.

'What's it for?' she asked, peering inside.

The professor's eyes twinkled, delighted at having impressed her. 'It's a priest hole, my dear. Centuries ago, being a Catholic priest in Scotland was a dangerous business. Those who dared to travel the country preaching to the faithful found refuge from Protestant inquisitors in this house. Then, when the school opened, it was no ordinary school. It provided free education for children in greatest need, the first of its kind in this country.' He turned, leading her through to the kitchen. 'I'm sure you can see from the thickness of the walls in here that this room is older than the rest of the house – or what's *above* ground, at any rate.'

Rossi nodded, fascinated.

'This room is all that's left of a watchtower that stood here hundreds of years ago. It guarded the shore against smugglers and ship wreckers.'

'Ship wreckers?'

'Yes. They'd shine lanterns out to sea on stormy nights, luring ships onto the rocks. The ships' captain's thought they were being guided to safety but once the ships ran aground, the wreckers stole their cargo, often murdering any surviving passengers and crew.'

He moved off again and Rossi followed, spellbound, to a low door beneath the main staircase. The professor twisted the old brass doorknob and beckoned Rossi to follow him down some worn stone steps, illuminated by a bare light bulb. At the bottom was a large cellar piled high with many years' worth of household goods that could easily have been thrown away, and in amongst the junk was a very old door. The professor reached for a flashlight before resting his hand on the door handle.

'We can't risk having a permanent electric light in here in case someone accidentally leaves it on,' he explained. 'The markings in this room have survived as well as they have because it's dark and the temperature is reasonably constant. Please be careful not to touch anything my dear. Even the oils occurring naturally on your skin can do irreparable damage to the paintings.'

Rossi nodded, unable to imagine what he would show her next in this extraordinary house.

He turned to her with a curious expression on his face. 'This is the Buckie House's most precious connection with the past, Rossetta, but even so this door is *never* locked.'

It was clear that he wanted some sign from Rossi that she'd understood, and so she nodded, despite having no idea why on earth that fact should be important.

The room was, Rossi saw as she entered, more like a cave than a cellar.

'Look, Rossetta.'

The professor swung the torch beam around the walls and over the ceiling, revealing ancient paintings of strangely dressed warriors and fierce creatures.

Rossi gasped. 'Who did these, Grandad? And how old are they?'

'That's the amazing thing, my dear. The paintings in this room are from different points in history, starting from the time of our most ancient ancestors the Selgovae, to the near ancients, the Picts who inhabited these lands almost two thousand years ago. You see, the people who lived here valued this particular site enough to paint their stories and spiritual symbols on these walls over many thousands of years.'

Rossi looked closely at the grotesque creatures in the paintings. Her eyes came to rest on a particularly gruesome figure with the body of a man and the head of a wild boar. 'But these things weren't real?'

The professor shrugged. 'Most likely they were pagan deities, like the Egyptian gods Anubis, who was part-man and part-jackal, and Isis, who was part-woman and part-hawk, but the truth is we don't know much about the life of our ancient ancestors as they left no written history. We have little to go on but these paintings and carvings found all over Scotland and, of course, the myths and legends told in Scottish folklore, which are full of magical creatures just like these, some good and some bad.'

'But why this place? Why was it so important?'

The professor's wry smile seemed almost ghostly in the torch-light. 'Well now, if I knew the answer to that one, my dear, and could prove it, I'd be off on some all-expenses-paid lecture tour!'

He shone the torch around the room again, and this time Rossi caught sight of a large and stunning image. A group of children knelt before a bright light encircled by a dragon, but the image was incomplete, cut in two by the rear wall of the cave.

'Did the cave go further back at one time?'

The professor shook his head. 'It looks like a false wall has been built in the middle of that painting, doesn't it? But in fact, that wall is solid rock. You'll find no bricks or join marks there. I'm afraid that image is just another part of the mystery of this place.'

He turned the torch off and led her out. 'You asked me what happened to you today, my dear,' he said closing the door behind them. 'You should know that there is much about this house that is unknown and perhaps unknowable, but what I do know is this: the Buckie House and the site on which it is built has been a refuge for people, a place of physical and spiritual asylum across all human history.'

He stared intently at her as though willing her to understand something he either could not or would not fully explain. 'What I want...' he hesitated as if choosing his words carefully, 'is to assure you that this house bears no ill will towards you or yours.'

Rossi was less reassured than he might have hoped, hearing him speak about the house as though it was a being with feelings and intentions rather than just stone and mortar.

She shivered. 'But what about now? It's just an ordinary home *now*, isn't it?'

'Perhaps,' the professor said, seeming to ponder the question carefully, 'perhaps…'

'I'm scared, Grandad,' Rossi admitted, moving closer to him.

He put his arm around her shoulders and hugged her close. 'Don't be, my dear, for as long as you are within these walls you are absolutely safe.'

Looking up at him, she saw that he was deadly serious.

'Always remember that, Rossi,' he said, using her pet name for the first time. 'Whatever happens…'

Out in the sunshine, the boys, unsettled by their grandfather's reaction to Rossi's claims, were at odds with one another and couldn't make up their minds about what to do with the rest of the afternoon. Drew wanted to go back down to the beach but Sean was in a contrary mood. Tired of arguing, Drew decided to get himself a snack, leaving his brother alone in the garden. Sean wandered down the side of the house eager to confirm for himself that he was right and Rossi was just being stupid. He found the blue and white china pattern on the wall and stared at it until he was cross-eyed. Satisfied that nothing was written there, he was just about to turn away when the words SEAN, ANDREW and ROSSETTA popped out at him just as his sister had described. And to his amazement beneath their names he saw RUAIRIDH roughly written on the grid in broken china and next to it STRUAN, also a Gaelic name, he assumed, although not one he was familiar with. Five names then, just as his grandad had warned there might be. But in addition there was another word, over-arching and more prominent than the five names below it, a word that sent his heart racing.

'Are you coming to the beach now or what?' Drew asked behind him, through a mouthful of roughly made sandwich.

Sean spun around, startled. He started to tell Drew about the names but stopped, thinking better of it. Drew would tell Rossi and she'd tell Grandad, or worse still Bridie, and they'd never be allowed to go there, when now he wanted to more than ever. For the over-arching word on the shell wall, the word that had made his heart race with excitement, was SCABINORY.

6

SCABINORY

The next day dawned sunny again but with a fresh, blustering wind blowing in from the sea. After breakfast the children debated what to do, agreeing it was too windy for the beach. No one mentioned the message on the shell wall and Rossi was grateful that Sean in particular seemed willing to let the events of the day before go without teasing her about it.

'Why don't we take a walk up to Scabinory,' Sean suggested casually. 'There isn't much else to do and I'm dying to see the stones up close.'

'I don't know,' Drew said, thinking of the weird experience he'd had the day before, although he was pretty sure now that he'd imagined the whole thing.

'I don't think I want to either,' Rossi said. 'Bridie says it's dangerous. Let's climb Largo Law instead.'

Drew shook his head. 'Grandad said he'd like to climb it with us, and he's busy today.'

'Oh come on, you two,' Sean said, trying not to sound too desperate. 'How dangerous can it be? We can all swim well and anyway I'm not planning on falling in the pond, are you? Besides, Bridie's not here to stop us, she's off playing golf and she's left plenty of sandwiches in the fridge. I say let's pack a picnic and go while she's out or we might never get the chance.'

They argued back and forth for a few minutes, but when Sean declared he was going with or without them, first Drew and then Rossi reluctantly agreed.

They packed a good lunch in two small rucksacks and headed out of town. As Rossi suspected, it was much further than it looked from the boys' bedroom window and by the time they reached the edge of the field where Scabinory stood it was almost midday and she was hot and tired.

'Let's stop here for lunch,' she begged when Sean stepped onto the stile that led to the field and a fairly steep climb to the trees at the top of the hill. 'It'll make our packs lighter and besides, I'm starving.'

They sat down in the lee of an old dry stane dyke, the higgledy-piggledy sort that scored much of the landscape of Scotland. *So much prettier than wire fences,* Rossi thought, munching happily on Bridie's delicious lemon curd sandwiches and admiring the magnificent view of the town and coastline.

Sean began packing up before the others had even finished, eager to reach their target now that it was in sight. 'Come on, you two,' he said. 'Only one last steep bit and we're there.'

A well-worn path ran across the grassy hillside to Scabinory, proving they weren't the only ones who'd trekked in to visit the historic site, but today there was no sign of another living soul. The wind picked up as they neared the summit, screaming through the trees as though threatening to tear the leaves from their branches, chasing clouds across the sun, turning the air chilly and casting ominous shadows over the ancient stones.

Drew stopped in his tracks, filled with an eerie sense of déjà vu.

Rossi too felt a growing sense of dread as she followed Sean through the trees to the first of the five great stones that stood guard around Scabinory's outer rim. Made of red jasper and standing over two metres tall, they must have stood proud and straight once, but time and weather had taken its toll so that some had sunk at awkward angles and all had corners broken off or worn away. They walked from stone to stone, looking for anything that might provide a clue to their origin.

'They're like very old men,' Rossi said softly, running her hand down the face of a lichen-covered slab, fascinated despite her misgivings. 'Old and wise and stern, don't you think?'

'How on earth did they get up here?' Drew asked, thinking of the hill they'd just climbed.

Sean looked back down over the steeply sloping fields around Scabinory. 'With great difficulty, and a lot of manpower. Come on,' he said, losing interest, 'let's find the Witching Stone.'

They scrambled down the sloping embankment to the pool at the heart of Scabinory and followed the path around the water's edge until they reached a large, flat slab of pink porphyry which seemed to sprout from the murky depths of the pool itself. Beyond it, further passage around the bank was made impossible by thick bulrushes growing well out into the water.

'This must be it,' Sean said, looking at the elaborately carved cup marks and spirals on the otherwise smooth surface of the stone. 'I wonder what these mean.' He traced his fingers around the patterns, but nothing spoke to him of magical powers connecting it to the message on the Buckie House wall.

Not much interested in the stone, Drew wandered away from the others and found a comfortable tussock at the water's edge. It was completely sheltered and strangely quiet in contrast to the howling wind out on the open hillside. Insects buzzed gently as the sun came out from behind a cloud and returned the warmth of the day, illuminating the soft grassy banks, wild flowers and bulrushes that furnished Scabinory's inner sanctum.

The scent of putrid flesh carried on the warm breeze, startling Drew; he sat up, seeking the source. There, rotting in the centre of the pool was a dead and bloated sheep. The buzzing came from flies swarming around the corpse.

'Yuck, that's nasty,' Sean said, joining him. 'I wonder how it got there.'

Rossi wrinkled her nose. 'Poor thing, maybe it drowned.'

Memories of these exact same smells and sounds got the better of Drew at last. 'Look you two, I think we should go,' he said, thoroughly spooked. 'There's something not right about this place and yesterday…' But his words were lost beneath the friendly attack of a large and familiar shaggy dog.

'Ted,' he groaned, knocked flat on his back. He pushed the dog away, laughing, and Ted switched his attention to Sean, jumping up on the other boy and whipping his legs with his tail.

'Down boy!' Sean shrieked. 'Ouch! Good boy. Your tail's a flipping lethal weapon, Ted. Where's your master, boy?'

They looked around for Ruairidh and saw him coming down

the slope towards them – his expression thunderous.

'Ted, here!' he said sharply before turning his fury on the others. 'So you're following me now are you, after I told you to leave me alone? How dare you follow me out here?'

'Hang on a minute, we didn't follow you!' Sean yelled back. 'Believe it or not, you're not that interesting.'

'Sure, then what are you doing away out here? Why would you even think to come here if you're not following me?'

'Grandad told us about Scabinory,' Rossi said, 'and we wanted to see the stones.'

'You've no business being here,' Ruairidh said, a little less sure of himself but unwilling to back down.

'We've just as much right to be here as you or anyone else,' Sean fired back. 'Scabinory's a national monument, and everyone has right of way on the land in Scotland, Grandad said so.'

'You don't know anything about Scabinory,' Ruairidh said vehemently, 'and you don't know *anything* about Scotland. Come on Ted, let's get out of here.'

He swung around looking for his dog. 'Ted,' he called again but there was no sign of him, 'Ted! Here, boy!'

The others watched, puzzled, as Ruairidh scanned the basin, yelling louder. When the dog didn't appear he began searching the bushes around the pond. As seconds passed and there was still no sign of him, his calls became increasingly urgent.

'Come on,' Rossi said running after him, 'something's wrong.'

'Ted! Ted! Here, boy!' they yelled, fanning out around Scabinory. A few minutes later Rossi and Sean met hot and breathless at the tallest of the Standing Stanes. Ruairidh was already there, desperately scanning the surrounding fields.

Drew arrived last, panting. 'He's definitely not on the other side of the hill, I looked everywhere.'

'I know,' Ruairidh said miserably, his anger with the others long forgotten, 'he's just disappeared.'

'He can't have disappeared,' Rossi said, reasonably. 'Are you sure he wouldn't run home for some reason?'

'Yes, I'm sure. He wouldn't leave me.'

'What if he saw a sheep or something? Wouldn't he run after it?'

Ruairidh shook his head. 'I've trained him not to chase live-stock, and anyway there aren't any sheep in the field at the moment and none anywhere in sight, except…' Frowning, he pushed past the others and ran back down the steep embankment to the pool. Without removing his clothes or his shoes he slid into the water and swam out towards the dead sheep. The others ran after him, coming to a stop at the water's edge.

'Ruairidh, I really don't think that's a good idea,' Rossi said, alarmed.

'It's the only place we haven't looked,' he called back, sinking down to feel around him in water made muddy by his own movement. 'Ted might be caught on something under the water.' Finding nothing near the sheep, he rounded a wide and densely packed crop of bulrushes and disappeared from view.

'Where is he?' Rossi asked, craning her neck, 'I can't see him.'

'He'll come out the other side in a minute,' Drew said confidently, but seconds passed and there was neither sight nor sound of the boy or his dog.

'Ruairidh!' Rossi yelled. 'You've had your fun, now come out.'

She stared anxiously at the bulrushes, unsure whether this might be his idea of a joke. Then, to her horror, Sean slid into the water, wading after their cousin until he too was forced to swim.

'No, Sean, come back!' she yelled, but Sean ignored her and seconds later Drew slipped over the edge of the bank after him.

'Drew don't you dare!' But with less than a moment's hesitation he followed his brother into the water.

'You don't know what's been dumped in there!' Rossi screamed. 'You might snag yourself on a branch or something and get pulled under. What if the water's poisoned and that's what killed the sheep. Oh for God's sake, come back!'

But neither boy spared her a glance as they disappeared from view behind the bulrushes just as Ruairidh had.

'Rossi, we've found something!' Drew yelled a few seconds later, his voice strangely muffled, and then…nothing.

'Come back!' Rossi screamed, panic really setting in. When there was no reply she reluctantly slid down to the water's edge and, muttering about all the ways she was going to kill her brothers, slipped into the cold, murky water and rounded the bulrushes just in time to see Drew's feet disappearing beneath the Witching Stone.

'Drew!'

His muffled voice came from underneath it. 'It's just a cave Rossi, it's all right, come on.'

Carlin Meg, the Witching Stone, jutted out from the bank so close to the surface of the pool that, from above, it was impossible to see the small gap between her underbelly and the water. Rossi sank up to her chin in the icky, murky water and cursed her brothers as she scrambled for purchase against the bank, pushing herself under the rock and up into the cave opening. She slid backwards, dunking her head repeatedly before two sets of hands reached down to pull her up. She lay sodden and spluttering on the cold earthen floor. It took a minute for her eyes to adjust to the small amount of light filtering in through the crawl space, but when her brothers' concerned faces came into focus, she scowled up at them.

'I told you not to go into the water, you idiots. Ouch!' she said, banging her head on the low roof as she sat up. 'Have you found Ruairidh and Ted?'

'No, but they must be in here,' Sean said. 'Come on, let's go further in and see if we can find them.'

Rossi didn't much like dark, enclosed spaces. 'I don't think we should,' she said. 'How do we know the roof of this thing won't collapse on us? I really think we should go back and tell someone.'

Sean sounded irritated in the gloom. 'You wait outside if you like. You too Drew, but I'm going on.'

'Not without me,' Drew said, unwilling to be outdone by his older brother.

Rossi hesitated, debating whether to turn back without them. Somehow sitting in the sunshine alone while her brothers crawled beneath the ground wasn't that attractive. 'Okay, okay,' she said. 'I'm coming.'

Wriggling on her stomach and trying not to think of what might be crawling beside her, she followed the boys into darkness. 'Careful,' she said crossly, hitting her head against the sole of Drew's shoe, but after only a few seconds more she came up against his back with a thud.

'The cave's bigger here, see, Rossi?' he said. 'You can kneel without hitting your head.'

'We can't go much further without a torch,' Sean said, frustrated.

Suddenly, a muted light appeared up ahead, casting a large shadow on the cave wall. The children gripped each other, unsure what it was for a second, then sighed in relief when they heard the pad of Ted's feet and felt his big curly head nudging them each in turn. The shadow reduced to a more normal size as Ruairidh drew closer holding a small LCD torch that was attached to his key ring.

'It's you!' he said, releasing a long breath. 'You nearly frightened the life out of me.'

'Likewise,' Sean said. 'Are you all right? Is Ted?'

'We're fine,' Ruairidh said, gruffly, 'but I'm pretty glad to see you guys. Can you believe this cave? I've been coming to Scabinory forever and I had no idea it was here, and there's something else really weird about it.'

'What?' Sean asked, mirroring his cousin's excitement.

'It gets bigger the further back you go, but it isn't going downhill like you'd expect, it's climbing, steeply.'

'But that's impossible,' Sean said, thinking of the view from the Standing Stanes. 'Scabinory is the highest point on the landscape for miles around.'

'I know, and can you smell something weird?'

The others sniffed the air, then immediately screwed up their noses.

'It's yucky,' Rossi agreed, 'what is it?'

'I'm not exactly sure. I've smelt it before but I can't quite place it. It's probably what attracted Ted in here in the first place, that and the water level in the pond. It's much lower than usual because we've had such a dry summer.'

He shone his torch on his cousins' faces. Sean and Drew's eyes gleamed with excitement but Rossi looked like she'd rather be anywhere on earth than there right now.

'Ted and I are going to explore a bit further,' he said firmly. 'Anyone coming?'

'Absolutely,' Sean said.

'Me too,' Drew said.

'Do you think we should?' Rossi asked. 'I have a really, really bad feeling about this cave. Shouldn't we tell someone before we just go exploring it?'

Ruairidh was more animated than she'd ever seen him. 'I've never heard of a cave at Scabinory, even though zillions of archaeologists have crawled over every inch of it. I think Ted might have discovered something completely new. It might just be an ordinary cave, but what if it's something more, something to do with the Standing Stanes?' His eyes gleamed in the torchlight. 'This could be our only chance to explore it. The minute we bring grown-ups here it'll be completely out of bounds for us, believe me I know. The last lot of so-called experts who came to see the cave drawings in the Buckie House cellar asked Grandad to ban me and Ted from going down there. He didn't of course, but that's what they're like.'

Rossi looked at the boys' eager, dirty faces. She nodded reluctantly, recognising defeat. 'Just a little bit further then, seeing as we have a torch.'

They carried on in silence, climbing steeply until Ruairidh suddenly came to a stop. He shone his torch up ahead, then back towards the others.

'Guys, there's a second tunnel up here.'

'Which one should we take?' Sean asked, peering past him.

Ruairidh shone his torch down one tunnel then up the other. 'Your guess is as good as mine.'

'We could split up,' Drew suggested.

Sean snorted. 'With one torch? Idiot!'

'Well, this one seems to go down roughly in the direction we've just come,' Ruairidh said, lighting the first few metres. 'It's possible it also comes out somewhere at or near Scabinory.' He swung the torch beam up ahead. 'This one keeps going up, which we know to be impossible.'

'I vote for the one that goes back,' Rossi said hopefully.

'I vote to continue up,' Ruairidh said. 'I want to know how on earth this tunnel can still be climbing, but as we've only got one torch, I won't force you to go if you don't want to.'

'I say let's keep going,' Sean said.

'Me too,' Drew put in.

Rossi nodded reluctantly, and with growing unease she followed the others, climbing steeply up what appeared to be a natural stone staircase. As they walked on, the air became increasingly rank.

'What *is* that stink?' Sean asked, pulling his T-shirt up over his nose.

'I know it doesn't make sense,' Ruairidh said slowly, 'but it smells like a mixture of bird pooh, from carnivorous birds like the falcons and kestrels I sometimes have in the aviary, and rotten meat, but I can't imagine why birds would be in a dark tunnel like this.'

'It could be bats,' offered Sean.

Rossi looked nervously up at the roof. She hoped not, she hated bats, but Ruairidh shook his head.

'Bats don't smell... *meaty* like this, but whatever it is must have another way out. The exit can't be far now.

They climbed on until they came to a wall of smooth rock almost two metres high. It took several attempts to hoist Ted and each other up and over, but having managed it, the cave floor from then on began to flatten out as if they'd reached a plateau. Ruairidh turned off his torch, revealing faint natural light filtering in from a distant opening.

'Come on, there's the exit up ahead. I can't wait to see what's outside.'

They pushed on, encouraged by the thought of reaching daylight and fresh air. The tunnel suddenly opened out into a large, dimly lit cave. The smell was now truly obnoxious and beneath their feet the cave floor felt loose, shifting and snapping with every step.

'What's that on the ground?' Drew asked.

'It's just sticks,' Sean said, bending to feel around his feet in the gloom. 'But who or what would bring so many sticks this far into a cave?'

Ted sniffed the ground with interest as Sean picked one up and held it towards the meagre light. 'It's not sticks,' he said, surprised, 'it's bones from some kind of animal, and a large one at that.'

Rossi moved closer to the boys. 'Does that mean something's living in here?' she asked, peering into the dark recesses of the cave.

Turning his torch back on, Ruairidh swept its narrow beam over the floor and almost dropped it. Rossi screamed and hid her head against Sean's back and Drew gripped her arm as the light revealed hundreds of skeletal remains littering the floor, some bleached white with age, others in various stages of decay, tattered flesh hanging from limbs and rib cages. But they weren't animal remains. They were human.

'It's okay,' Ruairidh said, trying to sound calmer than he really felt. 'It's some kind of burial place, that's all.' He racked his brain for some reasonable explanation as to why such a thing might be in use in modern-day Scotland but came up blank.

Rossi didn't care what it was. The hair on the back of her neck stood on end as her feet rolled on the loose bones of the dry and decaying dead. The urge to flee was overwhelming.

'I want to get out of here, quickly!' she said. 'Something's really wrong with this. Come on, I mean back the way we came. I don't want to go any further. Please Ruairidh, I'm scared.'

'We all want to get out,' he said, reasonably, 'but the exit is just over there. It'll be much further if we go back down the tunnel.'

Indeed, the cave opening was less than twenty metres away, although the light coming from it was still strangely dull. Drew took Rossi's hand and pulled her firmly onwards, stepping gingerly on the bones until Ruairidh came to a sudden halt.

'Wait,' he whispered sharply.

The others stopped, grumbling as they each bumped in to the one in front.

'Shhh!'

They held their breaths and above the pounding of their hearts they heard Ted growl. The growl turned to a snarl, and he leapt forward. Ruairidh caught his collar, restraining him tightly and at the same moment a voice from the shadows ahead called out in a fierce whisper.

'Hold that dog or I swear I'll put an arrow through its head afore it ever reaches me!'

7

STRUAN

A hooded figure emerged from the shadows, holding taut the string of a bow, with an arrow nocked and pointing straight at them.

'Speak yer names and yer business here,' he demanded in a Scottish accent that was thick and unfamiliar-sounding even to Ruairidh.

The children stood frozen and mute, too stunned to act despite the bizarre threat.

'I said, yer names!' The stranger pointed his arrow at first one, then another of them as he came closer. 'Speak or I'll run ye through!'

Ruairidh came to his senses first. 'I'm Ruairidh,' he said, 'and these are my cousins, Rossi, Sean and Drew.' He held his palm up towards the stranger and tried to sound unfazed by his odd behaviour. 'There's no need to point that at us. We don't mean you any harm. We're just exploring the cave.'

'Yer children?' The stranger seemed surprised, and they realised that in the gloomy light at the back of the cave, he could see less of them than they already had of him.

'No more so than you.'

'And yer explorin' the cave?' He sounded incredulous. 'Just explorin'?'

'That's what I said.'

'Then yer either fools or liars.'

Sensing Ruairidh's temper rising, Rossi laid a hand on his arm to quiet him and stepped forward.

The boy aimed his arrow straight at her. 'Drop yer weapons and step back!'

'We don't have any weapons!' Ruairidh said furiously, having had just about enough.

'Then yer fools indeed,' came the rude reply.

'Please let us explain,' Rossi tried. 'We didn't mean to disturb you. If you'll just put that thing down we'll go back where we came from and leave you in peace.'

But the boy made no move to lower his weapon. Instead he addressed Ruairidh again. 'Ye've a lass with ye, here?' he said scathingly. 'What do ye want here?'

Rossi's fear was overridden in that moment by indignation that he thought she in particular shouldn't be there. 'We've already told you,' she said crossly. 'We came on the cave by accident and all we want to do now is make our way back.'

The boy cocked his head slightly to one side, not for a minute relaxing the string of his bow. 'Back? Back where?'

'Scabinory,' Drew blurted. 'We want to get back to Scabinory.'

The boy lowered his bow and took another step towards them. 'What do you know of Scabinory?' he asked, his tone even more menacing than before.

'It's where we entered the cave,' Rossi said, 'it's where we came from.'

The boy slipped the arrow deftly into the quiver on his back and looped the bow over his hooded head. Drawing a short sword from beneath his cloak he approached them, but when Ted snarled and strained against Ruairidh's grip, he hesitated.

'Hold that dog, I said.'

'The dog won't hurt you if you stop threatening us,' Ruairidh fired back.

The boy edged past them to the rear of the cave, taking only a dozen steps before coming up against solid rock.

'The cave ends here,' he said, with an even harsher edge to his voice. 'Ye lie!'

Drew and Rossi rushed to the rear of the cave, mindless of the stranger's sword. Taken by surprise he let them pass, watching as they ran their hands frantically over the wall, but to their horror he was right. There was no tunnel behind them anymore.

'It's got to be here,' Rossi sobbed. The ill ease she'd felt ever since entering the cave at Scabinory finally giving way to terror. 'We came this way, we did. We must be able to get back.'

'Get down!' the boy whispered as a shadow fell over the cave entrance, further dimming the already meagre light.

The boys and Ted obeyed immediately, sensing some new danger, but Rossi hesitated, balking at the thought of lying amongst the decaying dead on the cave floor. Before she could protest, the boy and Ruairidh each gripped an arm and dragged her down beside them.

'Quiet!' The boy whispered fiercely. 'All of ye, if ye value yer lives!'

The shadow fell again but this time, amidst a flurry of wings, a giant bird of prey landed at the cave entrance. Stunned, Ruairidh recognized it immediately from its distinctive white tail as a sea eagle, but many times larger than those he had seen before – this creature's wingspan was at least five metres wide. It peered with large golden eyes into the dark recesses of the cave, cocking its head from side to side, its hooked beak slightly parted as though tasting the shadows. After a moment, it ducked and entered, taking one step toward the children then another, its long, lethal talons clicking sharply against the bones on the cave floor.

The children lay frozen, blood pounding in their ears, unwilling even to breathe. On one side of Rossi the stranger tightened his grip on his sword, and on the other Ruairidh silently wrapped his fingers around a long bone, but the eagle came no further. It listened for a moment more and then turned back to the entrance, spread its giant wings and launched itself gracefully into the air, quickly disappearing from view.

Ruairidh released the breath he held in a loud rush. 'That's impossible,' he whispered, voicing everyone's thoughts.

'Believe it,' said the stranger. 'Come, we can't stay here, not if ye want tae live.'

'Where on earth to?' Sean demanded, recovering from the shock of what he'd just seen. 'We're not going anywhere with you, not till you tell us what's going on here.'

The boy's reply was curt. 'Ye said that ye came from Scabinory, that ye entered this cave there?'

The others nodded.

'Well I know that tae be impossible. Scabinory lies many leagues from here and none have made that journey and survived it in a decade or more, although braver and stronger than you have tried. But whatever the truth o' who ye are and where yer from…' His eyes, barely visible beneath the hood, flicked across their faces in the dim light. 'Whether ye be friend or foe…'

The children opened their mouths to protest that they were neither, but the strange boy raised his hand. 'Whatever the truth, ye can't stay here else ye become food for the eagles. I'll take ye tae Turpie, he'll know what tae make o' ye.'

'Turpie? Who on earth is he?' Sean asked, thinking it was a ridiculous sounding name.

'The greatest druid that e'er lived,' replied the boy as if stating a simple fact.

'Druid?' Drew asked.

'A wizard,' Sean said. 'I thought that was Merlin. You're joking, right?'

But the strange boy didn't answer; instead he turned and walked away, hugging the shadows until near the entrance, where he dropped to his knees.

When the others caught up they realised that he knelt before the corpse of a man very recently dead. Rossi quickly turned away, covering her mouth, feeling like she might vomit.

Repulsed and fascinated in equal measure, the boys watched the stranger bow his head before the tattered body and mutter a few words in a language they didn't understand before taking the man's sword and sheathing it at his waist.

'You know him,' Ruairidh stated.

The boy nodded. 'His name was Enderlich and he was a good man, loyal tae my father for which he was honoured with this sword. It belongs tae his son now, and shall be returned tae him.'

He dropped to his stomach and beckoned the others to do likewise and follow him out of the cave. They did as he bade, fanning out beside him on the ledge where the giant eagle had perched only minutes before. Looking down they realised they were high on a hill far above a tree-covered valley that extended to the sea some miles away. In the centre of the valley, rising from the woods high up on a rocky crag, sat a great castle, dark and forbidding in an eerie twilight.

Rossi and the boys stared down at the scene.

'Where *are* we, Ruairidh?' Rossi asked.

He shook his head, completely at a loss. 'I've got no idea. None of this makes any sense.'

Two giant eagles glided effortlessly into sight below them, riding the warm air currents and they watched, tense and silent until they disappeared from view behind the mountain.

'Let us hope they've gone tae roost in one o' the caves on the other side,' whispered the stranger. 'Come, night will fall shortly and we must make good our escape before then. The highest paths are treacherous, one slip and ye'll fall tae yer death. Follow me closely, use whatever cover the mountain affords ye, and be silent. Yer lives depend on it.'

But when he looked at the others they were staring at him, their faces frozen in shock. He scowled, registering that something was wrong, and his eyes came to rest on Ruairidh. Ruairidh jumped to his feet, only to find the point of the stranger's sword at his throat. Ted snarled and sprang, knocking the sword from his hand.

'They're identical,' gasped Rossi, looking from her cousin to the stranger as they faced each other furiously.

And they were in stature, age and looks, though dressed very differently, the boy in woollen hose and a sheepskin tunic beneath a long hooded cloak and Ruairidh in jeans and a sweatshirt. The stranger's hair was longer, shaggy and ill kempt, but nevertheless they were indeed identical, right down to their hazel eyes and scowling brows and the distinctive blonde flash that ran across their scalps.

'What means this?' the stranger demanded. 'By the Gods, who are ye?'

Ted stopped growling and moved toward him, sniffing his hand, as confused as the others were by this boy who looked so like his master.

'I could ask exactly the same thing,' Ruairidh shot back.

The stranger stood straighter. 'I am Prince Struan, rightful, though as yet uncrowned, King of Alba.'

Sean started, recognising the name he'd seen on the Buckie House wall.

'My people are the Selgovae,' Struan continued, pointing to the valley below, 'and that castle down there is my home.'

'Alba?' Ruairidh repeated, unsure he'd heard him correctly. 'That's the ancient name for Scotland. I mean *really* ancient. And the Selgovae are the people Grandad thinks might have put the stones at Scabinory.'

'Listen, you guys,' Sean began, wanting to tell them about the shell wall, but his words were swept away in a fury of beating wings and clawing talons as an eagle attacked.

8

THE EAGLES ATTACK

To the cave!' Struan yelled, slashing wildly at the giant bird with the long sword so recently retrieved from his dead companion. Sean, Rossi, and Drew dived for the cave opening and he followed close behind.

'Ruairidh!' Rossi screamed, realising that the eagle had landed on the ledge, trapping him and Ted on the other side.

Ignoring Ruairidh and the madly barking dog, the eagle dipped its head beneath the cave roof and screeched, intent on the children within. Magnified by the echo in the cave, the noise was deafening. They retreated, terrified, covering their ears, while out on the ledge a second bird swooped, clawing at Ruairidh as if in a co-ordinated attack. Ted leapt at the bird, snapping and snarling, while Ruairidh dodged its wickedly sharp beak and lethal talons as best he could.

Corralled at the back of the cave, the others watched the attack with mounting horror.

'We've got to help him!' Rossi screamed, as the bird inside the cave seemed to lose interest in them and turned towards the battle on the ledge.

Struan reached for his bow then cursed, realising that the quiver was still on his back but his bow was on the ledge where he'd left it when he'd lain with the others. Thinking quickly, he threw Sean his short sword and the other boy caught it reflexively. He stared at it and at Struan as it dawned on him what was expected.

'Are you with me?' Struan yelled above the din.

Sean wiped his sweating palms against his jeans one at a time, grasped the sword with both hands and nodded. They ran after the eagle, yelling and slashing from both sides, drawing its attention away from Ruairidh.

'Find something to throw, Rossi,' Drew yelled, scrambling on the ground for missiles. Their hands fell on human remains, and without a thought they pelted the bird with skulls and bones. Gradually they gained ground, forcing it to the very edge of the ledge until Struan and Sean reclaimed the mouth of the cave.

'Here!' Struan yelled, kicking his quiver to Ruairidh.

Ruairidh scrambled for it, not daring to take his eye off the bird for a second. Grasping an arrow in each hand, he stabbed upwards as the eagle hovered close, finding its soft belly. Shrieking, the great bird lifted up, but gripped by madness, Ted jumped, grasping the tip of its wing with his strong teeth and holding on in a lethal tug of war. The eagle rose higher, lifting Ted off the ledge, desperate to dislodge him.

'Ted, let go!' Ruairidh screamed. In one fluid motion he scooped up Struan's bow, threaded an arrow and shot the great bird at close range through the chest. It gave a piercing shriek and twisted violently, shaking Ted loose before dropping like a stone to the valley below. Ted landed hard on the ledge beside him, winded but otherwise unharmed. Startled by the fate of its companion, the other eagle slipped into the air and away.

Ruairidh stared at the others across the ledge in shock. He opened his mouth to speak, but before he uttered a word an eagle swooped from nowhere. It grabbed his shoulders, lifting him a metre or so from the ground, hanging there for a heartbeat, struggling to gain height as Ruairidh whipped his body from side to side. Roaring with rage, the others threw themselves across the ledge, grasping for his legs, but with a deafening shriek and a furious beating of wings the eagle lifted him out of reach and away.

As the light failed, more eagles appeared from behind the mountain and flew after Ruairidh as if by unspoken command. Struan snatched up his bow and let an arrow fly, barely missing the great bird holding Ruairidh struggling in its talons.

'No!' Rossi screamed. 'It'll drop him!'

Struan lowered his bow. 'It would be a better death,' he said, bending past her to retrieve his sword.

They watched helplessly as Ruairidh, now just a dark shadow in the sky, fell slack and lifeless in the great bird's talons until the night closed in around him and they could follow his progress no more.

Ted wouldn't accept that Ruairidh was gone. He ran in a frenzy from one side of the ledge to the other, barking and leaping into the air at each turn, as though by his will alone he could follow his beloved master into the sky. He came to a sudden stop at the edge of the parapet and stared down into the dark abyss. Instinctively Rossi knew what he was thinking.

'Ted! No!' she screamed.

He turned, his eyes flashing, his mouth frothing with fury, bearing little resemblance to the gentle dog she'd met the day before – and then he jumped, disappearing down into darkness.

'Ted!' Rossi screamed, her voice breaking.

She ran to the edge with the others and looked over but it was too dark to see anything. They sat down in stunned silence, Rossi sobbing, Drew deathly pale, hitting the back of his head repeatedly against the cave wall, Sean staring into the darkness after Ruairidh.

'Come,' Struan said, 'yer friend is gone and we can't stay here. There will be time enough tae grieve when we reach the safety o' my camp.'

Sean gasped. 'Grieve! You think he's dead?'

'More than likely,' he replied without emotion.

Sean leapt to his feet. 'If there's even the smallest chance he's alive, we've got to do something!'

'What would ye have us do?' Struan shot back. 'Fly after him? Yer friend is lost and for that I'm sorry, but there are many here who have suffered the same fate.'

Rossi sobbed louder, thinking of the bones stripped bare on the cave floor. 'We have to get home, we have to get help for Ruairidh.'

'What if we can't get home?' Sean said, venting his own fear and frustration on his sister. 'What if we're the only hope for Ruairidh now?'

'We could wait here till morning and see if the way back to Scabinory is open again,' Drew said.

Sean shook his head. 'You heard Struan. The eagles will come back at first light and we'll be sitting ducks. I don't think we have any choice but to follow him for now. Once we're safe, then we can think about helping Ruairidh.'

The others hesitated. Following the strange boy seemed like madness, but staying on the mountain wasn't an option either. The decision was soon made for them as Struan began picking his way down the mountain in the dark and they realised he'd soon be lost from view. Reluctantly and in shock they left the shelter of the cave and followed him down the treacherous mountain path.

9

DRUID MAGIC

The moon, hidden behind thick cloud, gave them little idea of where they were heading as they stumbled down the steep slopes through thick heather and muddy bogs. By the time they entered the forest on the valley floor they were exhausted. Their clothes and shoes, fine for a summer's walk in the Scottish countryside, were completely inadequate for this terrain and, scratched, bruised and still damp from wading through the pool at Scabinory hours before, they straggled through the trees behind Struan without further question or argument.

At last they came to a rabbit trail of sorts. It was narrow and patchy but it made their going easier and they followed it for a while until they reached a small clearing. The moon came suddenly from behind the clouds, illuminating the forest in a ghostly silver light and revealing the castle they'd seen from the mountain. It was close now, perched high above them, black and forbidding like a giant crab crouched upon a rock.

Rossi stared up at the castle, then back at the silhouette of the mountain, trying to make sense of what she found familiar about the scene. 'What's the name of that castle, Struan?'

'It's Dyn Edyn,' he replied proudly, 'the largest in all Alba.'

'Dyn Edyn?' Rossi swung round to look at the mountain again. She gasped, realising what she was seeing. 'It's Arthur's seat!'

'What?' Drew asked, following her gaze.

'Don't you see? The mountain, it's Arthur's Seat. Dyn Edyn was the name of the early fortifications on the site that's now Edinburgh Castle, which makes that mountain Arthur's Seat.'

Sean frowned up at the oddly shaped mountain. 'Are you sure, Rossi? Edinburgh Castle and Arthur's Seat are a long way from Scabinory. We couldn't possibly have walked that far in a day.'

'Yes, I'm sure. Look.' She pointed from one rounded peak to the next. 'It's the shape of a sleeping lion, see. It's unmistakable.'

'Not a lion,' Struan said, 'a dragon.'

'What?' Rossi wasn't sure she'd heard him correctly.

'I said the mountain is shaped like a dragon. It's called Drachen Fels. It's the ancestral home o' the Dragon Lords, or at least it once was. Come on, we can't stop here, there are spies everywhere. There will be time enough for history lessons when we're safe.'

He led them back under cover of the woods, veering sharply to the right around the base of the castle.

'Where are we going?' Sean whispered, catching up with him. 'I thought you said the castle was your home? And what spies?'

Struan's reply was fierce. 'It is my home, or it should be. The castle is taken by my enemies while those still loyal tae me must hide like rabbits in the woods.' He lifted his finger to his lips, bidding Sean to be quiet. The forest was strangely still, made eerie by the pale moon lighting the trees. A blood-curdling howl suddenly rent the silence.

Rossi's hair stood on end. She laid her hand on Struan's arm. 'Tell me that's not a wolf. Struan, there aren't any wolves here are there?'

'Of course there are wolves,' he replied, tersely. He lifted his nose to the night air and his hood fell back, freeing his long hair so that it streamed down his back. He let out a plaintive howl, chilling Rossi to the bone. 'But not tonight,' he added as a heavily armed shadow stepped from the trees followed by two others.

Struan gripped the first man's forearm in greeting, and trembling with relief the man grasped him by both shoulders and pulled him in for a hug.

'Sire, we saw the eagles take someone and feared it was you.'

Struan's fondness for the older man was unmistakable. 'No, Merlich my friend, I am well, but the eagles did take someone.' He nodded back to the three children. 'Their companion.'

Merlich surveyed Rossi and the boys suspiciously. 'Who are they? If they're spies we should kill them here, Sire.'

Rossi clutched her brothers in alarm and felt them stiffen.

'They're my guests,' Struan said, laying his hand on Merlich's arm, '…for now. And the enemy night patrols?'

'The forest is quiet, Sire, strangely quiet, as though the creatures feel no need tae hunt us, and more, the castle is locked down tight, no one goes in, and no one comes out. We await word from our spies but 'tis obvious that something is afoot in there this night.'

Struan grunted by way of reply. He drew the sword he'd taken from the cave and, cradling it in both hands, held it out to Merlich. The other man said something softly to Struan as he took it and although the children couldn't hear what it was, there was no mistaking his sorrow and gratitude. Struan laid a hand on the man's shoulder in response. 'Come my friend,' he said, 'let us return tae camp.'

He signalled for the children to follow, and exhausted as they were, they gave no argument. In truth they had little choice when Merlich and his men closed in behind them.

They hadn't walked far before Struan stopped again, this time dropping to the ground in front of a hollowed out log and disappearing inside like a rabbit. In less than a second he looked up from a manhole, his face strangely ethereal in the moonlight.

'Come,' he said, 'there is food and shelter.' Then, as if understanding their hesitation, added gruffly, 'Yer safe here.'

Knowing they had little choice but to obey, Sean went first. Peering down, he saw Struan looking up at him from a tunnel some way below ground with his foot resting on the bottom rung of a rope ladder to steady it. He beckoned Sean in, then whispered for Rossi to follow next, and once Merlich joined them, the other men pushed a wooden cover over the hole. The children guessed that from outside the entrance to the log would look like nothing more than a well-worn rabbit trail.

Although dimly lit, the tunnel was dry and more than high enough for Merlich to stand upright. The rock walls, the children noticed, were pitted with millions of little air bubbles and pleasantly warm to the touch.

'What is this place?' Drew asked.

'Lava tubes created when Drachen Fels breathed fire many lives o' men ago,' Struan said. 'There are several vents like the one ye came through. They keep the air clean enough to breathe and although we can't burn wood for fear that smoke may lead tae us being discovered, there is a plentiful supply o' hot water for cooking from thermal spas that run beneath the rock.'

They reached a circular wooden wall that fitted the tunnel precisely. Hanging from hooks on either side of a stout door were long woollen cloaks like the ones Struan and Merlich wore.

'Put these on,' Struan ordered, handing one to Sean.

'Why?' Sean asked, just about tired of being told what to do.

Struan shrugged. 'Because I know not yer purpose here. Ye look and sound strange tae me and until I understand why, and that ye have no evil intent as ye claim, I would not have my people see ye.'

'Are you always this friendly to strangers lost on your lands?'

Struan locked eyes with him, his bearing strong and confident, used to exerting his authority and being obeyed without question.

'These are evil times. We survive here by caution and suspicion alone, our hiding place vulnerable tae a single careless word or action.' His eyes rested on Rossi and her brothers, assessing them. 'Many are in league with the Gododdin, their spies are everywhere.'

'The Gododdin?' Rossi searched her memory of the Scottish history book she'd read on the plane – it was only two days ago, though it seemed like a lifetime already. 'Weren't they constantly at war with the Selgovae?'

Struan regarded her with renewed suspicion. 'Ye know something of my people it seems. Come, stay close now and cover yer clothes and faces.'

When they were ready, Merlich knocked on the door. A view hole opened and a pair of sullen, watery eyes stared out. There was some scuffling before the door swung open. The gatekeeper bowed to Merlich as they passed through, barely sparing a glance at the hooded figures accompanying him, assuming they were part of the patrol.

Once through the gate the children heard voices, and to their surprise the tunnel widened into a large cavern bustling with people. Shoppers haggled at market stalls and tradesmen worked their crafts while women cooked and old men talked and drank.

Rossi watched, amazed, as a group of children ran past playing catch in the torchlight. They disappeared down one of the smaller tunnels off the main cavern where people appeared to live.

'What on earth are all these people doing down here Struan?' she asked.

'Years ago the Gododdin and their eagle army drove my people from their homes and fields,' he said, over his shoulder. 'Those who escaped the Gododdin's grasp fled with me to these tunnels. My people cannot go out by day, for the eagles hunt them. They are creatures of the night, but even then it is not safe, for we become the Gododdin's prey. We are prisoners here waiting for our chance to fight back.' His tone when he spoke next was determined. 'But that day is coming, I can feel it.'

Struan kept to the shadows and they passed through the cavern, drawing little attention from people used to seeing patrols coming and going. The smell of cooking hung heavy and delicious on the air and hunger and fatigue washed over the children – the promise of food and rest beginning to outweigh any concerns they had about their reception amongst these strange people.

Struan stopped at a fork in the tunnel and turned to Merlich. 'I bid you feed and water our guests, my friend, and then take them to the druid. I will meet you there.'

Merlich nodded, but when he turned to the children his expression was severe. 'This way,' he said, brooking no opposition.

The children hesitated. They knew Merlich disapproved of Struan's decision to bring them to the hideout, and they realised as the boy moved off that they'd come to feel safe with him. But when Struan disappeared, they followed Merlich in uneasy silence. He opened the door to a large kitchen where cooks were hard at work on the evening meal. The smell was delicious. It had been a very long time since the children had enjoyed Bridie's sandwiches in the lee of the dry stane dyke.

Bridie! Rossi thought of her for the first time since entering the cave at Scabinory. *What must she and Grandad be thinking?*

The cooks stopped work and stared at the hooded figures with open curiosity until Merlich motioned them to leave, which they did quickly and without a word. He himself served the children stew, bread and ale, which they sipped carefully despite their thirst, grimacing at the harsh taste. When they finished he ushered them out, this time leading them steeply downwards until they came to a small door marking the end of the tunnel. He knocked sharply and seconds later the door opened, revealing an odd little man and a faint smell of sulphur.

The man was tiny, almost gnome-like, and his body was badly deformed so that his back arched in an unnatural hump. His bright little eyes were set one higher than the other in his misshapen head and his large nose merged with his mouth in a wide V where his top lip should have been.

He has a harelip, thought Rossi, fascinated. She'd seen a documentary about it filmed amongst South American Indians. In the modern world, it was fixed when children were very young.

The little man's eyes darted keenly from one child to another, finally coming to rest suspiciously on Merlich. 'What brings you to my master's door at this unearthly hour, my Lord... *Merlich?*' he asked in a rasping whisper.

Merlich regarded the man with ill-concealed loathing and what Rossi could only guess was a little fear. 'Tell your master that Prince Struan has returned from Drachen Fels with...' he hesitated, searching for the right word, '*guests*. He asked that I bring them to the druid. I bid you let us enter.'

The little man didn't seem to care much for Merlich either. He surveyed the children once more, noting with satisfaction that they showed only curiosity at the sight of him and not fear or revulsion like the man beside them. 'Come in children,' he croaked, sweeping his arm before them.

The children filed past into a dimly lit antechamber barely big enough for them all to fit. Merlich made to follow but the little man raised his hand.

'I will take them from here. My master does not permit armed men in his laboratory and they have no more need of your protection.'

Merlich pursed his lips, not for the first time at a loss as to why Struan allowed this freakish creature to live amongst them, and with such authority. To his mind the little man's likeness was too

close to that of the Gododdin for comfort or safety. Everyone
knew that such deformity harboured evil spirits. He should have
been exposed to the forest beasts at birth, as was the way amongst
the Selgovae. And as for the jack-o'-nape's master, *the druid*, in
Merlich's view he was little better. No good had ever come from
magic – why, hadn't Struan's own mother proven that? But knowing the boy would always take the little man's part, he merely
scowled and turned back up the tunnel with a flourish.

The odd little man smiled lopsidedly with what could only be
described as glee as he squeezed past the children to open another
door, as though getting the better of Merlich had pleased him
greatly. He beckoned them into the strangest room they'd ever
seen. It was another lava tube, but this time running vertically so
that they stood inside a large cylinder, the roof of which towered
far above them. The circular wooden platform beneath their feet
had a large hole at its centre surrounded by an iron railing, cast
with mathematical shapes and planets. Peering over, Rossi and the
boys saw that the tube disappeared far down into darkness, rather
like a deep well. The walls, above and as far down as they could see
by flickering torchlight, were pitted with a myriad of little holes
from which poked parchment, roll upon higgledy-piggledy roll,
reachable only by a rickety ladder running around the room on a
dubious-looking rail.

Rossi shuddered at the sight of the ladder, no more keen on
heights than she was on small spaces. *No way would she ever climb
down there!* she thought.

The curious little man motioned for them to follow him around
the railing to where a sundial, piles of maps and an array of crude

chemistry equipment covered a number of large tables. As they approached, Struan rose from a wingbacked chair, freshly changed into a black tunic embroidered with a fiery dragon, his hands clasped behind his back and his feet apart as though ready for any challenge they might present. He nodded to the little man, who inclined his head slightly before turning to the children.

'Welcome to my laboratory,' he croaked, his currant eyes twinkling with keen intelligence. 'I am Turpie. Druid Turpie some here call me. Sit please and let us see if we can unravel this riddle.'

The children stared at him.

'You don't look like a druid,' blurted Rossi, which was exactly what the others were thinking.

The little man cocked his ugly head to one side. 'Is that so? And how do you suppose a druid should look?'

Rossi blushed and shook her head, at a loss. 'I... I'm not sure.'

The man grinned grotesquely, revealing a single tooth in the black chasm where the roof of his mouth should have been. 'Well perhaps, my dear, you can describe the other druids of your acquaintance?'

Struan's lips twitched and he cleared his throat.

'I don't know any,' Rossi admitted.

'*We* don't know any,' Drew said, coming to his sister's aid. 'Everyone knows there's no such thing as magic so there's no such thing as druids or witches.'

'Is that so?' Turpie replied, and before their eyes his gnarled body uncurled and elongated and his hair and features aged until the children's perfect story book wizard, complete with white beard and gown, stood before them. He smiled indulgently as they stared wide-eyed and speechless. 'Is this better? I see that it is,' he answered, laughing. 'Pity, though.' He waved his hand over his gown. 'It's just so very conventional, don't you think?'

He turned to Struan, whose grim face had almost cracked a smile at his antics. 'Perhaps you will be so good as to bring our guests some of my elixir, my boy. I'm sure it will do them good after their long journey.'

Struan disappeared to do the druid's bidding, his brow once more set in a frown.

So like Ruairidh, Rossi thought fleetingly. *Ruairidh! What had become of him?*

As soon as Struan had gone, the children tripped over each other in their eagerness to ask questions.

'Where are we?' Sean demanded.

'What are you going to do with us?' Drew asked.

'What about our cousin?' Rossi added.

'All in good time,' the druid said, not unkindly, pointing to some chairs around a long messy table, 'now why don't you sit so we can all explain ourselves in comfort. Ah, here's Struan with my elixir, good.'

The boy placed a goblet of thick steaming liquid in front of each of them before joining them at the table and helping himself.

Sean eyed his drink suspiciously. 'What is this exactly? How do we know it's not poison?'

Struan frowned in disgust. He grabbed Sean's goblet and drank deeply, pushing his own towards the younger boy.

'My elixir brings great comfort, my dears,' Turpie said, patiently, 'and I assure you no harm will come to you as long as you are under my roof. Now drink up and let's start at the beginning.'

The elixir was indeed very comforting and, feeling much better than she had since leaving the Buckie House that morning, Rossi took the role of storyteller. The druid listened, nodding occasionally as she described the long plane trip from Australia and other modern wonders in their world, while Struan sat grimfaced with his arms folded across his chest, as though he thought everything she said was total rubbish.

When Rossi came to the part where she saw their names on the shell wall, the druid leaned forward. Drew interrupted telling of his strange experience looking out his bedroom window at Scabinory and Sean admitted that he too had seen the names on the wall, including Struan's name.

Rossi's eyes flashed. 'You mean to say something happened to both of you at the Buckie House and you didn't tell me? You both just let me go on feeling like a fool?'

The two boys stared guiltily into their cups.

'It wasn't like that,' Drew said, knowing how bad it looked. 'Five minutes after it happened I was sure I'd imagined it.'

Sean shrugged defensively. 'And I would have told you, it's just that I knew you'd never go to Scabinory if I did, that's all.'

Rossi glared at him. 'Too right, then we might not be in this mess.'

'Tell me about Scabinory,' the druid said. His grey eyes brightened as Rossi described the Witching Stone and the disappearance of the tunnel and their shock at seeing Ruairidh and Struan together on the ledge.

'Then Ruairidh was taken by the eagles,' she said, stopping, too upset to go on.

'Ah,' the druid said. 'Perhaps I can give you some little comfort on that account. You see we've received news of your cousin. Indeed, he was seen alive and well at the castle this very night.'

Rossi and her brothers jumped to their feet.

'Someone saw him?' Sean asked. 'You're sure it was him?'

Turpie nodded. 'If he is indeed Struan's double then yes, I'm sure.'

The children whooped and threw high fives before hugging each other in relief.

'Where in the castle? Can we get to him?' Sean demanded. 'Come on, we've got to do something!'

'All in good time,' the druid said, waving them back to their seats. 'Suffice to say for the moment he is safe. Now as to the rest of your tale...'

Struan's scowl was even worse than usual. 'Ye can't believe them, Turpie,' he stated baldly. 'Their story is fantastical, surely?'

Rossi laughed, her good spirits returning with the knowledge that Ruairidh was alive and by all accounts well. 'You think our story is unbelievable? After everything *we've* experienced today.'

'Fantastical indeed, it is,' the druid said thoughtfully. 'Certainly much has changed since I was last in the future world beyond Scabinory. Why, passenger planes and flying to Australia were the stuff of science fiction for ordinary people when I was a lad. And that young rascal, your grandfather, *Bo* we used to call him, a professor at the university? Ha! Well there's a turn up for the books. He never paid much attention to his teachers when I knew him.'

Rossi and the boys stared, absorbing what he'd just said.

'You came through Scabinory too,' Rossi gasped, relief washing over her. Here was another like them – a grown-up from their own time, someone they could trust.

'Yes indeed, more than sixty years ago, my goodness I've lost count – and with your very grandfather, *the professor!* Ha!' He chortled on, enjoying the joke.

'Did you come through Drachen Fels?' Sean asked, eagerly. 'Why didn't you go back? *Is* there a way back?'

'Yes we came through Drachen Fels, and quite a shock it was too.' He regarded each of the children in turn, warming to his subject. 'There were dragons up there in my day, you know. Your grandad loved dragons, but I never cared for them myself. Big, smelly, temperamental creatures. Mark my words,' he said, leaning forward, 'you must never, ever cross 'em!' He pursed his lips as though remembering something distasteful. 'There were five of us of course, three from my world: your grandad, Aileen McBride and me.'

'Bridie?' chorused the children.

The druid nodded. 'And two more from here, long dead now both of them.' A shadow crossed his face and the children wondered what memories he chose not to share. 'But as to the way back, by no means can you return through Drachen Fels. No!' He shook his head solemnly. 'There are two ways through that we know of, although who's to say that there aren't more – Drachen Fels and of course Scabinory as it is in this time. The fates alone seem to decide where you will find yourself when you arrive, but there is but one way back. You have a purpose for being here my dears, just as your grandad, Bridie and I did, and that purpose will take you, just as it took us, to the Witching Stone at Scabinory. It used to be a journey easy enough made, but no more.' He shook his head again. 'No more.'

Drew stared at the druid. 'But if you're from our world, Turpie, how did you change your shape before?'

'Ah. Well, I can't explain the science of it but there seems to be something about the switch from the other world to this that creates an energy that could well be described as magic, hence *Druid Turpie.*'

Drew looked at him doubtfully. 'So we have it too?'

'No doubt, indeed some have multiple abilities, although I don't know why, possibly to do with their level of intuitiveness in the other world.'

'But what sort of abilities?' Sean asked, sure that he didn't feel any different from how he'd always felt. 'You mean like super powers?'

Turpie laughed. 'Not quite. More like exaggerations of abilities you've always had. Take me for example, as a boy I was always a great mimic.' He chuckled, remembering. 'Got your grandad and me into no end of trouble at school. The headmaster used to say I'd end up on the stage or in prison, one or the other. Then, when I came here, I discovered I could blend in with any crowd rather like a chameleon, and with time and practice I was able to completely change how I looked at will. Your grandad now, he could communicate with all manner of creatures, even dragons. He was mad about living things of all shapes and sizes and Bridie, well she could tell the truth from a lie just by looking at a person.'

'I think she still can,' Sean said, guessing not much got past her.

Turpie looked at Drew. 'I suspect you, young man, have a very useful skill indeed. What you described earlier is an ability to transport at least three of your senses to another place, and at some distance. That's not one I'm familiar with.'

'Maybe because I'm interested in old buildings and stuff?' pondered Drew.

The druid shrugged.

'What about me?' Sean asked eagerly. 'What do you think I can do?'

The druid smiled. 'That remains to be seen, my dear boy. No doubt all will be revealed in time.'

'This is all very well,' Rossi said, 'but what about Ruairidh?'

'Ah, yes, now there I think we may have been fortunate. The eagles have long searched for a lad with a distinctive white flash in his hair. It's my belief they've taken their prize to Crane, thinking he's Struan.'

'Who on earth is Crane?' Drew asked, lost. 'And what does he want with Struan?'

Turpie looked around at their confused faces. 'Perhaps I should start at the beginning. Here in Alba there are three nations: Struan's people, the *Selgovae* or nation of men; the *ferrishyn* you may know better as the *People of Peace.*'

The children shook their heads, totally unfamiliar with the term.

The druid tried again. '*The old folk*, then? *Faeries?*' he said at last, reluctantly, when they had still showed no sign of recognition.

Sean scoffed. '*Faeries?* This just keeps getting better and better.'

Turpie grimaced. 'That's exactly why I avoided using that term.

It has all sorts of silly connotations attached to it in your time –
pink frocks and gossamer wings and the like. Now, where was I?
Ah yes, the third nation, the Gododdin, composed of many tribes
held together by the war lords, Ghob and Ghom, from the black
lands to the North. They are gargoyles, cretins, hobgoblins and
toadies, banshees, ogres and nyaffs. The Gododdin are the arch-
enemies of both men and the ferrishyn.'

The old druid's expression suddenly darkened as he spoke. 'Long
have the Gododdin coveted the land of men, for it is in their nature to make war. Until just a few years ago, they were held back by
an alliance that stood between man and the ferrishyn, an alliance
guarded by the Dragon Lords of Drachen Fels and symbolised by
the Heart of Midlothian, placed in good faith by the ferrishyn at
Scabinory.'

'What's the Heart of Midlothian?' Rossi asked.

'The Heart of Midlothian, my dear, is precious beyond value to
all the peoples of this time, but most especially to the ferrishyn,'
Turpie replied vaguely.

'But what is it?'

Turpie cleared his throat and began again. 'The sacred Heart
of Midlothian sits at the centre of the great circle of ferrishyn life,
balancing all the other elements…'

'You mean you don't know,' Rossi said, shrewdly.

Turpie cleared his throat again. 'Well no, not exactly but I'm
sure I would know it if I saw it. Now, as to Crane, years ago four
children just like you also made the journey to Alba, but two did
not return. You know them I think,' he said, looking at Rossi and
her brothers.

Realisation lit Rossi's face. 'Our parents and Ruairidh's parents – Kate and Philip!'

Struan stiffened, angered by something she'd said.

Sean stared at Turpie, incredulously. 'Our parents? But why wouldn't they have told us, warned us about it, or Grandad and Bridie for that matter?'

Turpie shrugged. 'Well as to that I'm not sure, except to say that – as the secret of Scabinory is not widely known in your world and only children seem to pass through – perhaps when those children reach adulthood they simply forget about it.'

'Bridie and Mum and Dad may have forgotten but I don't think Grandad has, at least not completely,' Rossi said, thinking about what he'd said in the cellar.

'Then perhaps he wanted you to come,' Turpie said, thoughtfully. He smiled. 'Perhaps he knew this old fool was bound to be in trouble by now.'

'So Kate and Philip stayed here just like you did,' Sean said. 'Our parents returned home, but they stayed and had Ruairidh.'

Rossi looked at Struan's scowling face, so like her cousin's, and realisation dawned. 'Not just Ruairidh, they had twins!'

Struan shot to his feet, unable to contain his anger at her assumption a minute longer. 'Philip Crane is not my father, and as to whether this *Ruairidh* is my brother, that is not yet proven.'

Turpie shot him a sympathetic look. 'Now my boy, difficult as it may be, I think we can safely conclude that he is indeed your brother. His return, after all, is a possibility we've long considered.'

'Ye mean *you* have long considered it, Turpie. As far as I'm concerned my brother died with my treacherous mother in the forest o' Goyle-Na-Garg. For all we know this boy may be a *pooka*, such a thing is not unheard o' in these parts.'

Drew wrinkled his nose. 'What on earth is a *pooka*?'

'It's a creature found in the forests of Gododdin,' Turpie said, 'one that can take on animal and sometimes, though rarely, human form, but I think not in this case. If Crane had such a one – and they are known to be nigh impossible to catch – how many different ways might he use it rather than have you meet it by chance in the cave on Drachen Fels? No. The eagles have long guarded that mountain on his command, turning it into a graveyard to deter those who would go there and laying in wait for any that might try to enter from the other side.'

Drew stared at Struan. 'You and Ruairidh are brothers? Identical twins?'

Turpie nodded, while Struan's fierce scowl said he was yet to be convinced.

'If Crane isn't Ruairidh and Struan's father, then who is?' Rossi asked.

'When they first arrived here, Kate and Philip were indeed boyfriend and girlfriend as you describe it, until they met the fifth member of their circle, King Rannoch of Alba. I wasn't here to witness Kate and Rannoch's love affair. I had chosen a life with the ferrishyn many years before, where my differences are not feared or hated as they are in Alba.'

The children remembered Merlich's attitude towards the deformed man he thought was the druid's servant, and they thought they understood.

'But even in Elphame the great romance between the young

king and Kate of the Healing Hand, for that was her gift, was the stuff of legends. Crane seemed to take rejection well, and when your parents returned home he stayed, becoming an important and powerful member of the royal court. Kate and Rannoch married and in time had twin boys, but Crane watched them with a black heart. Oh, he charmed and gave all pretence of loyalty, but privately he schemed, waiting for his chance. It came one day when Kate asked to return home for a short time to show her family the little princes. Rannoch wouldn't allow her to take both boys, for the journey to Scabinory was always dangerous, though never so much as it is now, and he wouldn't risk both his heirs. He and Crane accompanied her and Prince Ruairidh with an escort hand-picked by Crane and that, I'm afraid, was Rannoch's fatal error.'

Struan interrupted. 'It is said my mother killed my father so she could return to her own land with her favoured son.'

'That's the story Crane tells, Struan,' cautioned Turpie. 'A story that gave him legitimate stewardship over the kingdom and Rannoch's remaining heir in the eyes of many of your people. The truth of how Rannoch died and what really happened to Kate, I suspect we'll never know. Indeed we have long thought that Crane murdered her and little Prince Ruairidh too. At least now we know they made it through Scabinory to the future, alive.'

'A fact that strongly supports her capitulation with Crane,' Struan argued, 'otherwise, why did she not return?' For a moment his bitterness at having been abandoned by his mother was clear for all to see.

'We don't know that she didn't,' Turpie said wearily, as though

Kate's actions and character were something they'd argued about before. 'For all we know her bones are amongst those on the cave floor at Drachen Fels, but that is of little import now. After Rannoch's death, by whatever means, Crane somehow connived to take the Heart of Midlothian from Scabinory. He had already built support amongst the disloyal and disaffected at court and had in place a secret pact with the Gododdin. With the Sacred Heart in his possession, the Gododdin Lords Ghob and Ghom mobilised their armies behind him and attacked Dyn Edyn. The eagles drove the dragons from Drachen Fels, where they had long protected Alba's western border with Gododdin, and Crane proclaimed himself king. I was here on a rare trip out of Elphame when it happened so I don't know why the ferrishyn didn't honour the old alliance and come to Alba's aid, but knowing the ferrishyn queen as I do, I can only imagine there was a very good reason. Unfortunately, as the road to Elphame is now barred, we cannot know it.'

Struan grunted, as though he didn't share Turpie's good opinion of the ferrishyn queen. 'It is only because o' Turpie's quick thinking that I am alive today. Crane ordered me taken tae Gododdin as a hostage, although it is my guess he would have murdered me rather than let me become a rallying point for the resistance. Turpie took the shape o' the one Crane entrusted with the task and stole me away and it is only thanks tae Turpie that we found these lava tubes.'

Turpie inclined his head modestly. 'A simple understanding of the workings of volcanoes – knowledge from our time comes in handy here sometimes.'

The three children sat in silence, digesting the story.

Turpie's eyes touched on each of them in turn before speaking again. 'And so five children come together in time and place once more. *Five*,' he emphasised. 'Four answering the call of Scabinory on a particular day and you, my boy,' his eyes gleamed as they came to rest on Struan, 'pulled irresistibly to the ancient lair of the dragons in the service of a friend at exactly the same moment. The power of five is great indeed!'

'Crane may already know everything,' Struan said. 'The boy may have told Crane that he is not me.'

'Perhaps... and perhaps not,' the druid replied, considering it. 'Either way the future of our nation rests with you children and the return of the Sacred Heart to Scabinory.'

'We're only kids,' Rossi said, weakly. 'We need to get back home so we can get help for Ruairidh.'

Struan scowled at her. 'Haven't you listened to anything he's said?'

'Struan,' the druid chided, 'it's a lot for the young people to take in.' He smiled kindly at Rossi but his next words, though patient, held little comfort. 'My dear, there is no help to be had for Ruairidh at your home, but you must indeed return there and in that task you share a common goal with Struan, for he cannot liberate his people and you cannot go home without first returning the Heart of Midlothian to Scabinory. Without it that place holds no magic in this time.

So, you must take the Sacred Heart to Elphame, as a symbol of our good faith, to beg the ferrishyn queen to honour the old alliance by providing you with an army. With that army you must re-take Scabinory, freeing the Dragon Lords held captive this many a-long-year by Crane, for he and the Gododdin cannot be defeated without them.'

He looked around at the children's horrified faces. 'I do believe,' he said, 'we have here the beginnings of a quest.'

10

THE BEGINNINGS OF
A QUEST

Sean stared at Turpie as if he was quite mad. 'Let's see if I've understood this right. We have to rescue our cousin from an impenetrable fortress, find the Heart of Midlothian although you don't know where it is or what it looks like, and return it to Scabinory, a place surrounded by demonic creatures that can only be defeated with the help of faeries and dragons.'

The druid sat back in his chair, a wry smile playing on his lips. He nodded. 'Yes. I think that sums it up really rather well.'

Sean threw up his hands in disgust. 'Have you any idea how we're going to do this?'

'Yes, in part,' Turpie replied, easily. 'You're right, we don't know where to look for the Sacred Heart, but we do know that Crane would never trust the Gododdin with such a prize, so it follows that he will keep it close. The castle is the most likely place, although over the years our spies have searched it thoroughly. Our best hope of finding it lies in an ancient prophecy.'

Sean shook his head. 'Oh, this should be good. Go on then, tell us.'

Turpie cleared his throat. *'The Sacred Heart once lost will find when five once more are joined in time.'* He paused for dramatic effect before continuing. 'So, it seems to me, we can't worry about the location of the Sacred Heart until we find your cousin, and for that we do have a plan.'

He crossed to the rickety ladder and pushed it partway around the room on its well-oiled rail before climbing up and selecting a parchment from a pigeonhole high above their heads. Muttering about not being as fit as he used to be, he climbed back down and unfurled the parchment on the table in front of them. They recognised it immediately as a map of the lava tubes.

'The possibility of *Struan's* capture is something we've had lots of time to think about,' he said, using their empty goblets to hold down the corners. 'These tubes run close to the base of Castle Crag. For years we've been digging towards the catacombs beneath the castle and for some time now a tunnel has been complete. Our proposal is this: you three must go into the castle to find your cousin and search for the Sacred Heart. Struan, lad?' he said, inviting him to continue.

Struan folded his arms on the table. 'Turpie thinks we have been fortunate in yer cousin being taken, and in that he may be right. Crane considers my rebel army a raggle-taggle bunch o' undisciplined and poorly armed serfs. He believes that with my capture, they will surrender without much o' a fight, and we will give him exactly what he expects.' His eyes gleamed at the prospect. 'Some o' my people will act as decoys, giving themselves up, while a larger force, much stronger and better armed than Crane expects, awaits my command to attack. Once we have the Sacred Heart, they will draw Crane's forces away, allowing us to take Sithbruaich Gate, the only land route between here and Elphame.'

'How will we know where to find Ruairidh once we're inside the castle?' Rossi asked, sure she'd find herself waking up from this horrible nightmare any minute.

Turpie and Struan looked at Drew.

His eyes darted from one to the other. 'Me? What can I do?'

'Much, I suspect,' Turpie said, rising, 'but come, we've tarried long enough. Crane thinks he has Struan and he'll be planning his next step. We must move fast but first we must do something about your clothes.' He looked pointedly at their jeans and T-shirts. 'Struan, lad?'

Struan lifted a cloth bundle from the floor and unfolded it, handing each of them servants' garb of simple woollen tunics, hose and sheepskin boots.

'These itch,' Drew said, clawing at the coarse wool as it slipped around his neck.

'Ach, yer just soft,' came Struan's unsympathetic reply. When they were ready, he surveyed them critically. 'Ye still look odd, but ye'll do.'

'Gee thanks,' Sean said.

Turpie opened a small trap door in the floor. 'Come, everyone. The entrance to the tunnel is concealed beneath us.'

They peered over his shoulder at the dark, bottomless pit below.

Rossi backed away. 'Oh no. No way am I going down there.'

'Come now, my dear,' the elderly druid said, placing his foot on the top rung of the rickety ladder. 'If an old man can manage, so can you.' And with that he slipped down a few rungs, just about giving the children heart failure, then swung around the railing at speed before jumping through a well disguised door, and pushing the ladder back to them.

The others joined him a few minutes later, Rossi still shaking, having ridden with Sean's arms around her and her eyes firmly closed. The tunnel they now stood in was man-made and much smaller than the lava tubes. Turpie had to bend and the children could barely stand upright as they picked their way over hundreds of metres of rough-hewn rock. After what seemed an age, the tunnel widened into a circular room where a dozen short, thickset men sat playing cards at a table. Seeing Struan they jumped to their feet and the two most senior among them quickly stepped forward.

'Alec, Archie,' Struan said, extending his hand to one then the other.

'Sire,' they replied, grasping his forearm.

'These are the bravest fellows in all o' Alba,' Struan said, for the benefit of Rossi and the boys. 'They have worked on this tunnel in secret for many years, voluntary prisoners if ye like, unable tae return tae their families, unable tae breathe the fresh air or see the night sky lest one o' our own people or Crane's should discover it.'

Alec scanned Rossi and the boys with open curiosity. 'Is it time, Sire?'

Struan placed his hand warmly on the man's shoulder. 'Yes, ma friend, at last it is time.'

He deals well with his people, Rossi thought, impressed by how devoted these men seemed to be to him.

Turpie laid a hand on Drew's shoulder. 'Drew lad, beyond this wall lies a vast network of storerooms, dungeons, and catacombs that form a veritable maze beneath the castle. We need your help to find your cousin. I want you to concentrate on that wall and summon the way.'

Drew took a deep breath and stared dubiously at the blank wall, trying to imagine what might lie beyond it. When nothing happened he squeezed his eyes tight shut, willing himself to see the rooms beyond, but still nothing.

Moments later, he released his breath with a frustrated sigh. 'I can't do it.'

'You must,' Struan said impatiently. 'Try harder.'

Rossi glared at Struan. 'How did you do it last time, Drewbie?' she asked kindly.

He shrugged miserably. 'I don't know… I just looked at Scabinory and wished I was there and suddenly I was.'

'Well, you want to find Ruairidh, don't you? So we can all go home? Why not wish to be with him and see what happens?'

Drew relaxed his shoulders, took another deep breath and focussed again on the wall. A moment passed, then suddenly the wall melted away and his senses rushed into the rooms beyond. He swayed unsteadily on his feet, his eyes fixed on some distant goal, seeming to the others as though he had fallen into a trance. Rossi reached out to steady him, but Turpie caught her, shaking his head.

Drew felt as though he were flying through rooms and passageways, past cellars and store rooms until he came out of the underground chambers and up into the castle courtyard. He flew across it and down some stairs to an ornate door that opened on to a well-furnished sitting room with a doorway to an adjoining bedroom, and a second door on the far wall. Beyond the door he saw Ruairidh surrounded by a white light so dazzling that it blinded him. The impulse to shield his eyes threw the process immediately into reverse, but this time he did his best to slow it down, noting rooms and landmarks along the way. He fell back into his physical self as though dropping from a great height, like the *Tower of Terror*, his least-favourite ride at a theme park back home. He swayed dramatically and Sean and Rossi rushed to support him.

'Did you see him?' Sean asked. 'Did you see Ruairidh? Was he all right?'

'Did you see the Heart of Midlothian?' Struan demanded.

Feeling woozy and nauseous, Drew shook his head. 'I only saw Ruairidh, but not clearly; there was a bright light behind him and it blinded me.'

'Do you know the way?' Struan asked.

'Yes, yes I think so.'

'Alec, Archie,' Struan commanded, and the men took their places at a section of wall marked with a large white cross, each holding a sharp spike against a shallow hole already made for the purpose. They placed thick wads of leather against the spike ends to absorb the sound and two others came forward with mallets wrapped for the same purpose. They struck the spikes in unison and with a dull thud, penetrated the thin shell of rock that separated the tunnel from the castle catacombs. As long cracks appeared in the wall, more men moved forward, pushing the rock inwards to make a fist sized hole and then pulling it towards them, carefully catching each piece and passing it silently backwards until the hole was large enough for the children to squeeze through. Once on the other side, Rossi and her brothers turned to Turpie and Struan.

Turpie smiled encouragingly through the opening. 'Good luck, children,' he whispered.

For once Struan's face was not quite so sternly set. He reached through the hole, grasping each one's arm in turn, fitting his hand around their forearms in the manner they were becoming familiar with.

'Ma forces await news of yer success,' he said. 'Go with good luck and the blessing o' the gods.'

Sean took a deep breath and turned to Drew. 'Okay, matey, lead the way.'

11

CREATURES OF GODODDIN

Ruairidh's last thought, before the eagle's vice-like grip on his neck rendered him unconscious, was of Ted barking insanely on the mountain ledge beneath him. Coming round, his thoughts were again of his beloved dog, quickly followed by the horrifying realisation that he was in the clutches of a giant eagle flying hundreds of metres above the ground. He searched the night sky for his cousins and saw three more winged shadows above him, their talons empty.

They've escaped! He thought jubilantly. *Or they're dead*, he was forced to acknowledge, stripped of their flesh and rotting in the cave with the other poor souls.

'We have the prince,' screeched a voice above him. 'We have him!'

'But not the others!' shrieked another. 'Crane fears the union of the five most of all. He will punish us, kill us!'

'Who will tell him?' called a third voice, shriller even than the one before. 'Not I, not I, not I.'

'Not I, not I, not I!' came a cacophony of cries.

Ruairidh looked around, seeking the source of the voices but could see no one. *It's the eagles!* He realised at last. *I can understand the eagles! How on earth?*

'Don't tell,' called another, its words taken up by the flock in an eerie chorus, echoing through the still night air. 'Don't tell, don't tell, don't tell…'

Prince? Crane? Ruairidh's mind raced, trying to make sense of what he was hearing. And where were the eagles taking him? *Think, damn it!*

He drew some deep breaths to calm his fiercely beating heart, and thoughts of Struan fighting furiously on the mountainside came to him. *Of course,* they thought he was Struan, Prince Struan he'd called himself. And Crane, who was he? Struan's enemy, that was for sure, someone to be feared even by the eagles. Someone who would kill to have Struan.

The great castle on the crag was getting closer; his destination obvious then, but what would this Crane do with him? He'd know right away he had the wrong boy just by looking at his clothes. Would he hurt him? Kill him? Should he admit he wasn't Struan? *And tell him what?* That he was most probably from another time? Would Crane think him a witch? What exactly did they do to witches here? Hang them? Burn them?

The eagle circled the castle's central courtyard, gradually losing altitude while the others remained high overhead and, believing him still unconscious, it dropped him less than gently onto a cart filled with stinking kitchen waste before landing gracefully in front of it. The courtyard filled noisily as lookouts announced their arrival and soldiers and castle folk spilled out of the keep with flaming torches, excited to see what the eagle had brought.

The bird screeched furiously as the crowd drew near, raising its wings in front of the cart to protect its prize. Shielded from their view, Ruairidh made a snap decision. They wanted Struan, so he would give them Struan. What use was he to them otherwise?

He tugged at the rubbish around him, pulling on a stinking rag. It wasn't much more than a sack but it was large enough to cover him, and he quickly discarded his watch, sweatshirt, jeans, and shoes, stuffing the evidence of his modern life far beneath the midden.

In seconds a line of guards formed in front of the eagle, stabbing at it with long spears in a bid to drive it into the air, but the great bird screeched fiercely and held its ground. Realising he was out of time, Ruairidh quickly smeared his body with dirt, paying special attention to his legs and feet to make it seem as though he really did walk around barefoot.

'It's no use,' said a guard. 'Stupid bird's no goin' tae let us anywhere near whoever it is. Ye'd better fetch the king.'

King? Hadn't Struan said he was the *rightful, though uncrowned King of Alba*? Had this Crane stolen his throne?

The other guard's reply was terse. 'I'm no fetching him, ah've seen Crane kill better than me for wasting his time.'

But there was no need to summon Crane. A loud commotion sounded in the courtyard, followed by men coming smartly to attention. Ruairidh arranged the rags over his T-shirt, covering it as best he could just as a loud menacing voice shouted over the din of the crowd.

'What the blazes is this? Eagle, what have you brought?'

For a second Ruairidh debated whether to keep pretending to be unconscious but then thought better of it. What was it Grandad always said? *'Know thine enemy.'* With his heart hammering in his chest, he took a deep breath and stood up, head held high, fists clenched on his hips, stance wide and proud as the eagle bowed its head low in homage to the man in front of it, revealing him to the crowd. They gave a loud collective gasp and the words, *'Prince Struan,'* rumbled around the courtyard.

Thankful for his elevated position, Ruairidh looked down imperiously on the man who'd spoken with such arrogant authority. He was short and stout but strong, *bullish*, thought Ruairidh, and his thin, fair, collar-length hair topped a broad, pasty face with pale blue eyes that pinned Ruairidh with an avariciousness and malice he had never encountered before. It was a sly, cunning face, he decided. He started, seeing an ugly brute of a beast at the man's side. It stood head and shoulders above the man, its thickset body heavily rounded in the shoulders as though it would walk more naturally on all fours. It wore armour, giving its body the appearance of a man's, but the likeness ended there, for its head was that of a wild boar. It lifted its snout and caught his scent, licked its long tusks as if finding it appetising, and surveyed him covetously with mean, beady eyes.

The blonde-haired man released a long breath of air. 'I have him!'

Grinning with evil satisfaction, he stepped closer, raking his cold eyes over Ruairidh. 'Welcome, Struan,' he said in a mocking tone. He turned towards the crowd with a conspiratorial smirk.

'I guessed you and your band of merry men would be scavenging like rats in the woods, but I didn't expect to find you quite so filthy and ragged.'

A murmur ran around the courtyard at his jibe but it contained only pockets of laughter. *This man is not wholly amongst friends*, thought Ruairidh, and he lifted his head higher, drawing comfort from the thought. By nature proud and stubborn, it wasn't much of a stretch to appear regal. He thought of the strange rhythm of Struan's speech, quite different from his own, and hoped he could pull it off.

'I am *Prince* Struan,' he said, his voice ringing out around the courtyard, 'rightful master o' this castle, rightful heir tae the throne o' Alba, and I demand ye step aside and restore ma keep and ma people tae me.'

An excited murmur reverberated around the courtyard. Ruairidh held his breath, praying he'd read the situation correctly and waiting for the cry of fraud, but the denouncement never came. Instead, the mean, pasty-faced man laughed a snide, weasely laugh. The creature at his side snorted with contempt, and those immediately around him took up the sound.

Ruairidh surveyed the large crowd now packing the courtyard. He was shocked to see that many of the soldiers were evil-looking creatures, some like the beast at Crane's side but others even more horrible, dark and skulking with grotesque features exaggerated by the torchlight. Tall, thin gargoyles leant eagerly towards him, their sharp beaky noses and pointy ears twitching with anticipation. Short, fat cretins with small heads and large, wide-spaced eyes grinned at him with glee and scrawny toad-skinned hobgoblins danced from foot to foot, hardly able to contain their excitement. Behind them stood Struan's people; those left behind when he fled with Turpie to the lava tubes, some staring at him shocked and silent, horrified by his capture, some looking at the ground in shame. One elderly man in particular caught his attention, staring up at him with unbridled admiration. He had friends here, he realised with some satisfaction – or rather, Struan did. He was not alone. The thought gave him strength.

'Oh, I don't think so, *Prince* Struan,' the man said, raising his mocking voice for all to hear. 'I have you now and soon your little group of outlaws will crumble into dust. I, Philip Crane, am King of Alba now.'

Philip Crane? Ruairidh fought hard to keep the shock from his face. His grandad thought Philip Crane, his mother's last known boyfriend, was most likely his father, although Bridie most certainly didn't. She always said Philip had a slyness about him that Kate would have seen through eventually.

But of course. He could see the likeness now between this man and the boy in the photograph at home. In that instant he knew with absolute certainty that this man was not his father. He turned his head to the side and spat insolently. A ripple of mirth ran through the crowd, this time directed at Crane.

Crane's face was a mask of fury when he turned back to Ruairidh. 'Seize him!' he thundered.

The crowd roared, those at the rear pushing and jostling against the Gododdin soldiers' backs. A nyaff, thin and weasely with close set eyes and large ears tried to pull Ruairidh from the cart, but his elevated position gave him the advantage and he kicked first it and then another away, punching wildly until his feet were pulled out from under him. They pinned him to the cart then swung him into a sitting position and secured his hands behind him. Crane came close to his face then, sneering – so close that Ruairidh could smell his rancid breath – but empowered by the knowledge that this man, whose shadow had hung over him all his life, was not his father, Ruairidh suddenly felt no fear. He stared him down and, unsettled by the boy's nerve, Crane dropped his gaze first, before stunning him with a vicious blow to the stomach. Ruairidh doubled in agony, unable to stop the tears that sprung to his eyes.

'Take him to the dungeon,' Crane ordered, satisfied. 'We'll see how long his pride lasts when his ragged, leaderless band surrender to me one by one. And hear this!' he said, turning to the crowd. 'If any man so much as tries to free him, I shall personally throw him, his wife and his children from the castle walls.' And with a great flourish of his cape, he turned to leave the courtyard.

'Sire.' Ruairidh heard the eagle squawk. 'What of my reward?'

Stealing a backward glance at Crane as he was manhandled away, Ruairidh was surprised to see the man pause though no one else appeared to understand.

'You found him where?' Crane barked.

'On his way up to the cave at Drachen Fels,' the bird lied.

Crane eyed the eagle shrewdly. 'What of the others?'

'There were no others.'

'I will say when a reward is due,' Crane growled, satisfied with the eagle's reply. 'Guard the castle from the air – the rebel fools will no doubt try to reach him.' And with that he disappeared into the keep, the boar-like beast and his personal guard falling in behind him.

The Gododdin guards propelled Ruairidh across the courtyard and down a steep flight of steps, barely allowing his feet to touch the ground. The door to a dungeon was thrown open, the ropes binding his hands cut, and he was tossed inside. There was no bed in the room, simply a pile of straw beneath a high, barred window. Ruairidh retreated to the straw, rubbing his wrists where the ropes had bitten painfully. Moments later the door opened again and two buckets, one empty for his use and one filled with water, were placed inside. Ruairidh immediately grabbed the empty bucket and turned it upside down beneath the tiny window. Standing on it he could see out fairly well. Although in the underbelly of the castle, he was still high up on the crag, which he could see in the moonlight. There was no possibility of escape that way, he realised, disappointed. His bravado of a few minutes before was gone now and he felt afraid, alone and suddenly exhausted as the adrenaline drained from his body. He felt something move in his T-shirt pocket beneath the old sack.

Hammy! He'd completely forgotten slipping her in there before leaving home that morning, as he so often did. He lifted her out and she stood on her hind legs on the palm of his hand, her whiskers twitching as she stared at him with her bright little eyes.

'Yes,' he said, realising with delight that he knew exactly what she was thinking, 'we have had a wild time of it, haven't we, and I'm hungry too.' He looked around the floor and saw some grains still attached to his bedding straw, which he guessed must have been beaten by hand. He lowered the little hamster to the ground and lay down, watching as she filled her pouches.

'I'm so glad you're here, Hammy,' he mumbled as he closed his eyes and let sleep carry him away.

12

THE SOUND
OF SILVER BELLS

The melodic sound of a young girl singing woke Ruairidh sometime later. He looked around the cell trying to get his bearings, then sank back, groaning when he remembered where he was. *He hadn't dreamt it!* The singing stopped for a moment, as if the girl was listening too, then began again, pure and clear like the sound of silver bells on a summer's morning. She sang in a strange tongue, but although he couldn't understand the words, somehow he knew that she sang of spring mornings and long summer days, happiness and laughter and the freedom of the woods. It was a song completely at odds with this bleak, barren place. Every bone in his body hurt but with an effort he got up and crossed to his cell door, seeking out the voice. There was a view hole big enough for him to stick his head through, designed to allow the guards to see him without opening the door. Outside, the torch-lit passageway was deserted. Strangely, the singing didn't appear any louder out there, nor did it seem to be coming from any particular direction.

'Who's there?' he called in a loud whisper.

The singing immediately stopped.

A guard appeared from a room further down the passage towards the courtyard. 'What do you want?' he growled.

Ruairidh was relieved to see that a man had been set to guard him and not one of the hideous beasts he'd seen the night before. 'I heard a girl singing.'

The guard looked genuinely surprised, then frightened. 'Ain't nobody singing down here 'less'n' it's ghosts,' he said, looking around as though a ghost might indeed jump out at any moment.

'But I heard it,' insisted Ruairidh.

'*Oooh!*' came a ghostly voice from inside the guardroom and a second man appeared in the passageway waving his hands, his eyes wide with mock fear.

The first guard jumped. 'Ach Cairdie, ye frightened me half tae death.'

'What's this about ghosts?' Cairdie asked.

'The prince, eh… prisoner, thinks he heard a lassie singing down here.'

'Ye don't want tae be hearing anything in here, not if ye know what's good for ye,' Cairdie said, folding his arms.

'What's this?' said the first, as an old man came down the steps from the courtyard carrying something draped with a cloth.

'Food delivery, that's all. Just the usual,' the man said. 'Yer new down here, eh? Part o' his highness' castle guard? There's no many o' the Selgovae that have made that grade.'

The guards stood a little straighter, pleased at having impressed him with their recent promotion.

'But there's food gets delivered down here just the same I should think,' he continued. 'Didn't hear his highness tell ye tae starve the laddie.'

The guards looked at each other, for a second unsure what to do. Then, keen to assert his authority over his mate, Cairdie made a decision. 'Lift the rag,' he commanded.

The old man did as he was bid, presenting the food for examination.

'Now search him,' Cairdie instructed his companion.

'God almighty, he stinks,' Ruairidh heard the other say.

'Nae need tae be personal,' the old man said.

'On ye go, then,' Cairdie said, 'and don't you speak tae the prisoner, mind.'

The old man's face appeared in the window and Ruairidh recognised him immediately as the same man who'd stared at him with such regard in the courtyard the night before. He held out a small chunk of bread and when Ruairidh took it, he leant through the window. 'Yer friends know yer here, Sire,' he whispered.

'Get back here,' yelled Cairdie, grabbing the man by the scruff of his neck and throwing him to the ground. 'I told ye not tae talk tae him. Now get out o' here!'

'Should we tell Crane he spoke to the lad, Cairdie?' Ruairidh heard the other fret as they returned to the guardroom.

'No way. Ye know what Crane's like when he's given bad news. There's no harm done, just forget about it, Mackie.'

Feeling desperately sorry about the old man's treatment but warmed by the news that someone in Struan's camp knew where he was, Ruairidh ripped the bread open, ravenous. To his surprise, out fell a tiny knife. He quickly covered it with his palm, checking the window in case the guards had seen it. Only when he was sure they'd returned to their room did he dare examine his gift. The knife handle was made from bone beautifully inlaid with mother of pearl, and the blade when he opened it glinted in the early morning light, streaming through the little window. It had been recently sharpened to a fine razor edge and was engraved with a tiny dragon woven around the letter R.

Ruairidh sat against the cell wall turning the knife over and over in his hand. So Crane hadn't run off with his mother after all. He'd come to Alba and by some means managed to overthrow the king. But surely he would have needed an army to achieve that, so how had he done it? Ruairidh felt light-headed as a tremendous realisation struck him. What if his mother *had* run away with Crane, not to London like other Scottish teenage runaways, but to Alba, and if his mother *was* here then the likeness between himself and Struan could make sense. It was possible, he allowed, that Struan was his brother!

He leapt to his feet and paced the small cell. If he was right and Struan was his brother then where was his mother? And who was his father? He kicked wildly at the cell door, yelling for the guards. A moment later Cairdie's disgruntled face appeared at the view hole.

'What's all this about? Yer not a prince in here, ye know. There's nobody here who's at yer beck 'n' call.'

'My mother,' Ruairidh demanded, unable to contain his excitement, 'is she here?'

Cairdie scowled. 'I don't know what you're playing at. Everybody knows she never came back. Crane say's it was her what killed them both when the old king discovered she was a witch and would have cast her out, and then she drowned herself. Good riddance, I say. She could do all manner o' unnatural things. A man in his position should never a' married the likes o' her in the first place.'

'Killed them both? Killed who?' Ruairidh held his breath.

'Why, the other wee prince and yer father, King Rannoch.'

'Where did she kill them?' Ruairidh asked, knowing that at least part of the guard's story was untrue.

'Everybody knows that. Didn't they tell you anything in that hide out o' yours? Why, she killed them at Scabinory, of course. Cursed place if you ask me,' he added, shuddering. 'Not that I've been there, mind.'

Ruairidh wasn't listening. His mother hadn't abandoned him, as he'd always believed. She'd taken him to his grandfather to save him from Crane, but what then? Had Crane killed her? It seemed certain his father was dead. He felt a pang of regret for the man he would never know, but at least now he had a name. King Rannoch of Alba was his father. *The R engraved on the knife,* he thought suddenly. The man had given him his father's knife. And he was a prince, *Prince Ruairidh of Alba,* and he had a brother. Had he survived the eagles' attack? Did he know they were brothers? Oh, he had to get out of there fast!

Realising Ruairidh was no longer interested, Cairdie stomped back to his guard room muttering about 'Bloody royalty.'

Wired with excitement, Ruairidh paced from the door to the window, wracking his brain for a way out. Hammy appeared under the door with her pouches full to bursting and he bent to her, unaware that she'd been gone. She ran across the floor to his outstretched hand and busily emptied her pouch with her front paws.

'Did you find her?' Ruairidh asked the little animal. 'Did she give you something nice to eat?'

Confirmation that Hammy had found the singer silently came back to him, but it wasn't food that she was working from her pouches. It was a small piece of cloth, and written on it were the words HELP ME.

13

A LOYAL FRIEND

Fury at having failed to protect his beloved master from the eagles drove Ted mad beyond reason. He needed to get off the mountain fast. His leap took him onto the scree that covered the steepest slopes and he slid on the moving mass of loose rock until, bruised and dirty, he found solid ground. Unlike the children, Ted knew exactly where he was. He often walked Arthur's seat with Ruairidh and the professor – it was a favourite outing for the three, usually culminating in an ice cream for Ted at the gates of Holyrood Palace, which in modern times lay close to the mountain's base. Unlike humans, who so often see only what they expect to see, the differences Ruairidh had seen in the tree-covered valley between the mountain and Castle Crag didn't have the same significance for Ted. He knew the scree on the slopes would break his fall and his superior night vision made it easy to follow the eagles from below. They were heading for the castle, a route he knew well. Of course it wasn't the same castle, but the silhouette was not so dissimilar to him.

He reached the village, spilling down the crag on its most accessible side in the same way that the street known as the Royal Mile did in his own time. Fires burned and the smell of roasting meat hung heavy in the air as the villagers prepared their evening meal, but Ted ignored it, thinking only of Ruairidh. He ran straight up to the castle gate's, wagged his tail at the guards and scratched to get in just as he did at the kitchen door at home.

'Away with ye, ye big brute!' yelled one of the guards, then when Ted curved towards him in friendly submission, he followed with a vicious kick to his ribs. Ted yelped in pain. 'Mangy brute, we've enough scavengers in here already. Go back to the village where ye belong!'

Ted hung back, waiting for the gates to open so he could dart past the guard, but visitor after visitor was turned away. No one was allowed into the castle that night on Crane's orders for fear that the rebels might attempt a rescue. Ted trotted back to the village and skirted around the cooking fires. He found exactly what he was looking for in a young girl sitting with her baby brother on her lap at the fireside while her mother cooked supper. He crouched down on his stomach and crawled towards her, cocking his head and whimpering softly.

'Oh look, Jamie,' the little girl said to the baby. 'Isn't he a fine doggy? Look, he's like a big woolly sheep.' She reached out to pat Ted and obligingly, he rolled onto his back, his bent paws suspended comically in the air.

She giggled, delighted. 'You're a good doggie, aren't you? Look at him Mama, isn't he sweet? Can we keep him, please?'

Her mother looked up from her cooking. 'He's a fine beast indeed,' she said thoughtfully. 'Not like the fleabags we usually see around here. I'll warrant such a fine animal belongs tae some noble man for a hunting dog, Ailie.'

Ailie's face fell.

'I tell you what, lass,' her mother said kindly, 'why don't we feed the beast tonight, and in the morning ye can take him up tae the castle when ye go tae see yer daddy. There might be a reward. Whoever owns him will surely be glad tae get him back, and if no one claims him then he's yours. We could do with a big guard dog with yer daddy away on duty most nights.'

With that she broke a hunk of bread into a bowl, spooned gravy over it from the pot on the fire and put it down in front of Ted. He gobbled it down and then lay beside Ailie, content to wait until morning.

Early the next day, after helping her mother with the baby, Ailie set off for the castle with Ted. It was a trip she made every day, taking her father clean clothes and meals and fetching supplies that as a member of the castle guard he could get while others could not. Things were tough in the village – Crane was more interested in fighting and his own personal fortune than the day-to-day plight of the people, and the eagles held them hostage as much as the rebels who lived in the lava tubes. They didn't care where their victims came from. Crane's subjects respected him little and feared him much.

Ailie passed the main castle gates and knocked on a small side door as she always did. The guards on the morning shift were used to seeing her, and her new dog was greatly admired. They hesitated for barely a minute before letting her in. After all, Crane's command to keep the castle locked down surely didn't apply to a familiar little girl and her doggy. Once inside, Ted's keen nose picked up Ruairidh's scent almost immediately. When Ailie noticed some friends amongst the children playing in the courtyard and ran to them proudly displaying her new dog, Ted allowed himself to be petted, but once their attention turned to another game, he simply disappeared. It didn't take him long to trace Ruairidh's scent down the steps from the courtyard to the dungeons below, and when he came to the guardroom and saw that Mackie and Cairdie were busy with their breakfast he slipped quietly past. At the door to Ruairidh's cell he stood up on his hind legs and poked his great hairy head through the view hole.

Ruairidh almost fell over in shock. 'Ted!' he gasped, barely remembering to whisper as he cupped the dog's head in his hands and nuzzled it against his own. To his delight he could understand Ted's thoughts as if they were spoken to him – words of regret at not having defended him better and of joy at finding him safe and well.

'It's okay, boy. It wasn't your fault. There was nothing you could do. Besides, I'm fine and I'm so glad to see you. What about the others?'

Ted was in the middle of telling him that they were well when he'd last seen them when the sound of chairs scraping across the floor and shuffling feet brought them both back to reality. Ted quickly trotted further down the passage into the shadows and moments later, Mackie peered suspiciously through the view hole.

'Who were ye speaking tae?' he demanded, looking around the cell and then both ways down the passage.

Hammy chose that moment to come back from one of her visits with the singer, running close to his foot. He sidestepped in disgust then stomped on the ground, just missing her.

'Ugh, horrible little rat,' he said as she scurried beneath the door.

Ruairidh bent to pick her up. 'I was just calling her back in,' he said innocently, 'she's a pet, aren't you little Hammy?'

Mackie shrugged off back to his breakfast. 'He's talking to a rat,' Ruairidh heard him tell Cairdie.

'There's no accounting for folk,' was the reply.

It was some minutes before Ted returned. Ruairidh was just beginning to wonder if something had happened to him when his woolly head appeared once more at the window.

'There's no way out of the dungeon that way?' Ruairidh repeated, understanding him. 'So we have to go past the guards, but how am I going to get out of this room? No, it's too dangerous,' he said when Ted revealed his plan to attack the two men. 'They have spears as well as swords. There's no way you can take both of them. Even if you could the noise would bring more running.'

Just then, a call came down from the courtyard, forcing Ted back into the shadows.

'Mackie are you down there?'

'Aye,' called Mackie, coming to stand in the corridor.

'Your lass, Ailie, is out here breaking her heart over her wee dog. She's lost it and she's in a fine state.'

'Dog? What dog?'

'Away ye go, Mackie,' Ruairidh heard Cairdie say. 'It'll only take ye a minute. The lad's no going anywhere.'

Ruairidh heard Ailie's father take the stairs out of the dungeon.

'This is our chance Ted,' he whispered. He waited a few seconds more to be sure Mackie had gone up above before calling out to the remaining guard for help and a moment later, Cairdie's scowling face appeared in the view hole.

'What is it?' Cairdie asked suspiciously, seeing Ruairidh doubled over on the ground. 'Mackie. Mackie!'

Ruairidh groaned. This wasn't how prison breaks played out in the movies. The man was supposed to open the door to check he was okay. Ted, seeing the precious few seconds available to them slipping away, bounded out of the shadows and knocked the man to the ground. He pinned him there with one large paw on either side of his head, snarling so close to the artery in his neck that saliva trickled onto his throat. Within a second the man dropped his weapon.

'Unhook the keys,' Ruairidh commanded.

The guard fumbled with the keys at his belt and Ted snatched them from his hands, then nosed them beneath the door. Quickly unlocking it, Ruairidh grabbed the man by his feet and dragged him in.

'Call him off me, call him off!' Cairdie begged, shielding his neck with his hands.

'Shut up or he'll rip your throat out!' Ruairidh growled.

Working fast, he shredded the man's cloak with his pocket-knife and bound his arms and legs before tying a gag firmly in place. Locking the door behind him, he and Ted ran down the hallway towards the guardroom hoping to reach the courtyard before the other returned, and they had almost made it to the bottom of the stairs when they heard footsteps above. They fled back down the passage, passing several cells beyond Ruairidh's before coming to a dead end. Ted was right, there was no escape that way.

They heard Mackie reach the empty guardroom and call out to his companion, then finding no one there, run down the corridor to Ruairidh's cell.

'We'll have to make a stand here,' Ruairidh said, searching desperately for some means of escape. Ted stood out-side the last door in the passage, his head cocked to one side, listening. Above the sound of his own heart pounding, Ruairidh heard singing again.

He frowned. 'If we go in there we'll be trapped for sure, boy.'

Ted whimpered and scratched the door.

'Okay, okay,' Ruairidh said, fumbling in near darkness to find the lock so he could try the remaining keys, but there was none.

Cairdie emerged from Ruairidh's cell shaking off the last of the ties. 'Don't fash yer self so, Mackie, he's down here somewhere. There's no other way out. We'll just take it slow and check every cell, locking each one behind us. We'll flush him out, you'll see, and the captain won't know a thing about it.'

'It's not just the captain I'm worried about,' came Mackie's panicked reply. 'Ye know what Crane said he'd do to anyone helping that lad escape, and I've a wife and two bairns tae consider.'

'Ye should o' thought o' that before ye left yer post.'

'Is that right? Well it wasn't me who got myself tied up in the prisoner's cell,' shouted Mackie, seeing that the other would pass the blame if he could.

As the guards argued, Ruairidh pushed desperately against the handleless door and, to his surprise, it swung silently open. He fell through, forcing Ted to jump over him, then quickly found his feet. As the guards approached, he and Ted backed inside.

'He won't be in there,' Mackie said, when they reached the door. 'It's false, it doesn't even open.'

Just to be on the safe side, Cairdie threw his shoulder hard against it and sure enough, the door shuddered but stayed firmly closed.

'He's got past us,' Mackie said, panic stricken, 'we're going tae have tae tell the captain.'

'No!' Cairdie was beginning to sound worried. 'We'll check the cells again. C'mon!'

Ruairidh heard the two men move back down the passageway and breathed a sigh of relief. The singing was quite loud now. How on earth had the guards not heard it, and what about that weird door?

'We could go back up the tunnel and try to slip past them, Ted,' he said, knowing they stood very little chance of getting to the courtyard that way. He felt for Ted's collar in the darkness ready to hold him back as he eased open the door, but Ted pulled him further into the cell.

'Okay, okay, boy. I see it's not just Hammy who's under her spell. We'll look for her, but she's obviously not in *here*, so first we have to find a way out.'

A strip of white light suddenly appeared at his feet and he jumped back, watching as it grew upwards in a shimmering wall like the liquid surface of a pool with sunlight dancing upon it. Through it Ruairidh saw a sparsely furnished room. Sitting at a table was a girl perhaps just a little younger than he was, boyishly dressed in a white shirt and grey calfskin hose. She was beautiful, her green eyes darkly fringed by long lashes, her skin the shade of creamed honey and her long flowing hair shining brown and gold in the torchlight like polished tiger stone.

Without thinking Ruairidh reached out to her and his hand passed through the shimmering light. She smiled, beckoning him in. He did as she bid, stepping tentatively through the mirrored surface without question as though pulled by an invisible string. Ted followed and went straight to her. He laid his head on her lap and she hugged him, laughing.

'Who *are* you?' Ruairidh asked, captivated.

'I'm Morag,' she said in a sweet, lyrical tone, like her singing voice. 'I'm a prisoner here like you.'

'I'm…' he hesitated, unsure whether to give up the pretence. 'I'm Struan.'

The girl cocked her head slightly to one side and a smile formed on her beautiful lips. 'I know who you are, Prince Ruairidh.'

Ruairidh's stomach flipped hearing his title spoken by this exquisite stranger. 'How do you know?'

'I've been waiting for you,' she said simply.

Hammy poked her head out of Ruairidh's T-shirt pocket and scurried down his arm to be closer to Morag, who stretched her hand out to the little creature, crooning.

'It's so lovely to see such a living thing. It's a long time since I walked in the woods, amongst wild things. How I do miss it.'

'You sent the note,' Ruairidh said, 'and it was you I heard singing, wasn't it? How come no one else heard you?'

'Only the pure of heart can hear the heart song,' she answered. 'No one but Crane knows I'm here, no one in the whole world.'

'But what could you possibly have done to warrant him putting you here?'

Morag's mouth curved wryly. 'You don't have to do anything to be thrown into Crane's dungeons. I'm a hostage of sorts, but you are come now and at last there is hope.'

'Me? But I thought you said you knew? What can I do to help you or even myself?' He cast his eyes around the bleak little room. 'So far all I've done is exchange one prison cell for another.'

Morag smiled, revealing white, even teeth. 'You are exactly who you are meant to be and who you are meant to be is exactly who I need.' She stood. 'Enough talk for now, it's time we left. The guards will search for you as long as they dare before telling Crane, and he will check on me as soon as he knows you are free. We have just a little time before he rips this castle apart.'

'But how do we get out of here?' Ruairidh asked, looking around the room. 'We'll never make it out the way I came in.'

Morag crossed to the back wall of her cell and just as before another shimmering doorway revealed itself.

Ruairidh stared at it, confused. 'But if you're not locked in how can you be a prisoner?'

'Crane used a powerful spell to hold me here. That's one of the reasons why he fears the five above all else.'

'The five?'

She nodded. 'Your cousins, your brother and you.'

Ruairidh's heart skipped. 'So Struan *is* my brother.'

'Yes, and now that the five are met the tide begins to turn against Crane and his containment spells have no power against me.' Her eyes gleamed green in the lamplight, beautiful eyes, sweet and strong, gentle and fierce. Ruairidh was reminded of Bridie's saying that eyes are the windows of the soul. Morag's was an old soul, he decided, old and completely without guile.

'How long did you say you've been here, Morag?' he asked.

She smiled. 'I didn't. But almost twelve years.'

'But surely you were just a baby twelve years ago?'

Morag's smile grew wider. 'Come, there will be time for explanations later, we must leave now or we will lose our chance.'

Ruairidh passed through the shimmering doorway first, checking the way was clear before turning back to Morag. 'Where does this passage go?'

'To Crane's private apartments, so he can come to me at any time without fear of others seeing him. He takes great pleasure in telling me no one guesses I am here, beneath their very noses.'

Ted trotted into the corridor behind Ruairidh but Morag hesitated.

'Are you scared Crane will hurt you?' Ruairidh asked.

She shook her head. 'No, he will not hurt me. I am far too valuable to him.'

Ruairidh met her eyes and reached for her hand. In that moment his heart was lost to this beautiful whimsical girl and he knew with a strange certainty that he would do anything to protect her. Morag took a deep breath and stepped out of her cell for the first time in twelve years.

'See, that wasn't so hard, was it?' Ruairidh said, keeping her hand firmly in his.

'You have no idea,' she said dryly.

They followed Ted along the passageway, looking and listening for any sign of guards in this part of the dungeon, but there were none. Presently they came to another shimmering doorway, but different from the others because they couldn't see through it to the room beyond.

Morag frowned. 'We should be able to pass through this one too, although it looks like there's a spell on the other side to hide it from prying eyes.'

Ted stepped up to the door, his head cocked to one side and his ears raised in question. He wagged his tail slowly at first, increasing in speed until it beat wildly.

Ruairidh looked at him, puzzled. 'What is it boy? What do you mean friends?' He stepped through the door and saw Rossi, Drew and Sean standing in the middle of Crane's sitting room.

'See, I told you there was a door in that wall!' Drew said, triumphantly.

14

SWORD, MACE AND AXE

Squealing with delight, Rossi threw her arms around Ruairidh, and Sean and Drew thumped him and Ted madly on their backs.

'Are you all right?' Rossi asked in a rush, relieved beyond anything at seeing him alive and well. 'First we thought you were in a dungeon then Drew saw you running through a passage beyond this room. He can see through things, it's amazing, but when we came in here we couldn't find the door. Who's this?' she asked, suddenly noticing the other girl.

'Morag,' Ruairidh replied, pleased and a little embarrassed by his cousins' welcome, 'she's a prisoner too and she's coming with us. And guess what, I can understand Ted, and Hammy too!'

But before the others could respond, Rossi froze. At her side Ted's hackles rose and he growled softly. 'Someone's coming,' she whispered. 'Quick, we have to hide.'

'This way,' Ruairidh said, turning back to the concealed doorway but when he tried to step through, his foot came up against it hard. 'Morag. How do we make this thing open?'

Morag's beautiful eyes were dark with fear. 'We can't from this side, not without the spell.'

Footsteps sounded in the corridor outside the apartment.

'This way,' Drew said, running towards Crane's bedchamber.

They crowded in just as the door to the apartment flew open and Crane strode in followed closely by the grotesque boar-like creature Ruairidh had seen at his side in the courtyard the night before. They held their breaths, praying Crane would have no reason to enter his bedroom.

'Everything is proceeding as you predicted,' growled the beast. 'The rebels began coming cowering from the forest this morning at first light.'

Crane threw off his cloak and took a seat in an enormous winged back chair. 'What sort of numbers?' he asked, sounding distinctly satisfied.

'Small groups so far, defeated and bedraggled and throwing themselves on your mercy just as you said they would.'

Crane's mouth twisted in a cruel smile. 'And they shall have it, until I have them all, that is, and then they'll pay dearly for their disloyalty. You can take them to Gododdin, Ghob my friend, as slaves… or meat, as you wish, every last man, woman and child.'

The creature grunted, pleased with the offer. 'And the boy?'

'I'll have him executed in the castle courtyard,' Crane said, relishing the prospect, 'and hang his corpse from the ramparts so the eagles can pick his bones clean. That should make a fine show for those still clinging to the hope that he will one day regain the crown – don't you think?'

'Give him to me and I will kill him slowly,' growled Ghob, 'much more slowly.'

Crane chuckled. 'Patience, my friend, when you've rounded up the last of the traitors there will be plenty for you to play with.' His expression hardened. 'We will teach those who still doubt who is king here once and for all.'

The children listened horrified, for the first time truly understanding what was at stake, both for themselves and the Selgovae.

A tentative knock sounded on the chamber door.

'Who's this?' Crane growled. 'The servants know never to disturb me here unless... Come in!' he thundered.

The door opened and the captain of the castle guard entered, falling immediately to his knees.

Crane leant forward menacingly. 'Speak, scum,' he growled.

'Y... Your H... Highness,' the man stammered, terrified, 'the p... prisoner, has escaped.'

'What did you say?' roared Crane. He reached for the man's throat, his eyes bulging so that it seemed they would pop from his crimson face. 'You stupid, stupid fool!'

'He tricked the guards, p... pretending tae be ill,' croaked the captain, 'a g... giant beast with huge fangs helped him.'

Behind the bedroom door, Rossi stole a glance at Ted's big soft teddy bear eyes.

'Fool!' screamed Crane. 'How long has he been gone? Where have you looked?'

'Only about one quarter o' an hour since, S... Sire. I came as s... soon as I was told. The dungeons have been s... searched and the castle is locked down. I've given orders to detain anyone wanting in or out. H… he's still inside the c… castle S… Sire, I'm sure o' it.'

Crane released him with a thrust to the floor. 'And what of the hounds, have the hounds been loosed?'

'N… no, Sire,' the man said, cowering at Crane's feet once more.

'Then do it! And that old fool, Critch, the one who keeps the history of the castle, bring him to me.'

The captain hesitated, surprised he was getting off so lightly. Crane had been known to kill those who failed him.

Crane bent so that he was only centimetres from his face. 'Now!' he screamed.

The children heard the man scurry out the door and up the corridor towards the courtyard.

'Ghob, see that it's done,' Crane said, harshly. 'Take this place apart brick by brick if you have to.'

Grunting, the creature bowed stiffly and followed the captain out the door.

As soon as they'd gone, Crane hurried to the concealed doorway. He muttered the spell and passed through, and the door closed behind him leaving a blank wall once more.

'Quick,' Ruairidh said, leading the others back into the main chamber, 'we've only got a few minutes before he realises Morag is gone.'

They raced into the corridor but hadn't gone far before a faint, blood-curdling howl sounded behind them.

Morag hesitated, visibly shaken. 'Perhaps it's better if I just go back,' she said, looking at Ruairidh.

He frowned. 'I thought you said he wouldn't hurt you?'

'He won't, but it will be much worse for you if he catches us together.'

Ruairidh took her firmly by the hand. 'Then let's make sure he doesn't catch us.'

They ran along the corridor, stopping at the bottom of a short flight of steps that led up to the courtyard. Sean crept up and peered out, looking for a chance to slip across unnoticed as they had on the way in, simply mingling with the many castle serfs as they went about their morning duties, but this time the courtyard thronged with guards and castle folk overturning boxes and carts and frantically sifting through piles of rubbish in their search for Ruairidh.

'Drew, are you absolutely sure we have to cross the courtyard to get down to the lava tubes?' Sean asked, coming back down stairs to join the others. But Drew had no chance to reply.

Crane had reached the corridor. He bellowed for his guard, throwing doors open with a loud crash as he searched each room in turn. Heavy footsteps sounded in the courtyard above as the Gododdin came running, forcing the children through the nearest doorway. Morag ran to a huge ceramic heater in a corner of the room. She felt it, praying it was cold. Relieved to find it was, she disappeared through an arch in the wall next to it and the others followed, watching as she prised at the wood panels behind the heater. One opened, revealing a crawl space designed to let serv-ants throw in wood without disturbing whoever was in the main room. There was barely enough space for them to squeeze inside, but squeeze they did, Ted sitting on top of them all. Ruairidh only just managed to pull the panel closed behind him before Crane threw open the door to the chamber and thrashed his way in, top-pling cupboards, chairs and tables in his rage.

'Search all the chambers in this passage again including mine,' he yelled as the guards joined him. 'Miss nothing. Search the chimneys and the latrines, the ceiling spaces and the servant holes. Where is that man Critch? He knows every nook and cranny in this damn castle!'

'Here, Sire,' came an old man's voice.

To the children's horror the panel to their hidey-hole opened and a man looked in, his eyes wide with surprise at finding them there. The children stared back, shocked to be discovered so easily, but to their amazement he simply closed the panel firmly once more.

'Nothing here, Sire,' they heard him say.

Crane stomped furiously out into the corridor and up the stairs to the crowded courtyard. 'Listen here, you scum,' he bellowed at the crowd. 'Everyone except the castle guard return to your quarters and do not move until I give the order. Search them well. If the prisoner is found there, you will be killed, whether you knew he was there or not. And Ghob, get those hounds in here now!'

Ruairidh quickly unfolded himself from the hole and helped the others out one by one.

'Why didn't that man give us away?' Rossi whispered, accepting his hand.

'He's a friend,' Ruairidh said, recognising Critch as the same old man who'd given him his father's knife the night before.

'Crane's a mad man,' Sean said, hearing Crane's threat as he clambered out last.

'Mad yes, but no fool,' Ruairidh replied. 'The fewer people there are wandering around the castle, the easier it will be to find us. Drew, you need to come up with another way out of here, and fast.'

Drew breathed deeply, trying amidst the chaos to focus his thoughts on the entrance to the lava tubes. This time it was much easier. In his mind's eye he saw the rooms along the length of the corridor leading to Crane's apartments and he flew through one then another to a weapons room, then beyond that to a cupboard, seeing in it a way down to the very bowels of the castle. Almost immediately he was back, rocking on his feet and fighting a wave of nausea. He headed for the door.

'This way.'

Bile suddenly rose in Rossi's throat as she followed Drew and the others out. 'Something really, really bad is coming,' she whispered. 'Run everyone, run!'

A bloodcurdling howl rent the air in the courtyard above and they ran, following Drew through the weapons room and beyond to the cupboard he had seen in his vision. He threw open the door and the others crowded around him, gasping as he lifted the lid of a latrine and peered down into the black, gaping hole below.

'Drew, you idiot!' Sean said, 'do you have any idea how far the drop is?'

'There's no other way,' Drew threw back, just as horrified as the others.

Ruairidh thought quickly. 'Sean's right, we might break our legs or worse our necks in there, and Ted will never make it. Come on, we'll have to try the courtyard again.'

But when they reached the weapons room the door on the

opposite wall opened, revealing Crane with Ghob behind him restraining two great snarling hounds on the end of a long leather leash. The hounds were black as pitch with eyes deep red in their massive heads and long fangs, more like a hyena than a dog. Seeing the children, they went berserk, foaming at the mouth in their eagerness to attack. Ted went mad too. It was all that Ruairidh could do to restrain him.

For a second Crane hesitated. His snake eyes darted from one child to another trying to make sense of what he was seeing, burning like hot blue coals when they came to rest on Morag.

'Spare the girls!' he howled as Ghob unleashed the hounds.

Utter fear and panic struck Sean as the hounds leapt across the room. Blood rushed before his eyes, threatening to burst from his temples, and a distant voice he didn't recognise as his own screamed in primeval rage. The others watched, stunned, as knives, spears, swords, mace and axes dislodged from the walls and flew full-force towards Crane and the hounds. Crane ducked, exposing Ghob who took a knife in the shoulder before his superior reflexes allowed him to yank Crane through the door and slam it shut, leaving the hounds to their fate. Weapons embedded in the door while others crashed to the floor around the bloodied hounds then rose again to renew their attack.

'The latrine it is, then,' Ruairidh said, recovering from the shock of what Sean had done. Rossi, Drew and Morag ran to it, bracing against the inner wall with their hands and feet to break their fall as best they could. Luckily the shaft hadn't been used for some time and was at least dry, allowing them some purchase.

'Sean!' yelled Ruairidh, realising his cousin was still in the grip of whatever energy drove the weapons. But Sean did not or could not respond, and things began to take on a new and frightening turn in the room as the weapons circled, hunting for a target.

Ruairidh ducked, narrowly avoiding an iron mace. 'Sean!' he yelled again, shaking him. 'Enough, Sean!' he screamed, centimetres from his cousin's face.

Sean's eyes met his and then scanned the room, taking in what he'd done. 'Random!' was all he managed as Ruairidh pushed him through to the latrine.

'I need to support Ted,' Ruairidh said. 'Help me get him on my shoulders then you go first. Ted, don't struggle, try to relax.'

They lifted Ted onto Ruairidh's shoulders and once he was sitting on the edge of the hole, Sean squeezed past, disappearing downwards at speed. The thud of weapons against the door in the other room continued, but more intermittently as the energy gripping them dissipated with Sean's increasing calm and distance. Ruairidh knew he didn't have much time. He swung his legs into the hole, braced his feet against the sides and let go. Ted's huge weight made it more than he could do to control his descent, and his feet scraped painfully against the walls as they dropped in what was little more than a free fall. The tube turned suddenly, separating boy from dog. Ruairidh shot out the bottom and four pairs of hands caught him and then Ted, breaking their speed before tossing them heavily onto the floor.

'What a ride, eh boy?' Ruairidh said, running his hands along Ted's woolly body and down his legs, checking for injury. The dog licked his face.

'This way,' Drew said, disappearing quickly down a passageway, and the sound of hounds baying at the entrance to the latrine above hastened the others after him.

'They're coming,' Rossi yelled, hearing first one then more hounds hitting the ground behind them as the entrance to the lava tubes came into view.

'We're almost there,' yelled Drew.

Archie and Alec leaned through, shouting them on and Drew dived head first into their waiting arms, quickly followed by Morag, Rossi and Sean. The hounds were almost upon Ruairidh when Ted slowed. Realising the dog meant to face them, giving him time to escape, Ruairidh grabbed him by the scruff of his neck and propelled him through the hole, then dived behind him with the hounds' fetid breath hot on the backs of his legs. The hounds leapt after him but Alec and Archie were ready with clubs and sent them crashing back with a sickening thud. Snarling, they sprang again, but more men ran forward, covering the hole with timber and bracing it with iron bars, and in seconds the rabid beasts were hidden from view. The timber shook and dust flew as their bodies thudded uselessly against it.

Ruairidh hugged Ted. 'What a rush!' he said.

'Totally!' Rossi said, her skin and clothes filthy and her hair wild. 'At least we know what Sean's power is now.'

'It's random!' Drew said enviously. 'You saved our lives, Sean.'

Sean's chest swelled with pride. 'You both did great too. In fact I can't believe what we all did.'

The timber behind him suddenly shook hard, hit by something much larger and heavier than the hounds, and the noise reverberated through the tunnel like thunder. As if answering the call, a band of heavily armed men came running down the tunnel from Turpie's laboratory. The first to reach them was Struan's kinsman Merlich. He stopped, letting the others run past to join the miners then stepped back, seeing Ruairidh.

'Sire?' he asked, mystified. 'But, I left ye in the woods, ye sent me here with a message for these children. How is it yer here?'

'I'm not Struan. I'm Ruairidh, his brother, at least I think I am,' Ruairidh said, awkwardly.

'The missing prince!' gasped Merlich, and the soldiers and miners turned to stare at Ruairidh, hardly able to believe what they were seeing.

The loud thud of a battering ram reverberated again and Merlich gathered himself. 'Prince Ruairidh, I'm told to bring ye all to your brother right away.'

Ruairidh nodded. 'Lead on.'

The children followed quickly as the thudding changed to loud cracking.

'Ready, men!' They heard Alec shout behind them. 'They're breaking through!'

'Let them come,' Archie growled, and was met with a chorus of 'aye!'

15

DECEIT AND DISLOYALTY

Crane retreated from the weapons room, shocked not only by the rain of weapons but by the other children with Morag and the boy he believed was Struan. He paced the floor, having no thought for the beast, Ghob, struggling to rip the knife from its shoulder or for the hounds lying dead in the room beyond. His heart told him that the others were most likely part of the five he had dreaded for the last twelve years. There was something about the red-haired girl in particular that was modern to his eye. But Morag couldn't possibly be the fifth, so who was?

Perhaps the five had not yet met. He brightened at the thought. Perhaps he still had time to destroy them before they could do him any real damage.

A knock at the door interrupted his thoughts and a guard entered, propelling a ragged servant clasping a sack in his filthy hands.

'Your Highness?' the guard asked, uncertain what his reception would be.

Crane's people mostly chose not to tell him anything if they could help it. He was renowned for taking his wrath out on whoever brought him news he didn't like, regardless of whether they were at fault or not.

'What?' Crane barked.

The guard pushed the servant towards him. 'This man empties the rubbish carts, and today he emptied the one that...' he searched for a word to describe Struan that wouldn't provoke Crane, 'the boy was in.'

Crane stepped towards him. 'Show me, scum.'

Shaking, the man opened the sack and pulled out Ruairidh's shoes, his clothing and finally his watch, which he held tentatively between two fingers and at arm's length as though it might bite him. Crane's face turned crimson. He stepped closer, recognising the significance of the clothing immediately. The servant quickly backed away but not before Crane kicked the clothes from his hands in a rage. Terrified, the man scurried out the door without looking back.

Blood beat loudly in Crane's temples as he stamped on the watch until it splintered and smashed. It was the other twin he'd taken, not Struan. This was worse than he'd imagined. Damn Kate! Somehow the child had survived and now he was back, the five had met, and Crane had two heirs to the throne to contend with. But how had she done it? He'd seen her throw herself and the baby into the fast flowing river with his own eyes, moments after he'd killed Rannoch. He vividly remembered the look of hatred and despair in her eyes as she'd jumped to her death. He'd set his guards to search for her and they'd sworn they'd fished both her and the child out dead, and buried the bodies. He hadn't wanted her to die, he'd always planned to keep her for himself once Rannoch and the two princes were disposed of, but she'd rejected him again, just as she had when she'd chosen Rannoch over him years before.

And how had those kids made it through Drachen Fels without getting caught?

The eagles! They'd lied to him just as his guards had all those years ago. He was surrounded by fools and liars!

Ghob entered, interrupting his thoughts. 'Sire, the hounds have tracked the children through a tunnel running into the woods on the east side of the castle, and our spies bring word of a rebel army massing to the South.'

Crane snapped from fury into action. 'Have you discovered their lair?'

'The entrance through the castle catacombs is braced from the other side, but we expect to break through at any minute.'

Crane paced the floor. 'Call the engineers and surveyors. I want that rat's nest found! Bring fire and oil – we will stick them like rats in a hole and then smoke them out. Send word to my horse guard, Ghob. We ride for Sithbruaich Gate!'

16

THE SACRED HEART

The children followed Merlich, running on and on up the long tunnel towards Turpie's laboratory. This time Rossi swung onto the ladder and circled the bottomless pit without a moment's hesitation, so keen was she to escape the battle now raging in the tunnel below. Turpie peered anxiously through the trap door, offering each of them his hand as they clambered up onto the platform.

'My dears,' he said warmly, embracing Rossi and then her brothers before reaching out to shake Ruairidh's hand, 'and Prince Ruairidh.' He bowed respectfully. 'Welcome. It's good indeed to have you back amongst your people. And you three have done so well to rescue him.'

'Not that well,' Rossi admitted, remembering for the first time that Ruairidh wasn't the only thing they were meant to bring back. 'I'm afraid there was no chance to look for the Heart of Midlothian.'

Turpie's eyes rested on Morag and he opened his arms wide. She went to him and wept silently there, as if letting go of all the fear and sorrow of the previous twelve years.

'It's been a long time for you alone in prison,' he said, stroking her hair, 'but you're amongst friends now, friends who'll do everything in their power to see you safely home.'

'You two know each other?' Rossi asked, surprised.

'We've never met, but I did say I'd know the Heart of Midlothian as soon as I saw it and here it is, manifested in this beautiful child.'

Ted nuzzled Morag's hand and Ruairidh instinctively reached out to comfort her. With that touch, twelve years of Crane's cruel rule played out in his mind's eye and he understood what the Heart of Midlothian was and what its removal from Scabinory had meant to the people of Alba. Silently, he found himself pledging to protect her, with his life if necessary.

Morag dried her tears and turned from Turpie's arms.

Her eyes really are extraordinary, thought Ruairidh. They seemed fresh now and lighter in colour, like spring leaves. Ruairidh saw in them hope for the future of Alba, and understood with absolute clarity exactly how important their quest was.

'You've had a tremendous stroke of luck finding her so easily,' Turpie said, 'and now you must move quickly to take advantage of it. Struan is waiting for you in the forest with his army, ready to attack Crane's forces and draw his eye away from Sithbruaich Gate. You'll need these.' He handed Ruairidh clothes and sturdy boots and each of them a sword and a bag of food to sling across their shoulders.

Rossi grimaced as she took the sword, certain she'd never be able to use it. 'Will you come with us, Turpie?' she asked slipping it awkwardly into her belt.

He shook his head. 'I'll go with you to meet Struan but will remain with the army. The road to Elphame is a hard one and these old bones of mine will only hold you back.' He smiled wistfully. 'But oh, how I'd love to see that land again.'

'Come,' Merlich said, impatiently. 'I must return tae our forces in the forest. We need move quickly. It's only a matter o' time before Crane discovers these tunnels.'

They followed him out of the laboratory and up through the tubes, eerily silent now that the women and children had fled and the men had gone to war. They soon arrived back at the main cavern, empty save for the scattered debris of people's lives, evidence of their hasty departure.

'This way,' Merlich said, heading across the cavern in the direction of the entrance they'd used before.

Halfway across, Ted came to an abrupt halt and growled up at the cavern roof. Loud hammering sounded, steady and measured as though something – many things – were being driven into the ground above their heads. Rocks and dirt suddenly rained down, as giant spikes appeared through the cavern roof, stopping less than a metre from the floor.

'Get down and run!' Merlich roared, just managing to dodge a spike as it came through.

They wove their way toward the exit tunnel but heard voices coming toward them. Crane's men rounded a bend, shouting as they spotted them.

'Turn back,' yelled Merlich, 'to the south exit!'

They fled back to the cavern and wove their way through the

forest of lethal spikes once more. Some began withdrawing, allowing small shafts of sunlight to stream into the cave from above and suddenly they felt drops of liquid falling on their hair and faces.

'Oil! yelled Merlich. 'They mean tae burn us out. Come on, faster!'

The drops of oil turned to streams, quickly followed by lighted embers that blazed, mixing with the oil as they fell. The upturned boxes and debris strewn across the floor quickly caught fire and within seconds the cavern filled with stifling smoke. Clutching each other, they wove through the fire and smoke behind Merlich, covering their faces as best they could, terrified their oil-soaked clothes would catch light, but the man's sense of direction was good and they quickly reached the south tunnel. They ran down it, coughing violently as the shouts of Crane's men rang through the cavern behind them, but the fire now burned so furiously that the soldiers could not follow. They ran on until they came to a rope ladder hanging from a manhole in the roof. Up they climbed, Merlich draping Ted's great weight around his neck until they all popped out into the cool, clear air.

Struan was waiting for them with a group of some twenty archers, in dark green cloaks, hooded and perfectly camouflaged against the forest. Turpie was last out of the hole and he took Struan's hand gratefully, puffing and groaning as his old body told him what it thought of all of this running and climbing.

Struan's eyes ran over them all, his expression inscrutable as his gaze came to rest on Ruairidh. 'And the Heart of Midlothian?' was all he said.

Morag stepped forward. 'I am the Sacred Heart.'

His eyes lit up and he stepped towards her, placing his right hand over his heart. 'Milady, it is an honour. You have done well,' he said to the others, without looking at Ruairidh.

Ruairidh reached out his hand. 'Brother...' he said, awkwardly.

Struan looked down at his hand for a second but didn't take it. Instead he turned to Merlich and grasped his arm in the traditional way. 'My friend, our army awaits your order to attack. I have chosen this band to help me take Sithbruaich Gate.'

Merlich nodded, watching the interplay between the two princes with interest. 'You have news of Crane's forces there, Sire?'

'Yes, our luck holds. Much of the division was called back to guard the castle last night and only a small force remains. I am confident we can take it. My friend, when Crane realises we have reached Elphame he will amass the armies of Gododdin and make for Scabinory by sea. The day of our victory over Crane is upon us. Take the fight all the way to the castle gates.' He gripped Merlich by the shoulders and locked eyes with him. 'I entrust the welfare of our people to you until my return.'

Merlich bowed with his right fist clenched over his heart. 'I will honour that trust with my life, Sire. You have my word on it. Come,' he said, turning to the druid, 'we must join the army.'

Turpie smiled reassuringly as he hugged each child in turn. 'Remember me to the Queen of Elphame. Good luck my dears, and Godspeed.' His eyes were full of emotion as they came to rest on Struan. 'Struan, lad,' was all he said, nodding once to the boy before disappearing into the forest with Merlich.

Struan signalled to the archers. 'Come,' he said to the others, 'we must move quickly. We can assume from his poor defence o' Sithbruaich Gate that Crane does not yet know the five are met. When he finds out, what little advantage we have will be lost.'

17

TO SITHBRUAICH GATE

The clash and cries of battle rang out in the distance as the children followed Struan and his archers for many kilometres through the forest towards the sea. Struan stopped often, listening to every lull or rise in the sound, anxious to gauge how his army fared.

It was obvious, thought Ruairidh, how much his brother wished he could turn back and join the fight. *His brother!* It was still such a weird idea and one that Struan, he knew, hadn't yet accepted as fact. Indeed, his brother had made a point of avoiding him during their long walk through the woods, eyeing him with suspicion and clearly preferring the company of his men. Even saying his name seemed more than Struan could bring himself to do.

Ruairidh frowned, not understanding why his brother displayed such enmity towards him, but he thought about Struan's passionate commitment to his people and the ease with which he took command, and had to admit that he'd make a great king. He was born to it, but so, it seemed, was Ruairidh. What would the future hold for him if they made it to Scabinory? Would Struan expect him to slip quietly back to where he came from and forget all about his brother and the Selgovae? And what did *he* want now? Was there a place for him here in Alba? What exactly did spare heirs to the throne do?

Ruairidh didn't know the answers to any of these questions. The only thing he knew for sure was that everything in his life had changed. He was no longer an only child, carelessly abandoned by his mother. He had a brother, a brother who would be King of Alba one day.

'What's he saying?'

Ruairidh turned absently to Drew. 'Who?'

'Ted, what's he saying?'

'I don't understand his dog sounds, if that's what you mean,' Ruairidh said, watching Ted snuffle noisily in the bushes. 'I seem to know what they're thinking, but for some reason they only understand me when I speak.'

'They?' Sean asked, falling in beside them.

'Ted, Hammy – all animals I suppose, and birds.'

'So, what's he *thinking* then?' Drew asked.

'He smells pig. Wild boar, I guess.'

'And what about Hammy?'

Ruairidh gently patted his chest pocket. 'She's fast asleep, and before you ask, no, I can't understand animal dreams.'

'Ask Ted something for me.'

'Ted, here boy,' called Ruairidh.

Rossi listened as Ruairidh translated Ted's happy dog thoughts. *Just one more bizarre moment among so many*, she thought. The last couple of days were like some random dream. She stole a glance at Morag who walked a little apart from the others, gazing at the forest around her, as though drinking in every sight, smell and sound. She was perhaps the most bizarre thing of all. *The Sacred Heart of Midlothian*, whatever that was.

As though reading her thoughts, Morag stopped to let her catch up. 'You're curious about me?' she asked.

'You're a faerie, the most important faerie there is, but you look like just an ordinary girl. Of course I'm curious.'

Morag smiled. 'I'd give anything to be just an ordinary human girl.'

'In my time faeries aren't real. They belong in story books and have magical powers.' Rossi looked at her quizzically. 'They can fly.'

Morag laughed. 'Not me! But the ferrishyn are indeed magical – at least to your way of thinking, I imagine. They live long, have wonderful powers of insight and healing and are fleet of foot and hand. But although *of* ferrishyn kind, I'm not *exactly* ferrishyn. I don't belong to any one race. I'm…' she hesitated. 'The ferrishyn queen will explain it better.'

Struan and his men came to a sudden halt at the edge of a sunny glade where seagulls soared in the open sky, their cries mingling with the calls of woodland birds. At the centre of the glade stood a gnarled and mossy hill, blanketed in daisies, blue forget-me-nots, and soft, fluffy dandelion clouds. The scene looked so warm and inviting after the cool, gloomy dankness of the woods that Rossi longed to lie down amongst the flowers and soak up the afternoon sun. She made to push past Struan but he stopped her.

'Stay back,' he whispered, 'it is Sithbruaich, the ferrishyn hill, and it is well guarded.'

'And here I was, thinking faeries lived in grottos,' Sean said, dryly.

The others smiled – all except Struan, who was, not for the first time, unsure whether Sean was serious or not. 'Everyone knows that where the ferrishyn live amongst humans they dwell in hills,' he said, deciding the other boy was probably just dim-witted.

Before Sean could come back at him, two Gododdin guards appeared around the northern end of the hill. Rossi, Drew and Sean froze in horror, seeing the ghoulish creatures clearly for the first time. Struan dropped down, pulling Rossi with him, and the others followed, crouching low with their heads bowed so that their green hoods covered their faces. The guards passed so close to their hiding place that Rossi held her breath, sure they were bound to see so many archers this close to the glade, but hiding in the forest was a way of life for Struan's men and they had simply melted away.

'What were they?' Drew asked once the guards disappeared around the southern end of the hill.

'Gargoyles,' whispered Struan. 'Their tribe numbers the largest of the Gododdin – nasty brutes. Come, stay close and quiet, the gate is on the far side.'

The children and Ted pulled back from the edge of the glade and skirted around the hill behind the trees, treading carefully through the dense undergrowth so as not to make a noise. As Sithbruaich Gate came into view so did the army encampment, where some fifty Gododdin soldiers mulled around the clearing at their ease, some cleaning weapons while others gossiped. Just two cretins stood smartly to attention, guarding either side of the gate itself.

'Good, it's as I hoped,' whispered Struan, surveying the defences.

Rossi stared at the camp, terrified by the large number of hideous, heavily armed creatures standing between them and the elaborately carved wooden gate some thirty metres away. 'This is good? Struan, you said this was the only way to Elphame by *land*, does that mean we can get there by sea?'

Morag's face drained of colour. 'No Struan,' she said, grasping his arm. 'Please, you must know, I cannot cross the Lothian Sea.'

'It's all right, Milady,' he said gently, covering her hand with his, 'not unless there was no other choice would I take you that way.'

'But why not, Morag?' Rossi asked, puzzled by her reaction and feeling sure the sea crossing couldn't be any more dangerous than this.

'Morag is ferrishyn kind,' Struan answered for her. 'Like all her race she fears the Lothian Sea above all else. The crossing is extremely dangerous and would most likely prove fatal for us all. We *must* take the road through Sithbruaich Gate.'

Rossi wanted to argue further, but Struan had already signalled to his men and was heading off again, motioning for the children to follow. He finally came to a stop on the north side of the gate directly opposite his men's position.

'Get ready to run for the gate when my archers draw the soldiers' fire,' he said, drawing his sword.

The others drew their weapons too, Rossi praying she wouldn't have to use hers. Struan pursed his lips and the sweet echoing song of a blackbird mingled with the calls of other woodland birds and from nowhere, or so it seemed to the unsuspecting garrison, a hail of arrows rained down. Chaos erupted in the camp. Some of the

Gododdin fell where they stood while others dived for shelter and returned fire, shooting wildly at the trees, without knowing the exact source of the attack. Struan saw their chance.

'Now,' he whispered.

They left the shelter of the trees, creeping as fast and as low as they could across the clearing, passing unnoticed behind Crane's men. They made good progress and were more than halfway to the gate when a horn sounded in the distance, stopping Struan in his tracks. The horn sounded again, this time accompanied by the unmistakable sound of horses, many horses crashing through the undergrowth towards the clearing. Recognising the sound of reinforcements, the Gododdin cheered loudly, and emboldened, they rallied, drawing swords and charging from their bunkers towards the archers. Struan cursed, knowing his men stood little chance trapped between Crane's foot soldiers and advancing cavalry. The sound of steel on steel replaced the rain of arrows as the archers met the Gododdin hand-to-hand, leaving the children exposed. To Rossi's horror, Struan continued on until forced to stop, when the two cretins guarding the gate ventured out from behind a large wooden shield. Seeing them, Ted snarled and strained hard against Ruairidh's grip, eager to have at them.

'Hey, you!' called out the first guard, immediately spotting them.

His shout drew the attention of some soldiers at the edge of the woods and they turned to see what was going on behind them. Struan hesitated, reluctant to give up on reaching the gate even though the odds of their making it without the archers were no longer good, but Ruairidh had no such difficulty deciding what to do.

'Run!' he yelled, grabbing Morag's hand and racing back with her towards the trees. Ted and his cousins ran after them for all they were worth, leaving Struan no choice but to follow.

The cretins gave chase, but at the edge of the clearing the first stopped, pulling the other back. 'No,' it said, struggling to catch its breath. 'We've tae stay at the gate – *pain o' death* – them's Crane's orders. If that's him coming, he'll kill us for disobeying him.'

The pair resumed their positions just as Crane and Ghob thundered into the clearing, followed closely by a dozen horsemen and three demon hounds dragging a cretinous creature from Ghob's command on the end of a long leather leash. Crane pulled his powerful warhorse to a jerking halt at the gate and it towered over the cretins, stamping impatiently.

'You men!' he bellowed, 'have you seen children?'

'Aye, Sire!' cried the cretin who'd followed Crane's orders to the letter. He pointed to the spot where they'd disappeared into the forest. 'We caught them trying to reach the gate and chased them to the woods, but we returned to our post. Following orders like,' he added proudly.

'You let them go?' Crane thundered. 'Fools! Imbeciles!' With that, he jerked his horse's head violently around and kicked it on into the woods, followed closely by Ghob and six others.

The children and Ted ran through the trees, not daring to look back as hooves thundered behind them and the baying of Ghob's hounds froze their hearts. The forest thinned, then gave way to tall sea grass and sand dunes, which they scrambled across knowing that Crane would be upon them any minute. They scanned the beach desperately and seeing a small fishing boat bobbing in the water a little way along the shore, tore across the dunes towards it. Struan reached it first and leapt through the surf and over the edge, going straight for the sail. Sean, Drew, and Rossi were right behind him. Ted and Ruairidh reached the water's edge just seconds later with Morag, but when Ruairidh tried to pull her into the surf her fear of Crane gave way to her terror of the sea and she drew back, snatching her hand from his. Ted stood up to his chest in the surf, barking madly and Rossi and her brothers screamed Morag's name, reaching over the edge of the boat as Struan laid his sword to the rope.

'Come on Morag!' yelled Ruairidh reaching out to her, as the boat broke free of its mooring, but she stepped further away from him.

'I cannot,' she said, trembling. 'The sea is murderous; we'll die if we set sail on it.'

Crane and his horsemen erupted onto the dunes. Seeing the children, Ghob dropped his arm and the hounds were loosed, overtaking Crane's horse and speeding along the stretch of sand towards Morag and Ruairidh.

'We'll die if we don't,' yelled Ruairidh, lifting her off her feet and throwing her into the bottom of the boat. He pushed it out as hard as he could, and jumped in, dragging Ted over the side.

They drew their swords and braced themselves, knowing the hounds had only to leap over the shallow breakers and they'd be torn to pieces, but to their amazement they pulled up at the water's edge, snarling and pacing furiously along the sand as though held back by a wall of glass.

'Why aren't they coming after us?' Rossi yelled above the crash of the surf.

'They were once ferrishyn kind too,' Struan shouted. 'They won't set foot in the Lothian Sea.'

Crane charged towards the hounds, his expression fierce and his long cloak billowing around him. He pulled hard on the reins and his great black horse reared and then galloped through the shallows after them, but it was too late, the little boat had caught the breeze and was already too far out. The other riders gathered on the beach and began setting arrows to their bows but Crane raised his hand as he galloped back through the surf toward them.

'Hold your fire! You'll injure the girl!'

The creature, Ghob, pulled his horse sharply around to face Crane. 'But we're losing them!' he snarled.

A cruel, self-satisfied smile played on Crane's lips. He stared at the little boat, muttering something lost to all but the breeze. The wind rose from nowhere, blowing clouds over the sun and chilling the riders on the beach and a ripple ran across the water from the foot of Crane's mount, gathering momentum as it rolled towards the boat.

'Relax, my friend,' he said. 'They will never make it to Elphame. The demons of the sea will drown them, and the dark haired girl... Morag,' he said, careful not to identify her to Ghob – perhaps especially to Ghob, 'will be returned to me.' He stilled his horse with a sharp word and a brutal tug on the bit, then drew a crudely made telescope from his saddlebag and fitted it to his eye, content to enjoy the children's demise from the shore.

The children watched Crane and his men grow smaller and smaller as a strong breeze sped the little boat out to sea. The wind turned chilly despite the warmth of the day and Rossi moved closer to Morag. A large wave swelled below them and the boat rocked, forcing Ted to step back from the prow and the others to grasp the sides.

'Where did that come from?' Drew asked, casting his eye over the otherwise calm water.

'I don't know,' Struan said, frowning as he watched the rogue wave race out to sea, but there were no more such waves and it was soon forgotten as the sun came out from behind the clouds again, warming the children's backs and lifting their spirits.

Drew scanned the distant shore. 'Where are we heading Struan?'

He pointed to a spot in open water some way ahead where white horses lapped on the surface of the sea as if washing against a small island. 'There,' he said, adjusting the sail.

'Not far then,' Drew said, relieved. He suffered quite badly from motion sickness and wasn't fond of boats as a rule.

As the little boat made swift progress across the sparkling sea and Crane and his men faded to dots on the shore behind them, Ruairidh relaxed and turned his attention to Morag. Unlike his cousins and his brother, who had taken up positions around the sides of the boat, Morag remained ashen faced on the floor where he'd thrown her, hugging her legs to still the trembling that gripped her whole body despite the warmth of the sun.

'It's okay, Morag,' he said, moving to sit beside her. 'Look, we've left Crane far behind and you're safe and dry in the boat. There's no need to be frightened.'

She looked up at him, her beautiful eyes brimming with tears. She shook her head before burying it against her knees once more.

'It's not Crane or getting wet she's afraid of,' Struan said, resting his hand lightly on the tiller, 'it's the murdhuacha.'

'Mur-hoo-cha?' Ruairidh asked, struggling to copy his brother's pronunciation.

'Sea demons,' Struan said.

The others looked at him blankly, having no idea what he was talking about. He frowned, racking his brain for the term he'd heard Turpie use and tried again. 'Mer-people,' he said.

Rossi's face lit up. 'Mermaids? Seriously? I'd love to see a mermaid.'

Struan's scowl told her she might as well have wanted to pet one of Ghob's hounds. 'Pray we don't,' he said, vehemently. 'The murdhuacha are demons. They'll drown ye and drag yer body to the dark depths, where they'll devour yer flesh and use yer spirit as a candle tae light the kelp forest, where in time it too will wither and die. For the ferrishyn, it is a fate much worse than death. Their spirits, ye see, burn for all eternity.'

Morag whimpered and crossed her hands over her head, burying it even deeper in her lap.

'So we'll be avoiding them, then,' Sean joked weakly, shifting away from the edge and checking out the sea around the boat. 'But how come people fish here if it's so dangerous?' he asked, thinking of the owner of their little vessel.

'It's said the fishermen on these shores are selkies, more seal than human, and that they pay their way with the best of their catch. Even so, if the murdhuacha are dissatisfied, the selkies too can fall victim to the siren's song. Fishing in these waters is a dangerous trade.'

The children sat in silence as the boat sailed on, thinking about what Struan had said. A pod of bottle nosed dolphins surfaced, riding the swell and criss-crossing beneath the prow as though challenging them to a race. Rossi loved dolphins and was used to seeing them in the surf near her home in Australia and despite Struan's warning about the murdhuacha, she couldn't resist peering over the side of the boat to watch them play. The water was crystal clear and strangely bright as if lit from below as well as from above. As she watched, a large, pale, shadowy form glided into view far below the dolphins, sailing through the water as effortlessly as a bird sails through air. It passed out of sight but then another came into view followed by another until several glided gracefully far beneath the boat.

'What are those?' she asked, pulling back from the edge.

Drew leaned over to look. 'What? Jeez,' he said, spotting the giant creatures. 'Struan, are those mermaids? Look, a long way down over there.'

Struan looked over the side. 'No, I don't think so. Turpie says they don't attack in clear water. They keep tae the cover o' the kelp forests.'

'Awesome,' Sean said spotting the creatures. 'Whatever they are their wingspan is enormous. Maybe they're giant manta rays.'

'Not in these waters, it's too cold,' Ruairidh said, crossing over from the other side for a look and causing the boat to dip alarmingly.

'Watch out, we'll overbalance!' Struan yelled.

'Sorry,' Ruairidh said, embarrassed at showing such poor sea-manship in front of his brother. He redistributed his weight to-wards the prow, gaining a sympathetic lick from Ted before the dog cocked his great hairy head over the water next to him.

Ruairidh gasped. 'Yes Ted, I think you're right. Ted thinks they're birds. Look at their heads and wings, not like manta rays, like birds.'

'But that's impossible,' Sean said, craning his neck as far over the side as he dared. 'Sea birds can dive and swim quite well, but they can't glide through water with their wings spread wide open like that.'

'They are birds,' said a small voice from the centre of the boat.

The children turned to Morag, whose haunted eyes were just visible above her knees. 'Giant birds of Elphame, like the sea eagles corrupted by Crane, but they aren't swimming, they're flying in the sky beneath us.'

The children looked over the side of the boat again not at all sure they believed her, but far below where the seabed should have been lay a patchwork of green and gold fields, villages and lochs as easy for Rossi and her brothers to identify as the Scottish landscape had been from the plane they'd travelled on only days before.

Rossi looked around at the others, her eyes shining. 'Absolutely amazing.'

Drew nodded unable to take his eyes off the wondrous scene below. 'Totally! But how can it be, Morag? Why doesn't the water fall in on the land? What's holding it up?'

Morag shrugged. 'What holds the sky up above us now?'

Ruairidh opened his mouth to explain what he knew about it

but thought better of it. Understanding the science didn't really make that phenomenon any less fantastic either. They continued to stare over the edge of the boat completely lost in the scene below the sea, none so captivated as Struan, who had no flight in a plane or movie images to prepare him for such a view. So transfixed were they, they didn't realise the little boat now skirted the edge of a vast kelp forest on its starboard side, nor did they see the dark shadows gliding silently beneath them, until it was too late.

18

THE MURDHUACHA

Grotesque human-like heads burst through the surface of the water near the children's faces, sending them scrambling away from the edge of the boat. Rossi grabbed Morag, screaming while the other girl wailed in terror. Ted went berserk, charging around the boat as more gruesome heads popped up but came no closer; they bobbed in the water, eyeing the unfamiliar barking creature and snorting blasts of wet air from slits in their faces that opened and closed like a seal's. Veins pulsed beneath their pale, translucent skin, feeding a writhing mass of blood-red worms atop their heads, which seemed to taste the air around the children like the tentacles of a sea anemone.

Struan drew his sword. 'Protect Morag!' he yelled and the other boys immediately raised their weapons in a protective circle around the girls.

Rossi wrapped her arms around Morag who rocked silently there, the ability to utter sound now completely lost to her. The murdhuacha's round, shark-like eyes rotated in their heads. They seemed to be monitoring the boat but still they kept their distance, unsure what kind of threat Ted posed. Seeing their advantage, Struan suddenly yelled and beat the wooden hull with the hilt of his long sword. Realising what he was doing, the other boys joined him. The little boat rocked violently and the noise was deafening, but the murdhuacha didn't back away. Instead, they opened their thin pouting lips, revealing multiple rows of small sharp teeth, and let out a scream so piercing that Ted pawed madly at his ears and the others gripped their heads in agony.

When they thought they could bear it no longer, and as suddenly as it had begun, the noise stopped and the creatures sank beneath the waves, lost to their view beneath the dark sweeping kelp forest. The children shook their heads, groaning, for the moment simply relieved that the pain was gone.

'They'll be back,' Struan said, grabbing an oar from where it hung inside the boat and tossing it to Ruairidh before taking another for himself. Sean and Drew stationed themselves on opposite sides of the boat, their swords raised.

'Here, Morag,' Rossi said, drawing the girl's sword and wrapping her fingers around it, 'you've got to protect yourself.'

But Morag was beyond word or reason and the sword slipped uselessly to the floor. Rossi picked it up and knelt protectively behind the other girl, holding a sword in each hand. The silence seemed to stretch on and on as they stared at the water, hardly daring to breathe. Suddenly the surface broke and a murdhuacha, male or female the children couldn't tell, leapt over the boat in an arc, revealing the fullness of its body. The creature was at least two metres long and its torso was indeed human-like, but its skin was more like the flesh of a squid. Along its back a series of lethally sharp barbs splayed open as it arched its spine. Its grey tail was smooth and sleek, making up two thirds of its body length, narrowing to a sharp triangle, again more like the tail of a large shark than the pretty gold fish fans Rossi associated with story-book mermaids. It reached for Morag with razor tipped claws on the end of long webbed fingers. Horrified and mesmerised by the sight, the children froze.

The murdhuacha let out another ear-piercing scream, startling Rossi into action. With a scream of her own she thrust both swords upwards, stabbing the creature in the belly with more strength than she knew she possessed. Shrieking, it drew back its claws, leaving deep gashes on Morag's neck and shoulders and falling with a gigantic crash into the sea. Another leapt from the water and another, arching over Morag, clawing until despite the children's furious attempts to hold her, they ripped her from the boat, disappearing with her beneath the waves.

Pausing only to drop Hammy into Rossi's lap, Ruairidh dived into the sea after her and Sean followed right behind. The two boys turned strongly beneath the water, pushing kelp fronds aside in a desperate bid to locate Morag while on the surface the murdhuacha circled the boat at furious speed, pounding it with their tails. The boat rocked wildly, gaining momentum with every hit. Rossi, Drew and Struan clung to its sides, desperately trying to prolong the inevitable until at last the little boat went over with a sickening thud, throwing them out into the churning sea.

19

TEARS OF REGRET

Ruairidh surfaced, treading water as he scanned the open sea for Morag. Seeing no sign of her, he dived again. Sean came up too, sucking in air, then, spotting his brother and sister in the water, immediately swam towards them.

'Stay with the boat,' he yelled, terrified their only lifeline might sink altogether.

Rossi and Drew were strong swimmers and had no problem reaching the upturned hull, but Struan was nowhere to be seen. Sean dived, cursing the dense seaweed that reduced visibility beneath the water to almost zero. When he came up for a second time he saw Struan break the surface close by, his arms flailing as he fought to get a breath. 'Can't swim,' he gurgled before disappearing beneath the kelp again.

Sean grabbed his shirt, pulling his head above water then dragged him, coughing and spluttering, to the boat where Rossi caught his flailing hand and slapped it firmly against the hull. They clung on for dear life, Hammy perched on the upturned hull and Ted paddling beside them, their teeth chattering as they treaded the freezing water only too aware of what swam beneath them. Cold, slimy kelp fronds slipped across their bodies, tangling with their legs; Rossi kicked them away, hating the feel of them. She looked around and below for signs of the murdhuacha.

'Where are they?'

'I don't know,' Drew said. 'They disappeared when we hit the water. I think they're still scared of Ted.'

'Then let's stay close to him.'

Ruairidh surfaced again some metres away, still unable to find Morag above or below the surface.

'Have you seen her?'

'No, she hasn't come up at all,' Sean called back.

Taking a deep breath, Ruairidh dived again, pushing apart the thick kelp fronds. Cold dread settled in his heart – she was gone, drowned, perhaps already taken to the dark depths. The kelp was so thick there was no way of knowing. He remembered her terror on the beach at the prospect of losing her soul to the murdhuacha for all eternity. She'd preferred to return to Crane rather than meet that fate. He'd forced her onto the boat, and for what? So he and his cousins could return home? How selfish it all seemed now. Hot angry tears mingled with the seawater as the gravity of what he'd done to Morag hit home.

A wave swept past, parting the kelp forest and suddenly he saw her, limp and pale in the grasp of a murdhuacha as it sped not down to the dark depths, but inexplicably up toward the surface. He swam towards them beneath the water but the creature was much faster. It broke the surface and turned on its back, cradling her on its chest like a seal or an otter might cradle food, unaware of Ruairidh's presence in the water. He surfaced beside it and reached out to grab her, but missed. Startled, the creature hissed furiously, spraying him with water from its nostrils. He reached out again but was pulled violently from below. He struggled hard against the murdhuacha's pull, kicking until his feet and legs bled against the barbs on its back and its razor sharp claws. Fighting to reach the surface, he saw Ted's feet in the water above him. The dog dived, biting his clothes and pulling against the murdhuacha with all his might until Ruairidh broke free and sped to the surface beside him, sucking in air. He barely had time to register that there was no sign of the others, and Morag was being towed unmistakably back towards the shore, before the murdhuacha had him again, this time taking him deeper, too deep for Ted to reach him although he dived repeatedly. In that moment Ruairidh knew that all the murdhuacha had to do was keep pulling him under and fatigue and oxygen deprivation would eventually do the rest. It was a game of attrition he could not win.

The fronds parted and he saw Struan struggling against a murdhuacha some metres below him, going deeper by the second. He knew with grim certainty that their time was up. Acting purely on instinct, he called out to the dolphins.

Suddenly dark flashes shot through the water around him. Their voices clamoured in his ears as they repeatedly rammed the murdhuacha and beat them with their tails. The murdhuacha were bigger and stronger but outnumbered three to one, they were soon forced to release their prey. Ruairidh surfaced, sucking in air. His cousins were already there, their chests heaving, but there was no sign of Struan. He filled his lungs and dived again, seeking the spot where he'd seen his brother moments before. Struan was some metres further down, free from the clutches of the murdhuacha but fighting the dolphins, his oxygen starved brain unable to recognise that they were trying to help him.

Ruairidh swam to him, but in his panic, Struan wrapped him in a strangle hold that his brother knew would drown them both. He shot his elbow hard into Struan's stomach, forcing him to release the last of his breath, grabbed his hair and swam strongly upwards. They broke the surface together and Ruairidh towed his gasping, vomiting brother to the upturned boat. To his relief, Rossi had Morag, the dolphins having already towed her back.

The battle between the murdhuacha and the dolphins continued to rage in the water around and below them, but they had no thought for anything but Morag.

'She's not breathing and there's no pulse,' Rossi shouted above the din, 'we have to get her into the boat.'

Sean stared at the upturned vessel, channelling his panic at the thought of losing Morag, and the energy of the battle, towards it.

'Get away from the boat,' yelled Ruairidh, grabbing Hammy as he realised what Sean was about to do.

The little boat flew out of the water like a toy, landing some metres away and the right way up. This time Sean came back to his senses quickly. He swam to the boat and clambered in. Struan was next, then Drew, and together they took Morag from Ruairidh and Rossi.

Struan fell to his knees beside her, pressing his ear to her chest. 'She's dead. It was all for nothing, we've lost her.'

Sean pushed him out of the way. He scraped his long wet hair from his eyes and crossed his hands over Morag's chest then waited for Drew to pinch her nose and breathe short, shallow breaths into her mouth before pumping her chest several times. Struan tried to pull Sean away, incensed that he should assault her dead body so, but Rossi grabbed his arm.

'Wait!' she said.

Morag's chest heaved and she turned, vomiting water and sucking in air with great heaving sobs. Sean rolled her gently on to her side and Ted and Rossi lay down next to her, sharing their warmth as shivers of shock and cold wracked her bloodied body. Struan stared at her, stunned by what he'd just witnessed.

Ruairidh slapped Sean and Drew on the back. 'That was fantastic. Where did you learn to do that?'

Sean grinned. 'At *Surf Life Saving Club*. Not that we paid that much attention. We were only in it for the ice cream. Never thought we'd ever actually have to do it, did we, Drew?'

Drew shook his head, too exhausted to speak. He sat down on the wooden bench to catch his breath and almost jumped ten feet in the air when at least a dozen dolphins popped their grinning heads out of the water beside him.

'Thank you!' called the children, reaching out as the dolphins leapt from the water then raced beneath the boat and out to sea.

Ruairidh scanned the sea around the boat, puzzled. 'They said this is as far as they go, something about a dangerous current. What do they mean, Struan?'

Struan took the tiller and pointed across the prow on the starboard side. 'It's the way down tae Elphame.'

The white horses they'd seen dancing on the water before were very close now and the others realised with mounting horror that it wasn't an island that caused the sea to froth and foam at its surface, but a giant whirlpool.

'Struan!' Ruairidh yelled. 'Quick! Steer the boat away.'

Struan shook his head. 'It's the only way down to Elphame.'

'You'll kill us all, Struan, no!'

But it was too late. The current had them and they spiralled downwards, slowly at first then faster and faster until all sense of time and space was lost and they knew nothing but the thundering in their ears. Merging with the swirling, foaming water, the boat broke and spun into a million pieces until the world stopped.

20

ELPHAME

The sun, hot on the back of Rossi's neck, woke her from a deep, restful sleep and she stretched luxuriously, allowing warm sand to trickle through her fingers. The familiar call of seagulls overhead and the roar of the surf crashing against the shore confirmed that she'd fallen asleep on the beach near her home in Australia.

What an incredible dream she'd had, about dolphins and killer mermaids or some such nonsense. The boys would laugh when she told them.

The sun really was very hot. She was surprised her mother hadn't already reminded her to cover up. Her strawberry blonde hair, blue eyes and fair skin meant she burned very easily and she wasn't usually allowed to lie in the sun without a hat and sun shirt. She really should apply some more sunscreen or maybe move under the beach umbrella. She groped around for her beach bag, reluctant to move from such a comfy spot but her hand fell instead on a familiar but unexpected shape. Her eyes flew open, coming level with the toes of a pair of green boots made of the softest suede and totally out of place on the beach. She raised her eyes, following the boots slowly upwards until they gave way to black calfskin trousers and a sword hanging from a silver belt, ornately decorated with elaborate patterns she vaguely recognised as Celtic in style.

She scrambled quickly backwards, taking in the body and face of a tall, startlingly handsome teenage boy. His bright green eyes were ringed by long dark lashes and his dark, tousled hair fell rakishly over his angular face. He grinned down at her, as though amused by her reaction, revealing perfect teeth that added even more' to his exceptional good looks. Ted appeared over her, wagging his tail and spraying her with sand. He licked her face lavishly before curling towards the stranger with a look of adoration he usually reserved for Ruairidh. The stranger ruffled Ted's ears and laughed, but his eyes remained fixed on Rossi.

Realising he thought she was admiring him, Rossi quickly pulled her gaze away and scanned the beach for the others. They lay close by, unconscious or perhaps just asleep, as she had been. Behind them, some distance offshore, a giant waterspout twisted furiously from the surface of the pale grey sea to the silver sky above. It was the roar of the waterspout she'd heard, not waves breaking on the shore. The events of the morning came rushing back to her. They'd escaped the murdhuacha and made it through that tornado from the sea above. *Amazing!* And there were others on the beach. Four men close by, similarly dressed and also unusually good looking, though older and none quite so handsome as the teenager who stood directly over her. Rossi realised that despite their nearness and their weapons, like Ted, she wasn't at all afraid.

She looked back at the boy. 'Who *are* you?' she asked.

The others stirred, hearing her voice. They sat up one by one and stared around the beach just as disorientated as Rossi had been. Ted immediately ran to Ruairidh, lavishing him with licks and raining sand down on him too, and the sleepy boy groaned.

Struan quickly stood, brushing sand from his hands before crossing the short distance to greet the teenager.

'I am Struan, Prince of Alba,' he said, extending his hand. 'These others are visitors from beyond Scabinory. We are all o' us friends o' the ferrishyn.'

'Welcome to Elphame, Prince Struan,' the stranger said warmly as he grasped Struan's proffered arm strongly below the elbow in the manner Rossi was becoming accustomed to, '…and Prince Ruairidh,' he said, reaching out to him.

Ruairidh stood, brushing the sand from his hair and face as best he could before accepting his hand.

'I am Ernissyen, Crown Prince of Elphame, and these are my kinsmen and esteemed members of the Queen's Council, Lord Affric, Lord Suilvan, Lord An Teallach and Lord Elphin.'

The men bowed graciously and Struan returned the gesture with ease. Ruairidh rather more awkwardly followed suit.

'And who is this goddess of the sun?' Ernissyen asked, his eyes shining with teasing humour as he looked down at Rossi.

Rossi blushed and looked away, unsure what to make of him saying such a thing.

'My cousin, Rossi,' Ruairidh said, noticing only that the ferrishyn prince had accepted him immediately as Struan's brother even if Struan hadn't introduced him as such, 'and these are her brothers Drew and Sean.'

Ernissyen shook hands with each of the boys in turn then bowed chivalrously as he held out his hand to Rossi.

'Beautiful Princess of Alba, if you are ready, I will guide you to my mother, Queen Maeve.'

She hesitated for a moment then accepted it, grinning over his head at her brothers. They grinned back, immediately getting the significance of what Ernissyen had said. If Struan and Ruairidh were royalty then so, it would seem, were they.

Ruairidh whipped around, realising one of their party was missing.

'Where's Morag? Did she make it?'

The others scanned the beach, shocked they hadn't missed her before.

'Be at ease, Prince Ruairidh,' Ernissyen said. 'We found Nyu beside you on the sand weak and terribly injured, but alive. She is already taken to my mother. It is truly a miracle that you have brought her back to us. We had despaired of ever seeing her again.'

'Nyu?' Rossi asked, as Ernissyen helped her to her feet.

'Nyu is the name given to her by the ferrishyn,' he explained, leading her up the beach to where a white, open-topped carriage waited, elegantly painted with scenes from a stag hunt, and drawn by four of the finest pure white horses she had ever seen. 'Come, my mother will explain everything.'

He helped her into the carriage and then held the door for the others before jumping up to the bench behind the horses. The Lords of Elphame mounted white stallions and followed behind like a guard of honour, while Ernissyen moved the horses on with a gentle word in his native tongue. They travelled for some time through lush countryside, past grass-covered hills that they guessed were houses, their arched doors painted in jaunty colours, each window sporting a brightly-painted window box spilling over with summer flowers. Villagers ran out to greet them as they passed, waving and calling their good wishes, and sweet-faced little poppets with rosy cheeks and hair that fell in fat curls danced alongside the carriage, each child and adult more beautiful than the last.

'I've never seen so many gorgeous people,' Rossi said, delighted. 'Does everyone in this place look like they belong on the cover of Vogue?

'I don't know what vog is,' Struan said, then frowned as the others laughed at his mispronunciation, '…but if ye mean are they all beautiful, then the answer is yes. It is a trait o' ferrishyn folk. They are as beautiful as the Gododdin are ugly, like two sides o' the same coin.'

'Are the Gododdin faeries too?' Drew asked, surprised.

'They were once ferrishyn kind, until the witch, Carlin Meg, cast her evil spell on them, corrupting their spirits and turning them into dark and twisted things.'

'*Carlin Meg* is the name of the Witching Stone at Scabinory. Is the witch still there?'

Ernissyen shook his head. 'She retreated deep into the heart of Gododdin, amongst the most grotesque of her creations at the end of the Great War, and has stayed there, powerless, ever since – as far as we know.'

They rounded the brow of a hill overlooking a lush valley. Stretching out below as far as the eye could see was a city of pointed spires, sparkling and dazzling so that it seemed to be made of glass. At its centre, on the banks of a great lake that shimmered beneath the metallic sky like polished silver, stood a magnificent palace whose tall twin towers dominated the city skyline.

'Shyleaoch, City of Light,' Ernissyen said proudly, stopping to allow them time to drink in the view, 'and at her heart, the Grand Palace of Aristaine, the jewel in the crown of Elphame and the most civilised and cultured place in all the world.'

'Her?' Rossi asked, watching, captivated as a flock of giant swans, perhaps those they had seen through the bottom of the sea, rose from the lake and flew off into the distance.

'Shyleaoch is our mother, our heart and our home,' he said, reverently. 'She stands at the centre of all that the ferrishyn hold true and dear.' His emerald eyes turned suddenly dark as he gazed down on the city. 'She must be protected at all costs,' he added, almost to himself.

'She's beautiful,' Rossi said.

Ernissyen smiled and the intensity in his eyes of just a moment before was replaced with good humour. 'That is indeed a compliment coming from you, Princess.'

Rossi blushed again, then frowned, annoyed with herself. She had to stop doing that around him. This time his flirting didn't go unnoticed. Drew and Sean exchanged looks with Ruairidh, who grinned back while Ted dragged his paw over his eyes in mock embarrassment. They all burst out laughing seeing him. Even Struan's lips twitched.

Ernissyen spoke to the horses once more and without the use of reins they moved off down the hill towards Shyleaoch.

City of light indeed, thought Rossi, for the city, down to its cobbled streets, was built of softly gleaming marble and white polished granite that sparkled with a million shards of silver. It bustled with beautiful people, elegant in white cloaks embroidered with silver thread and decorated with glittering crystals. But, as they walked, their cloaks parted, revealing silks and satins in dazzling colours. Even the women's hair sparkled, held in place with fine silver nets sewn with crystals and circled by a silver headpiece.

The streets bustled with carriages, many even more elaborately painted than their own, drawn by pure white horses, while white carriage dogs ran obediently alongside, adding to the picture of elegance and splendour. But despite the beauty of the ferrishyn and their city, the mood amongst the citizens of Shyleaoch seemed sombre as they bowed low to the children.

'They are honouring you,' Ernissyen said, over his shoulder. 'It is customary to return the compliment.'

'They seem so sad,' Sean said, wishing his hair wasn't such a mess as he bowed awkwardly to a group of the prettiest girls he'd ever seen.

'They're grateful because you've brought our light back to us, but terribly afraid, for Nyu is gravely ill and we don't know as yet if she has slipped so far into shadow that she cannot return.'

They arrived at the Palace of Aristaine on the banks of the glittering lake they'd seen from the hilltop. It reminded Rossi of a gothic cathedral, although not made of the grey sandstone so typical in Europe, but of white marble polished until it gleamed. Two massive central doors ornately carved from pale birch wood sat between tall twin towers, delicately filigreed and crusted with stone spikes that sparkled in the silver light like snow-covered branches.

'The Royal Court,' Ernissyen said over his shoulder, as a dozen stunningly dressed mature and distinguished-looking men and women filed from the entrance to greet them, 'and within, Aristaine, my home.'

He bade the horses stop and jumped down, then opened the carriage door and held out his hand to Rossi. The lords and ladies of the court bowed and curtsied as one as she descended and the words 'Welcome Princess and Princes of Alba, welcome,' reverberated around the courtyard. A fanfare of silver horns sounded as they crossed into the colossal hall, its great vaulted ceiling supported by rows of gleaming red granite pillars, and its black and white stained-glass windows depicting the story of Elphame.

Ruairidh and his cousins had seen such magnificent buildings on TV and still the Palace of Aristaine took their breath away, but Struan had never seen anything like it and was almost overwhelmed by the grace and beauty of the place. They reached a hexagonal platform beneath a huge silver dome where the queen sat on an ornate silver throne, her beautiful face graciously aged, her expression strong and regal.

Maeve, Wolf Queen of the Ferrishyn. Here indeed was a warrior queen, acknowledged Struan, hope rising that his people might yet be saved. Ernissyen bowed low before his mother and the others followed suit.

'Welcome all of you,' she said.

Her strong yet gentle voice wrapped comfortingly around Rossi's heart like warm honey and she felt herself relax, as though the responsibility of the world had been lifted from her shoulders.

'You have my people's heartfelt thanks for returning Nyu to us, but you are weary and hungry after your long journey. Come, sit with me, eat and we will talk.'

Struan stepped forward, boldly. 'Your Majesty, my people stand in desperate need of your help. I have come…'

'We've come,' interrupted Ruairidh, heartily sick of Struan's habit of excluding him and the others.

Struan frowned. 'The Selgovae,' he said with authority, 'are in dire need of your assistance. They battle as we speak against Crane and the Gododdin with inferior numbers and weapons. We entreat the ferrishyn to honour the old alliance that has long existed between our two great nations. Your Majesty, you must take your armies and storm the gates of Sithbruaich. For ourselves, we require an armed escort for our onward journey to Scabinory with the Sacred Heart.'

Ernissyen stiffened, and the queen pursed her lips. She rose from her throne, immensely tall and straight, towering over them, and Rossi, her brothers and Ruairidh shifted uncomfortably at the change of atmosphere in the hall.

'You speak passionately of your people's plight and the hazards of your onward journey,' she said, 'but there is, I am afraid, no question of the ferrishyn armies taking the road to Sithbruaich. But come, we will speak of this in time.' Her tone brooked no opposition. 'First you shall sit with us and eat.'

Struan made to argue, but seeing the dark look on Ernissyen's face, Rossi laid her hand on his arm, certain that antagonising their hosts would achieve nothing.

'For the moment, there is nowhere to rush to,' the queen added firmly, leading them to a banquet table laid with the most wonderful array of foods they had ever seen.

'What about Morag, I mean Nyu?' Ruairidh asked. 'How badly wounded is she? She will recover won't she?'

The queen shook her head sadly. 'I wish I could say yes with certainty Prince Ruairidh, but I cannot. Nyu's mortal soul dims by the hour, even as our ferrishyn healers fight to bring her back to us.' Her grey eyes rested on Struan. 'You risked much bringing her here by sea. The murdhuacha are lethal to our kind. We fear them as we fear nothing else. It is they who have forever kept my people from the sea above the sky.'

'We had no choice, Your Majesty,' Ruairidh said earnestly, seeing Struan bristle at the criticism. 'Crane's hounds almost had us. He'd have her now if we hadn't come by sea.'

The queen nodded. 'Then you made the right decision young prince, for she is better dead than in Crane's hands.'

'Dead?' Rossi asked, alarmed. 'She won't die will she?'

'We can't pass back through Scabinory unless she's returned there. Isn't that right, Your Majesty?' Drew added, then immediately felt terrible, realising how selfish he sounded.

The queen gave a slight smile. 'Yes, but let us not dwell on such dark thoughts yet, for Nyu is not dead. Her physical injuries were terrible but they already heal with the arts of our physicians. It is Nyu's fear that now keeps her from returning to us.' Her silver grey eyes rested knowingly on Ruairidh as though she could see into his heart. 'I can see you all value her life as much as we do.'

Struan remained impassive while the others nodded.

The food looked so appetising and they were all so hungry that despite the sobering news about Morag it was all they could do to hold themselves back but, following Ernissyen's lead, they waited until the queen was seated before sitting themselves. The queen offered a prayer of thanks for the safe return of Nyu in a strange and lyrical tongue and raised her goblet. The children raised theirs too and as soon as the queen chose some bread they pulled food onto their plates in a frenzy, while Ted wolfed into a large bowl at Ruairidh's feet.

Whether because they were so hungry or because the food was ferrishyn and cast with some spell, everything they tasted was delicious. The strawberries were the most sweet and strawberry-flavoured they had ever tasted, as was all the fruit on the table, and the meats were succulent and cooked to perfection.

When she'd taken the edge off her thirst and hunger, Rossi felt able to offer some polite conversation. 'Your palace is very beautiful, Your Majesty,' she said, shyly, 'as are your people.'

Queen Maeve laughed, the sound reminding Ruairidh of Morag's singing – like silver bells.

'The ferrishyn love their finery, my dear, and will decorate themselves as well as their surroundings if they have the opportunity.'

'You talk like you aren't one of them,' Drew said, munching on a chicken leg. He stopped, seeing Struan scowl at what he obviously thought was an impertinent comment, and sat back.

The queen laughed, not in the least insulted. 'It is true, Prince Andrew. Even though I am queen here and much loved in my late husband's stead, I will never really be of ferrishyn kind. My father was a ferrishyn prince but my mother was a wolverine –' at his blank look, she laughed again, '– a wolf able to take the bodily form of a woman when she so desired, hence Maeve, meaning *of the wolves*. Ernissyen's father, King Ludd, fell in love with me and brought me from my mother's home in the forest and here I have stayed, guardian of what was a secure and peaceful nation until Nyu was stolen from us.

'It will be so again, mother,' Ernissyen said passionately.

Struan leaned forward, unable to bear the casual table talk any longer. 'Not if you won't fight! Have the ferrishyn, the great warrior race, forgotten how to fight for what is good and just? Does the old alliance between our two nations mean nothing here anymore?'

Ernissyen's emerald eyes locked angrily with Struan's and he leaned towards the other boy. 'Long was there an alliance between the old folk and the new as you have said, and long was it honoured by my people and the Kings of Alba until your father took a bride from beyond Scabinory and that bride provoked the envy of one whose evil and cunning has outdone us all!'

Struan jumped to his feet. 'My father was not responsible for the loss of the Sacred Heart!'

'And neither is my mother, yet she bears its terrible burden just the same,' Ernissyen growled, pushing his chair noisily aside as he stood.

The queen put her jewelled goblet down on the table with

a bang. 'Sit, both of you. Nothing will be gained by fighting amongst ourselves. Ernissyen, what was done in the past is done and Prince Struan, I must tell you, it is by no means certain we can return Nyu to Scabinory, but we will find a way to try nonetheless – together,' she added, looking pointedly from one boy to the other.

'Why is Nyu so important to the ferrishyn?' ventured Rossi. 'What will change here in Elphame when she's returned to Scabinory?'

The queen relaxed a little, appreciating the diversion. 'Nyu, my dear, is *spirit*, the centre of all things, not just living things, but the mountains and the rivers, the sea and the sky.' She looked around at the children's blank faces, realising what she'd said meant little to them. She smiled and the tension in the room lifted. 'In your world, as in ours, there are four elements. You know them I'm sure. They are earth, fire, air and water. Nyu is the fifth element. Imagine, if you will, the four revolving around the fifth in a circle like the planets revolve around the sun. Without Nyu the four spin into chaos as if the sun were taken from the centre of the planetary system, do you see?'

The children nodded, not sure whether her analogy was literal or not.

'You speak of all the kingdoms, Your Majesty,' Ruairidh said, fascinated.

'Three great kingdoms,' she agreed, 'Elphame, the most ancient of the three. Alba, so lately overtaken, and the evil Kingdom of Gododdin ruled by the tyrant Lords Ghob and Ghom who are now in alliance with Crane.'

'We met Ghob at the castle,' Ruairidh said.

The others nodded, remembering only too well.

'Ghob is ever at Crane's side, I am told,' the queen said, 'for the wolves skirt the edges of the forest between Gododdin and Alba and still reach our borders with news of what goes on there. He does Crane's bidding while his brother remains behind, Lord of the Gododdin tribes.' She pursed her lips distastefully, reflecting on what she'd said.

'Long, ago, an alliance between the ferrishyn and the Selgovae was made, driving the Gododdin back behind their own borders in a great war meant to end all wars. At its end, the two great and victorious nations pledged to protect one another and the ferrishyn placed Nyu at Scabinory as a sign of their commitment to defend the alliance with all that they held dear. The Selgovae, on their part, agreed that the dragons could return to Drachen Fels, their ancestral home long before man walked upon the earth. The witch, Carlin Meg, had imprisoned them at Scabinory, where she milked their blood to fuel her powers. The Selgovae fed the dragons and gave them the treasure they crave and in return the dragons protected Alba's western border with Gododdin. Then came Crane, who murdered good King Rannoch and conjured Nyu from the stone at Scabinory, carrying her away in her mortal form.

'Nyu was a stone?' Rossi asked, entranced. 'One of the stones at Scabinory?'

'Yes, a stone of great magic, an anchor to our civilisation, solid and strong, Heart of Midlothian, Nyu, these are her names.'

'But she calls herself Morag? Why's that?'

'It means *great one* in the old tongue, a fitting name, and what

more fitting for the embodiment of *spirit* than a pure and inno-
cent child? Since Nyu was stolen, the ferrishyn have been trapped
in Elphame as sure as if this beloved kingdom were an iron cage.
And as for Scabinory, it is once more absorbed into the lands of
Gododdin, open for all manner of evil creatures to roam its forests
unchallenged.'

Struan frowned. 'Trapped? What do you mean?'

The queen rose. 'Come, I will show you.'

Her long silk skirts rustled on the ground as she turned behind
her throne and beckoned them to follow her through a door into
a park at the edge of the lake. Some forty metres from the palace,
two men hammered a post into the ground, one of hundreds that
stretched out into the distance behind them. The men stopped
work and bowed to the queen.

'New markers again today?' she asked.

'I'm afraid so, Your Majesty,' said the man closest to her, 'every
day now, as if the movement gains speed.'

Nodding gravely, the queen turned to the children. 'We know
little about Crane, where he is from, what makes him the powerful magician that he is, but that man commands the elements as
only the witch Carlin Meg has before him. You see, Prince Struan,'
she said, holding his gaze, 'it is not only the land of men that has
been cast into chaos and misery by the death of your father. This
post marks Elphame's southern border. Now watch.' She took a
step across the boundary and her body began to fade and distort –
like a television signal in bad weather, Ruairidh thought, fleetingly.
Ernissyen reached across, pulling her back, and she took solid
form again, leaning dizzy and disorientated against him.

When Ernissyen spoke, his voice was raw. 'You see Prince Struan, it is not our will to fight that is lacking, but we cannot fight as near ghosts without form or substance, and it is worse still. Every day this chaos creeps closer. Soon our fair city will become but shadow and mist.'

Struan nodded. 'Forgive me, I was wrong to doubt your honour. My father would be greatly shamed by my words.'

Ernissyen inclined his head.

'I entreat one of you to cross the boundary as I did,' the queen said, recovered enough to stand unsupported. 'Let us see if there is indeed hope for the peoples of Alba and Elphame.'

The children hesitated and then, before Ruairidh or Struan could act, Sean strode to the spot beyond the markers where the queen had stood. He closed his eyes tightly, bracing himself for what he imagined would be a horrible sensation, but nothing happened. The queen and Ernissyen gasped in relief.

Sean opened one eye. 'What?'

'It is as we barely dared to hope,' Ernissyen said. 'Humans can still pass out of Elphame.'

'Then there is still a chance for our two nations,' the queen said, her eyes touching on each of them in turn. 'You must indeed take Nyu to Scabinory, and then the ferrishyn armies shall be released. And when the Dragon Lords return to Drachen Fels, the rightful heir will once more sit upon the throne of Alba.'

The queen paced, her mind working fast. 'But the way to Scabinory is perilous. Crane will know by now that the murdhuacha failed and you have doubtless made it through the waterspout to Elphame.'

'Crane is in league with the murdhuacha?' Struan asked.

The queen nodded. 'The sea birds tell of it. Crane made a terrible pact with the murdhuacha when he barred Sithbruaich Gate, trapping some of my people in Alba. He gifted them to the murdhuacha in return for their promise to deliver Nyu to him should she ever venture upon the sea.'

Ruairidh nodded, understanding now why the lone murdhuacha had surfaced with Morag instead of taking her to the dark depths. It was delivering her to Crane.

'So we must take Morag and go,' he said, turning towards the palace.

The queen laughed. 'Not so fast young prince, the moment may come for swift action, but it is not now. The next few hours will tell us what the future holds for Nyu. In the meantime you must rest if you are to be of any use to her.'

They returned to the palace and were met at the door by two servants.

'Your Majesty,' Ruairidh said, realising they were expected to follow the servants away, 'I must see her.'

'Me too,' Rossi said, and the others agreed.

The queen inclined her head. 'Very well, we shall all go to her.'

They followed her back to the great hall and from there through corridor after corridor until they came to a doorway where servants bustled in and out. A tall, distinguished looking man with kindly grey eyes met them in the antechamber.

'Your Majesty,' he said, bowing.

'How fares the Sacred Heart, Doctor?'

'Her decline has slowed, Your Majesty, but there is still no sign that her mortal soul has turned back towards the light.'

The queen nodded sadly. 'Her friends would see her, if they may.'

The doctor bowed again before turning to address the children. 'Our Lady Nyu lies within this chamber. Please when you enter do not try to talk with her. Her mortal soul is transported away by our medicines, far away from the pain and fear of the attack to a place where it can rest and heal and we hope, come back to us.'

The children nodded and he opened the chamber door and led them inside. Rossi drew a deep breath remembering the terrible wounds inflicted upon Morag by the murdhuacha and prepared for the likelihood that with swelling and bruising she may look even worse now than she had in the boat. But as they approached the bed, she was astonished to see that Morag's face and arms, which had suffered the worst of the murdhuacha's attack, were flawless. She lay peacefully on the bed, propped comfortably against large feather pillows, her eyes open and her body completely at ease in a clean white gown. Rossi heard the others breathe in sharply, equally surprised at seeing her apparently so well. The doctor raised a finger to his lips, reminding them to stay silent. After a minute they turned and followed him out the door, which he closed quietly behind them.

'How can she have healed so quickly?' Ruairidh asked, barely waiting for the doctor to turn.

'She looks so perfect,' agreed Drew.

'Healing her physical wounds was easy,' said the doctor. 'Our medicines work quickly on flesh, but the soul...' he shook his head sadly, '...that is a different matter. Nyu was so afraid that her mortal soul retreated to a deep dark place and I fear that it will take one with greater healing powers than I possess to bring her back. All I can do is provide her with a peaceful place to rest.'

"Take care of her, Doctor,' Ruairidh said as they left the sombre chamber.

They parted company with the queen and Ernissyen. The boys were taken to a bathing room with a large pool where they plunged into warm water, languishing in the heat. Rossi was taken to a smaller room where she washed with fragrant soaps in a large wooden tub, but afterwards she sought out the boys for she didn't wish to be alone. They were given sweet hot tea and left to fall into huge feather beds, feeling safe and secure for the first time since leaving the Buckie House.

21

PRISONER OF THE STONES

The distant sound of music and laughter woke Rossi sometime later. The sky outside had turned to starless black and she realised she'd slept the afternoon away. She looked around, seeing her brothers still fast asleep, but Ruairidh, Struan and Ted were already gone.

Seeing her wake, a servant approached. 'The feast in your honour is already underway, Princess,' she said. 'It's time you dressed and went to meet your guests.'

Rossi shook Drew and Sean. 'Come on, sleepy heads. The party's started without us.'

The servants dressed them in fine clothes, Rossi in green velvet and silver satin, perfectly complimenting her hair and skin, while Sean and Drew wore sky blue. Ready, and done admiring themselves and each other, the children followed a servant to the main hall. As soon as they entered, Sean and Drew were swept onto the floor by some young dancers and, left alone, Rossi looked around for her cousins. She saw them dressed just as richly and talking earnestly with the queen. She started across the hall to join them but Ernissyen intercepted her.

'Leave them, please, Princess,' he said. 'Let the heirs of Alba speak with the Queen of Elphame. They have much of import to discuss ahead of your journey.' He smiled, seeing how annoyed she was that he should think her less important to their plans than her cousins. 'You will each have a role to play in the days ahead, and your time to speak with the queen will come, but for now will you do me the honour of partnering me in the next dance? I confess it is a favourite of mine.'

Deciding there was nothing to be gained by arguing about a meeting to which she hadn't been invited, Rossi took his arm and allowed herself to be led onto the dance floor. 'I'm afraid I don't know the steps,' she said, embarrassed. 'I'll probably stand on your toes.'

Ernissyen grinned. 'Then my toes will be honoured indeed,' he replied, sweeping her up.

Rossi needn't have worried, her feet seemed to know the steps though her mind didn't, and the prince held her firmly in his arms, swirling her around the dance floor until she felt she would drop with dizziness and laughter.

'Come,' Queen Maeve said to Ruairidh and Struan on the other side of the ballroom, 'I would speak with you privately, away from this crowd.'

The two boys followed her through tall glass doors to a large balcony.

When she turned to them, her expression was grave. 'I have very bad news for you young princes.'

'What?' Ruairidh said. 'Is it Morag? She's not... ?' he couldn't bring himself to say *dead*.

The queen shook her head. 'Nyu, or that part of her that is mortal is not yet dead, but that end now seems all but inevitable. While you slept, she sank further from the reaches of our physicians. There is now no possibility of her making the journey to Scabinory with you.'

'Then all is lost,' Struan said. 'It has all been for nothing.'

The queen hesitated. 'Not necessarily… Many years ago, *spirit* was given to be cast in stone at Scabinory but with one condition: that she would have the mortal soul and body of a girl and the freedom of the woods in that earthly form if she so desired. And so while *spirit* was cast in stone, Nyu lived amongst the forest birds and beasts. By what means he was able to do it, we do not know, but Crane drew *spirit* from the stone and placed it wholly in Nyu's mortal body. It is possible to part *spirit* from that mortal body once more and to transport it to Scabinory, but to do so requires that we make a very difficult decision.'

'Whatever it is we must do it at once,' Struan said. 'My people's future depends on it.'

'Hold on a minute,' Ruairidh said. 'You want to take *spirit* from Morag's – I mean Nyu's body? But what will that do to her?'

'I'm afraid that as you saw, Nyu is now merely a shell, a vessel if you like, surviving only because *spirit* dwells within her – while *spirit* can exist without Nyu, Nyu can no longer exist without *spirit*,' the queen said, gravely.

Struan shrugged. 'Then *spirit* will survive while Morag's mortal body and soul do not, but ye've already said that Morag's death is inevitable, so the outcome is the same. Besides, what does it really matter if the girl lives, beyond our group being sorry not to see her again?'

'But that's every bit as bad as Crane keeping her locked in a dark dungeon, or the murdhuacha taking her for all eternity to the depths of the sea!' Ruairidh said, furiously. He thought of Morag's longing for the world outside her cell and her love of living things. 'We're no better than they are if we do that to her.'

'There are greater things at stake here than Morag,' snapped Struan. 'The fate o' two nations hangs in the balance. Have ye no care for yer people?'

It was Struan's first acknowledgement that Ruairidh was indeed a Prince of Alba and his brother, but at that moment Ruairidh didn't care.

'There must be another way,' he said, adamantly.

The queen regarded him thoughtfully. 'There is perhaps a way, young prince, but it is by no means certain and will require a great deal of luck and courage.'

Ruairidh didn't hesitate. 'Tell me!'

'There was one, once, whose healing power was even greater than the ferrlshyn's. One who might yet be able to heal Nyu's mortal soul as we cannot. Perhaps then, when *spirit* is once more cast in stone at Scabinory, Nyu may live again.'

'Who is this person and where can I find them?'

'She is known in these parts as Buitseach.'

'Buitseach!' hissed Struan, his face suddenly pale. 'Buitseach is dead!'

Ruairidh looked from one to the other. 'Who or what is Buitseach?'

'A witch, an evil treacherous witch with unnatural powers. Buitseach is tae blame for all o' this,' spat Struan. 'If she were still alive, I for one would kill her if I saw her. She is no more my...'

'Perhaps you should not be so hasty in your judgement, Prince Struan,' interrupted the queen, 'for all we know Buitseach may be as much Crane's victim in all of this as any of us.'

'I don't care who she is or what she's done,' Ruairidh said. 'If she can help Morag I'll find her. Just tell me where.'

'I will place *spirit* and Nyu's mortal soul into two stones while her body remains here with us. The stones must be cast into Scabinory at precisely the same moment if Nyu is to live once more as a girl. You, Prince Struan, will carry the spirit stone directly to Scabinory and cast it into the vent whether your brother succeeds in his quest to save Nyu's mortal soul or not. The queen laid a hand on his shoulder. 'It is all that is needed to save your people and mine. Do not fail us.'

Struan nodded.

'You, Prince Ruairidh, will carry the stone embodying Nyu's mortal soul into Goyle-Na-Garg forest with the others, but there you will take a different road, through the Pass of Gore.'

Struan scowled deeply. 'The Pass o' Gore borders the lands o' the Gododdin; there is nowhere more dangerous in all the forest surrounding Scabinory.'

'Go on, Your Majesty,' Ruairidh said, ignoring him.

'The birds whisper of a voice on the breeze from within the pass, though they dare not fly near. Buitseach was known to sing to the creatures of the forest. Perhaps it is her they hear.'

Struan's expression was nothing short of incredulous. 'And that's all ye've got, whispering birds? This is madness. It will be suicide tae go there.'

'But I'll go anyway,' Ruairidh said, his eyes locking with Struan's.

Struan's scowl turned even darker and Ruairidh braced himself for another attack, but when his brother spoke it wasn't what he expected.

'Ye saved my life in the sea and I owe you a debt o' honour. If you are determined on this course then I will go with ye.'

'No,' Ruairidh said, appreciating how hard it must be for Struan to feel beholden to him in such a way. '*Spirit* must be returned to Scabinory whether I succeed or not and besides, Alba cannot afford to lose her future king.'

'Good,' the queen said, before Struan could argue any more. 'Now that's settled, let us turn our thoughts to the battle that will follow should you both succeed.'

'One more thing, Your Majesty,' Ruairidh said. 'I think it would be best not to tell my cousins about Buitseach – they'll only try to stop me…'

Struan snorted, as though that was a gross understatement.

'…or want to go with me,' Ruairidh said, ignoring him, 'and I won't have them risk themselves any more than is necessary. I must and will do this alone.'

Ted whined at his side.

'Not completely alone then,' he said, scratching the dog's head.

22

FERRISHYN HEARTS

Sometime later, Ernissyen took Rossi's arm again. She smiled, expecting to be escorted onto the dance floor, but instead he guided her through the crowd to his mother before taking his leave.

The queen beckoned Rossi out onto the balcony overlooking the city, where they looked down at the white, twinkling lights of Shyleaoch.

The queen smiled kindly. 'I feel great fear and uncertainty in you, child.'

Rossi nodded, avoiding the queen's eyes, worried she might disgrace herself by crying in front of this magnificent woman.

'I don't want to go to Scabinory,' she admitted. 'I wish I was brave like the others but I'm not. I'm terrified of the Gododdin and I can't imagine going into battle against anyone, let alone them.'

'And yet you would not have your brothers go without you and you would save Morag's life.' She smiled when Rossi looked up at her, surprised.

'I saw it in your eyes at her bedside,' explained the queen, 'and of course, you would never disappoint your cousins.'

Rossi nodded miserably.

'Then you are indeed a hero and the bravest of them all.'

Rossi stared up at her, confused.

The queen smiled. 'The others go for duty or adventure but you, you go for love and so your sacrifice and thus your courage is the greatest.'

'But I feel like I'm always harping on about being careful. I'm always pulling the others back.'

'Do not mistake caution for cowardice, my dear. It is the perfect balance for arrogance and impulsive heroism. Without your temperance the others would be lost, and as to the creatures that dwell in Goyle-Na-Garg forest, there are good ones there still, as well as bad.'

'But how will I know the good from the bad?'

'Why, you will use your good sense, my dear.'

Rossi understood then that her keen sense of danger was more than just skittishness. In the castle she'd known the hounds were coming even before Ted had sensed them, just as she'd known on the beach that Ernissyen and his fellows posed no threat. She looked up at the queen in wonder. The notion that she wasn't just a worry-wart, that her fears might serve some special purpose, felt incredibly empowering. The queen smiled back and a feeling of deep calm and resoluteness about the journey ahead swept over Rossi. Without thinking, she threw her arms around the tall woman's waist.

The queen seemed shocked for a second and then she laughed

and hugged her back. After a few moments, she lifted Rossi's chin.

'Go in strength, my *ferrishyn daughter*,' she said, warmly.

Rossi returned to the dance floor with her head held high.

Ernissyen crossed to meet her. 'You look different,' he said, examining her from head to toe.

'I am different,' Rossi said, 'decidedly different. Ernissyen, your mother called me her *ferrishyn daughter*. What did she mean by that?'

Ernissyen drew a deep breath – he looked surprised and strangely pleased.

'She pronounced you a Warrior Princess of Elphame, Rossi, which means she has great confidence in your strength, your courage and your honour, and...' He hesitated, staring out across the dance floor.

'And what, Ernissyen, what else does it mean?'

For once it was Ernissyen's turn to blush a deep shade of red. '...and she has proclaimed you a suitable match for me,' he said, meeting her eyes.

Rossi looked away, surprised and embarrassed by the faerie prince's admission.

'Let's dance,' he said, taking her hand, and they did until the small hours of the morning.

23

BORN TO GREATNESS

As dawn approached Struan rounded up the others and led them to the palace stables where Ernissyen and the queen's guard waited, mounted and ready to escort them to the city's northern border. Only Ruairidh was missing.

Struan paced the stable impatiently, his frown so like his brother's. 'Where is he? He knows we must make the most of the daylight hours. The creatures of Goyle-Na-Garg are none so dangerous as they are at night.'

'I think I know where he might be,' Rossi said. 'I'll go and check.'

She ran back through the wide gracious corridors of the palace until she came to Morag's room and sure enough, standing by her bedside deep in thought was Ruairidh. Ted was at his side, his head resting soulfully on the covers.

Rossi hesitated, hating to disturb him. 'Ruairidh, it's time to go,' she whispered.

Ruairidh took one last look at Morag's beautiful, peaceful face before turning away. He inclined his head briefly to Rossi as he strode past, his expression firm with resolve for the journey ahead. Rossi couldn't help reflecting on how well her cousin had made the transition from the haughty boy she'd met in the garden at the Buckie House to a Prince of Alba. *Born to greatness*, she thought, remembering something she'd read once.

When they were all gathered in the stable, the queen came before them.

'Do you know the use of weapons?' she asked Ruairidh and his cousins. When they shook their heads her response was firm. 'Then you must be suitably armed with weapons that know their use.' She beckoned Sean forward first, handing him a beautifully engraved silver short sword and a gleaming bow. 'You, young man, already have a knack for getting yourself and others out of trouble. Focus all your intent when you shoot this bow and your aim will be true.'

Next, she invited Drew to step forward, handing him a sword like his brother's and a beautifully balanced spear, smiling at his uncertainty as he took them.

'Andrew, use your gift to think of your target and this spear will find it no matter what obstacle lies in its path.'

It was Rossi's turn next and the queen handed her a harness for her back containing two exquisitely carved, silver-handled swords.

'To you my child I give these twin swords, for you have shown already how well you can wield them in the service of a friend. Mark her warnings well, you others, for her instincts are sure.'

The others were only momentarily surprised at the announcement of Rossi's special ability, remembering the occasions when she'd warned them about danger even before Ted had sensed it.

'Prince Ruairidh, Prince Struan,' she said, inviting them forward together. 'You, young princes, need only weapons that can inspire you to the greatness that is already yours by birth.' She signalled for a servant to approach and lifted the most magnificent long sword from his hands. Its black scabbard was beautifully engraved with Celtic patterns and a dragon coat of arms etched in silver and its handle was a mastery of filigreed steel. 'You recognise this I think, Prince Struan, even though you were so very young when parted from your father.'

Struan's face lit with wonder. 'It bears the royal coat of arms.'

'Indeed, it is the sword of the greatest warrior that the nation of men has ever known, your father King Rannoch.' She handed it not to Struan, but to Ruairidh. 'May it guide you to even greater fortune in battle than it did him.'

Struan's brow creased in a deep scowl and the queen laughed. 'I have not forgotten you,' she said, handing him an equally magnificent bow polished to a high sheen and a quiver of the finest leather, embellished in silver with the same coat of arms as the scabbard.

Struan turned his father's bow over in his hands, feasting his eyes on it. 'But where did ye get these?'

'Water sprites found them near Scabinory on the banks of the River Leven, where we believe your father was killed. They brought them here when they fled the Gododdin, and I have kept them, hoping that one day I would have the pleasure of passing them to his sons, as he would have wished.'

At last, mounted on chestnut mares and draped in dark green cloaks, they were ready to go. Ernissyen took Rossi's hand and placed a pale blue band on her middle finger. When it touched her skin it pulsed as though alive.

'To light your way, Rossi,' he said. 'It will take the hues according to your mood and need and comfort you through the worst of what lies ahead, and…' he hesitated, seeming a little unsure of himself, as any teenage boy might presenting a gift to a girl he admired, 'lest you forget me.'

The ring glowed blue, pink, yellow and green until all the colours of the rainbow seemed contained within it. Just looking at it made Rossi's heart soar.

Ernissyen and the queen's guard escorted them as far as the city boundary. As Struan led them away, Rossi turned to see Ernissyen watching them until he grew small and disappeared from sight.

'I hate this scenery,' Sean said, breaking the gloom they all felt. 'It's so infernally green. Give me a sunburnt country any day.'

'Tell me about this sunburnt land o' yours,' Struan said.

'Well,' Sean said, grinning, 'should I start with the sharks, the crocs or the snakes?'

He chatted on about Australia and the others listened, grateful for the distraction as the open fields of Elphame gave way to the rocky foothills of a great mountain range so high that the tops disappeared through the silver sky. Glad of their mounts, they picked their way up onto the highest slope of the tallest peak, coming at last to a giant cavern that cut deep into the mountainside.

'*Deamhans Beul – The Devil's Mouth*,' Struan said as they stared up at the towering cave entrance where, to Rossi's disgust, hundreds of bats soared. 'Through this mountain is the way back through the sea to the world above, and to Scabinory.'

They paused briefly to rest their mounts before entering the cavern, then climbed through the echoing gloom, coming out at last at dusk on the edge of a great forest.

'Goyle-Na-Garg,' Struan said, his tone grim. 'The border with Gododdin runs through it and there are many enemies within. Go quietly and keep your wits about you.'

Night fell abruptly, the full moon casting Goyle-Na-Garg in an eerie silver light as they followed Struan along a well-worn path, causing them to wonder what manner of creatures trod it regularly enough to maintain it so. They travelled in silence, reluctant to speak above the sound of the horses' hooves lest the noise mask approaching danger, but the forest was deathly still except for the intermittent hooting of an owl and the scurry of rats in the bushes beside the path. Far in the distance a wolf cried long and plaintively at the moon. The sound chilled them, forcing them deeper into their cloaks.

After a while, the path dropped steeply and they descended into dense mist rising at least a metre above the ground.

'The centre of the forest,' Struan said for Ruairidh's benefit. 'The Pass of Gorc is on the other side of this basin.'

The horses slowed as they picked their way through the mist, unable to see where they trod, and the children sat tense and anxious on their backs. Rossi's ring pulsed like a living thing, glowing red for the dread that had gripped her ever since entering the forest. She kept her eyes front, having decided long before that she wasn't going to look anywhere but at her horse's head, but even so, from the corner of her eye she saw a shadow.

'Struan,' she whispered.

He raised his hand, letting her know he'd seen it too. They passed another, skulking in a tree next to the path, and more appeared, staring silently from the branches overhead. The horses whinnied skittishly and shied away and Ted growled uneasily at Ruairidh's side. The children whispered along the line, spotting a shadowy creature crouching on a log, up ahead – brown, squat and misshapen with large hands and feet on the ends of unnaturally long limbs. It regarded them with wide, expressionless eyes before stealing into the trees like an ungainly ape.

'Brownies,' Struan whispered. 'They're not known for attacking humans. I think they might only want tae watch us.'

'Creepy little blighters,' Sean whispered and the others silently agreed, wondering what else less benign than brownies might be watching them.

The brownies were their constant companions, slipping from tree to tree alongside the path as the horses stumbled through the mist, their numbers increasing alarmingly until it seemed that many tens of pairs of eyes observed their progress.

Suddenly the hair on the back of Rossi's neck rose stiffly and a cold dread seeped into her bones. The brownies seemed to sense something too and melted into the trees as quickly as they had come. Ted growled low in the back of his throat.

'What is it?' Ruairidh asked. The dog lifted his nose to the night breeze, sensing, but as yet unable to define the threat.

'Something's coming,' Rossi whispered, sure of it, 'something bad, something wicked. It's tracking us. It's coming closer.'

Ted's growl turned to a snarl as the distant sound of baying hounds reached them on the night wind.

'It's the slaugh,' Struan whispered, urgently, 'their hounds have our scent.'

The children's hearts leapt with fear. The queen had warned them about the slaugh, once close relatives of the ferrishyn but long ago corrupted by Carlin Meg. Hunting humans was their favourite sport, although they'd had to make do with brownies and bears in the years since Crane took Scabinory. Excited voices rose above the baying of the hounds – they knew the scent they'd caught was not brownies.

Struan leapt from his horse. 'Free your mounts. We must leave the path. Let's hope the horses lead them away.'

Sending their horses charging down the path with a sharp slap, the children followed Struan's fleeing shadow running, careless of what lay at their feet beneath the mist, and the screaming pain in their lungs, thinking only of the need to get away. There was no thought of stopping, of being able to go no further – they knew there would be no mercy from the hounds and even less from their masters if they were caught. The baying rose to fever pitch as the first of the hounds streaked down their left hand side, so black against the forest that its blood red eyes and ivory fangs seemed disembodied. The children swerved from its path but it fell alongside them again, snarling at their heels. Another streaked in on their right and another appeared up ahead until completely surrounded they were forced to stop.

'Make a circle!' yelled Struan. 'Sean, climb a tree, we have need o' yer arrows.'

The children did as he said, bracing themselves for the coming attack. The dark hounds gathered around them, snarling and salivating in anticipation, and Ted snarled back, straining against Ruairidh's grip, desperate to have at them.

'Not yet Ted, not yet,' Ruairidh said, his voice steady and strong, giving confidence to Drew and Rossi beside him. Struan fitted an arrow to his bow and held ready, back-to-back with his brother as the demon hounds paced and snarled, snapping viciously at each other in their bloodlust and keeping the little group pinned tight like sheep in a paddock.

'What are they waiting for?' Drew asked, unable to bear the suspense. 'Why don't they attack?'

Struan didn't take his eyes off the pack for a second. 'They await their masters.'

In moments, three lithe figures appeared, running through the forest. The first to reach them threw back his hood and Rossi felt a flicker of hope. He was beautiful like the ferrishyn folk of Elphame, although unlike their ebony hair and honeyed complexions, his hair was pure white, as was his skin, and his eyes shone silver in the moonlight. Perhaps this was someone who could be appealed to. But as his pale eyes met hers she recoiled. Beautiful he was, but his eyes, filled with bloodlust from the thrill of the hunt, were cruel – this was no Ernissyen. He turned excitedly to his fellows and they danced in glee around the edge of the hounds, talking in fast, animated terms as though unable to believe their luck.

'They will take us alive if they can,' spat Struan, 'as sport for their torturous games. Don't let that happen, Sean,' he called, without turning. 'Rather you kill us all and yourself.'

Startled by his words, Sean accidentally let fly an arrow. As the queen had promised, true to his thoughts, the arrow found its target, piercing one of the slaugh through its heart. Sean gasped as it fell and its fellows screamed in fury. The hounds sprang and Ted broke free, roaring into the pack with a ferocity Ruairidh never guessed the gentle pet he loved possessed, bringing one hound down by the throat as another sprang at his back. It never reached him – Drew aimed his spear, impaling the animal in mid air as Sean and Struan fired into the pack, praying they wouldn't hit Ted. A hound flew at Struan, grasping his arm and knocking his bow to the ground. He drew his sword with his free hand, thrusting it at the animal while the others cut and slashed wildly without skill or thought, guided only by their will to survive. Still more came at them, biting and ripping their clothes, seeking to subdue rather than kill. First Drew then Rossi hit the ground, their arms gripped in vice-like jaws, forcing them to release their weapons. Sean fired arrow after arrow, hitting first one hound then another but the slaugh, until then pacing the edge of the action like spectators at a dogfight, sent their own arrows flying, forcing him from the tree and he was soon subdued. Struan went down next, cursing, until only Ruairidh was left standing.

It was all but over when the wolves shot from the darkness like silver bullets firing into the writhing pack of devil hounds. Forced back, the slaugh directed their arrows at the wolves and then, realising they were outnumbered, they turned and ran, leaving the hounds to their fate. Struan and the others regained their feet, as Ruairidh ran towards Ted, slashing at the writhing mass of hounds and wolves until the hounds turned tail, disappearing into the forest after their masters with the wolves on their heels, leaving the children alone. Ruairidh knelt beside Ted, who struggled to get up in a battlefield thick with the bodies of wolf and hound alike.

'Ted, are you all right?' he asked, anxiously checking his many wounds. 'Can you walk?'

The dog's reply came back strong and sure as he found his feet.

'Then this is where we go it alone,' Ruairidh said, turning to Struan. 'The slaugh will be back, so go now. Take the others and run. I'll meet you at Scabinory.'

Rossi and her brothers stared at him in shock.

'What do you mean?' Rossi demanded, relief at their success against the slaugh quickly turning to alarm. Both boys ignored her.

Struan nodded to his brother as he retrieved his weapons. 'Come,' he said, 'yer cousin has chosen a different path and there is no time tae debate it now. He's right, we're too valuable tae the slaugh for them tae give up on us this easily. They'll be back in greater numbers, and soon.'

'No!' screamed Rossi, making to run after Ruairidh as he and Ted turned away.

Struan caught her. 'He would spare you this danger. We must carry on. If luck is on all our sides, we will meet your cousin at Scabinory.'

The howl of baying slaugh hounds sounded in the direction that Ruairidh and Ted had taken. Struan hesitated, staring into the forest after his brother before turning away.

'But we can't just let him go!' screamed Rossi, turning desperately to Sean and Drew as they too picked up their weapons and made to follow Struan.

'I think we have to, Rossi,' Sean said, reaching for her arm. 'I don't understand it either but Struan hasn't led us wrong yet.'

'We've got to trust him, Rossi,' Drew said, sensing the import of what had passed between the brothers, 'and we've got to trust Ruairidh.'

When Rossi turned back, Ruairidh and Ted were already out of sight. Reluctantly, she allowed Sean to pull her away.

24

HAIRY GIANTS

Excruciating pain in his right shoulder brought Ruairidh brutally back to consciousness. Feeling confused and disorientated, he tried to ease the pain by drawing his hands closer, but face down in the dirt, with his arms and legs fully stretched and secured to stakes in the ground, he could barely move. He lay still, letting the pain subside and then, taking a deep breath, he pulled against the ropes until his right shoulder screamed and burned as though a red-hot poker were being held against it, but still the ropes would not budge. Groaning, he flopped helplessly against the ground.

Where on earth was he?

As the pain ebbed, he tried to make sense of what he remembered. He'd made good progress through the pass after separating from the others – Ted was at his side.

Ted! He vividly remembered the dog falling with a slaugh arrow in his neck, then excruciating pain when an arrow pierced his own shoulder, the hounds' attack and then nothing. A tear ran down his cheek at the possibility that his friend was dead.

The little stone in his trouser pocket pressed against his hip-bone as though seeking to remind him of Morag, fading as every minute passed and he sniffed hard, gathering himself. This was no time to wallow in self-pity. He had to think!

He froze, hearing movement and voices close by. He raised his head, trying to locate the sound, and his right shoulder burned like nothing he'd ever felt before. He was hot all over, feverish from the wound despite the damp earth beneath him and the cool night air. He lifted his head higher, attempting to look at his shoulder. The arrow was gone, removed by someone or something, but a river of blood oozed from the wound, slick in the moonlight. There was nothing else to see on that side but dark woods at the edge of a small clearing. He eased his head slowly around the other way, the effort taking all his remaining strength. The others didn't appear to be here, wherever here was, at least not as far as he could see. The thought gave him comfort as his head hit the ground with a painful thud.

In his limited line of vision he saw a large, round hut made from rough-hewn stones and sheltered in the lee of a cliff. Smoke curled from a crude opening in the black thatched roof and the smell of roasting meat hung heavy in the air around it. From the corner of his eye he caught sight of something fluttering in the trees near the hut. *Skins,* he thought, horrified. Slaugh or human, he wasn't sure. The queen's warning that the slaugh did unspeakable things to their captives came immediately to him.

Did the slaugh have him? He shuddered at the thought. What hope for Morag now?

When saving Morag and the Selgovae had become more important to him than returning safely home he didn't know, but it had. In truth, for some time now it was all he cared about.

The voices inside the hut grew louder and he listened carefully, trying to make sense of the unfamiliar dialect. A heavy pelt draped across the door swung to one side and two of the strangest creatures he had ever seen emerged, turning sideways and ducking low through the doorway to accommodate their huge height and bulk.

Although one was perhaps a little bigger than the other, to Ruairidh's eye they were identical in every other way. Both had big queerly shaped heads sitting squat on their broad shoulders and long, black, thickly matted hair that merged with their bushy beards and eyebrows on their fat faces. Both had thick bristles sprouting from their nostrils, so that only the purple-veined skin on their bulbous noses and their dark beady eyes were discernible amongst the hair. Their massive arms protruded from sleeveless vests made of animal skin that hung over high-waisted kilts, so dirty that if tartan was present, the pattern was no longer discernible, and beside their boar head sporrans hung huge wooden clubs.

'The slaughses nearly had it, Bochel,' one said to the other in a deep, gravelly voice.

'But what fer did the slaughses not set their nasty hounds at its throat, Boggin?' replied the other, its voice duller than the first. 'What fer, Boggin, what fer?'

Boggin sighed at the other's stupidity. 'Cause they wants it fer they's nasty business, that's what fer, Bochel. They likes it alive when they hurts it.'

'We wants it too, Boggin,' Bochel said, eagerly. 'We wants tae skin it, an' eat it, an' hang its skinses in the trees. Hooman skinses is pretty, Boggin. We've not had hooman skinses for the longest time. Not since the slaughses came tae the woods and Ma went tae Gododdin on her holidays have we had hooman skinses, Boggin.'

'Aye,' came Boggin's growled reply, 'that's why I got it away from the slaughses fer ye Bochel.'

'Slaughses yuk! Tastes nasty, Boggin.' Bochel spat emphatically on the ground as if he could taste the yucky slaughses.

His brother nodded. 'Aye they do, very nasty. There's nothing good for eating in the woods anymore. No more spriteses in the Puddocky Well.'

'Spriteses is tasty,' Bochel said, wistfully.

'No more wee folkses o' the moonbeams, they's all gone to the ferrishyn now, Bochel.'

'Och, they's got good eating then, they ferrishyn.'

'A don't think they eats any o' them Bochel.'

'Not even the juicy ones?'

Boggin spat on the ground in disgust. 'Nut. No even thon fat wee elveses.'

'What a waste o' good wee folkses,' Bochel said, dismayed. 'Ma hates waste, don't she Boggin?'

'Aye, she does Bochel. She never wasted a scrap o' anybody!'

The creatures reached Ruairidh and squatted down on their huge haunches for a closer look. Boggin poked him painfully in the ribs with a big, fat, hairy finger.

'No much meat on it,' he grumbled. 'Just a tasty bite that's all.'

'It's looking at me Boggin,' Bochel said, shuffling away as though Ruairidh was an especially creepy little spider. 'A don't like they hooman eyeses looking at me. They's eyeses is far too daiglin hogney like for me. Let's pluck em out, Boggin.'

'Ach away with ye, hoomans is not like daiglin hogneys at all. They's cunning wee besoms, always thinkin'.'

'Thinkin's not for daiglin hogneys,' Bochel said, shaking his head sagely. 'Thinking does daiglin hogneys no good at all. That's what Ma says.'

'Humph,' came the considered reply. 'Any-ways, if I cuts its eyeses out it'll bleat all night and we'z'll never gets our sleep.'

'I needs my sleep,' Bochel said, alarmed. 'I gets the grumbles if I don't gets my sleep.' He reached eagerly for his great club. 'I could just kill it now then, Boggin.'

Ruairidh squeezed his eyes tight closed and held his breath, waiting for the blow, but Boggin shook his head.

'I gots it for yer birthday treat, Bochel. I don't want tae kill it yet.'

'But my birthday's not till the day after the morrow,' whined Bochel. 'Why don't we kill this one and keep the other fresh for my birthday. Its skinses is pretty too, Boggin, all curly and golden-like, once a cleans the blood off o' it, that is.'

Ruairidh's heart leapt. They had Ted somewhere here, and alive!

Boggin shook his head again. 'The other one has sharp toothies. If we keeps it fresh with Buitseach's magic it'll bite us, and we don't want that.'

Buitseach! They had Buitseach here too? The little stone in Ruairidh's pocket pressed more acutely against his flesh as if in understanding.

'How about we fix this one, then eat the other for our breakfast the morrow?' Boggin said and he stood, kicking Ruairidh's leg for good measure.

Ruairidh let out a moan as pain ricocheted from his thigh to his shoulder. The pair argued amongst themselves for a little longer about what to eat first but Boggin eventually got his way and Bochel disappeared, returning in less than a minute with a bucket. Freezing cold water cascaded over Ruairidh and he jerked involuntarily against the ropes, adding horribly to the throbbing pain in his shoulder.

'No all o' its,' growled Boggin, snatching the bucket from his brother in disgust. 'Ye'll make it frisky if you use all o' its. Remember what happened with thon slaugh yon time?'

Ruairidh fell back against the earth shivering, and Bochel leaned in for a better look.

'Hasn't done nothin,' he said.

'Give it time,' growled his brother.

A moment passed and the pain in Ruairidh's limbs began to ease. His shoulder stopped throbbing and the dog bites on his arms and legs soothed into nothing until even the shivering abated and he felt amazingly fit and rested.

'See,' Boggin said.

'Humph,' was Bochel's reply. 'What about thon curly wolf?' he asked, eagerly. 'Can I finish him off? Can I skins him now Boggin? Can I?'

Ruairidh held his breath waiting for Boggin's reply.

'Aye Bochel,' he said, indulgently. 'Ye can have him, but I tell you what. Our dinner smells nearly ready tae me. Let's hang him up tae bleed while we eats, then skinning him will be less messy like.'

That settled, the two creatures waddled out of Ruairidh's view.

Moments later he heard puffing as though they lifted something heavy.

'I'll hold it Bochel, and you tie it up,' Boggin rasped. More grunting followed before the two thudded off to the hut to eat their dinner.

Ruairidh's mind raced. He had to get himself free before they came back for Ted, but no matter how much he twisted and pulled at the ropes the stakes held firm. He fell back, exhausted. Something tickled at his wrists and he looked up to see Hammy investigating the ropes. She stared back with her bright intelligent little eyes.

'Oh, Hammy, you survived the attack, am I glad to see you! Can you chew it, Hammy?'

Ruairidh lay still trying to be patient while she gnawed the rope as best she could.

'It's no use, Hammy,' he said at last. 'You'll never get through it in time.' He suddenly remembered the small pocket-knife, the one he'd been given in prison by old Critch.

'Hammy, inside my boot there should be a little knife. God, I hope it's still there.'

The little hamster ran down his leg and disappeared inside his boot, re-appearing in seconds with the small folded knife poking comically from her pouches in the same way she might carry a carrot stick at home. The knife wobbled precariously as she made her way up Ruairidh's legs to his hands. Straining to raise and twist his head enough to see what he was doing, he carefully pulled the little pocket-knife from Hammy's pouch and prised it open with his thumbnail. Willing himself not to drop it, he sawed awkwardly at the rope between his hands. Seconds later his hands were free and he bent to release his feet. Then, popping Hammy into his tunic pocket, he leapt up, mindless of the lack of circulation in his limbs, and turned to where the daiglin hogneys had been busy before. He saw Ted hanging upside down from a tree just a few metres away, dripping blood, and he ran to him, taking his full weight on his shoulders before cutting the rope. Lowering his friend gently to the ground, he bent to examine him, shocked at the extent of his injuries. The slaugh hounds had taken their toll before the daiglin hogneys interceded, ripping at Ted's throat and tearing his front legs to shreds. Ruairidh whispered words of comfort but Ted was far beyond hearing.

Loud burping and slurping noises sounded from the hut and he knew they had very little time left. He fetched the bucket the daiglin hogneys had used before and poured every last drop of water left in it over Ted, desperately hoping it would be enough. For a few seconds nothing happened, then before his very eyes the wounds foamed and healed, the matted blood on Ted's woolly coat dissolved away, and he raised his gorgeous golden head and licked Ruairidh full on the face. Ruairidh hugged him back. Hearing the daiglin hogneys slurping noisily inside the hut, Ted growled against his cheek.

'Come boy,' Ruairidh whispered, 'we need them to think we've gone.'

He scraped the ground from the tree to the edge of the forest with the side of his boot, dropping rope remnants along the way, then drew his hood over his head and tiptoed between the hut and the cliff face to wait.

It wasn't long before the daiglin hogney's came waddling out to do their skinning. Seeing Ted and Ruairidh gone, Bochel cried out in dismay.

'They's gone Boggin! Me birthday dinner, they's gone!'

Boggin examined the spot where Ruairidh had cut Ted down and the boy held his breath, willing the giant to follow his crude trail. 'They's gone this way. Look here, the hooman pulled the wolf in tae the woods. It's heavy Bochel, they won't have got far.' With that, the daiglin hogneys plodded into the forest, their huge bodies crashing through the branches as they went.

Ruairidh relaxed his hold around Ted's neck, breathing easy at last. 'Come on Ted, they have Buitseach here somewhere.'

As he stood, a hand fell on his shoulder and he almost yelled in fright. He tried to pull away but the hand grasped his clothing in a tight fist. He saw immediately that it didn't belong to a daiglin hogney. It was filthy, its fingernails long like ragged talons, but it was unmistakably the hand of a woman – a woman who had grabbed him from a hole in the wall of rock behind him no larger than an apple.

He twisted hard, breaking free. The hand snaked back inside the hole and was replaced by a wide manic eye. There had once been a cave in the cliff he realised, examining the wall in horror, but someone had bricked it up, all but for this tiny hole. And they'd bricked it up with a woman inside. His skin crawled at the thought.

'Who are you?' he demanded.

'Help me,' begged a voice from within. 'You have come to help me, haven't you?'

The crazed, unblinking eye and hysterical voice unnerved Ruairidh. 'I'm looking for *Buitseach*, the *Witch Buitseach*,' he said, uncertainly.

'If I am she, will you help me? I have been in here for so long. I sing to the birds in the hope that they will bring someone to help me. The daiglin hogneys caught me in the woods, you see, long ago. They would have killed me but one had a wound on its foot that would not heal and I made it better, so they kept me walled in here in the cold, cold darkness. So long I've been here, so often I've wished that I were dead. Everyone I loved is dead, my husband, my sons. Please help me.'

Pity for the poor, wretched creature washed over Ruairidh. 'I will help you, but first you must do something for me.'

'You must hurry,' Buitseach said, seeming not to have heard him. 'The daiglin hogneys are stupid and they have no patience. They will give up their search soon enough.'

Ruairidh took a piece of cloth from his pocket and carefully unwrapped the little amethyst stone.

The eye pressed closer to the hole and peered at it greedily. 'What is that? What is that shiny stone?'

'It is the mortal soul of one dear to me and important to many others. She is dying.' He looked at the stone and the light within was so faint that he couldn't be sure if it shone at all. 'She may already be dead.'

When Buitseach replied her voice was raw with sorrow and regret. 'I have great powers of healing, but I cannot help the dead. If I could, I would not be here now and a good king would sit on the throne of Alba still.'

'Who *are* you?' Ruairidh demanded, his heart racing.

'They call me Buitseach. It means witch, you know? It is no name at all, like calling you boy. Once I was loved by a nation. I was queen and a healer, not a witch. I was loved by a wonderful man and by two sons but I longed to go home to see my father and brother just for a little while. My husband wanted to please me. He agreed that I could take just one of my boys. They were heirs to the throne, you see. The risk, I thought, was small, but a king in those times wouldn't chance both his heirs and besides I could only carry one. I'd take the other the next time I visited, turn about, do you see?'

The eye stared at Ruairidh, willing him to understand. 'We went to Scabinory in secret because my husband's subjects didn't know I wasn't from their world. They're superstitious and wouldn't have approved his marrying me if they'd known. One trusted by my husband… and by me,' she added bitterly, 'accompanied us with his personal guard. He betrayed us. On the banks of the river he set a dagger in my husband's back.' Her voice faltered. 'My husband was a great warrior, but even the great can be betrayed. When I reached him there wasn't a drop of life's essence left in him. There was nothing I could do. I had no time to weep. I saw in the fiend's eyes that he wanted me and would kill my baby. I jumped into the river and it swept us far down stream. We hid behind thick rushes for many hours.' She paused, remembering how she'd crouched in the water with her child, frozen and terrified. 'When his men stopped searching, I ran beneath the Witching Stone, all the way to my father's house. There was no time to explain, I just left my baby there. I had to save my other son, do you see? I knew

Crane would kill him as soon as he returned to Alba. But when I came through the Witching Stone the fates brought me back to Scabinory. Still, I almost made it through Goyle-Na-Garg, past the slaugh and the hounds and the other beasts. I was close to El-phame when the daiglin hogneys caught me in their stupid snare and brought me here.'

She paused sadly, a tear sliding from her eye. 'My husband and the son I left behind in Alba are both dead, my other son must surely think I abandoned him without love, without care.'

Ruairidh bent so that his face was level with the hole. He pushed back his hood, allowing the moonlight to touch upon his white-streaked hair. His voice caught in his throat as he spoke. 'Mum, it's Ruairidh.'

The woman gave a great wailing sob. 'Ruairidh? Is it really you? I can't believe it. What about your brother, what about Struan?'

'Fine, when I saw him a few hours ago.'

She wept with joy. 'It's a miracle! I didn't dare hope that he was still alive, let alone here with you, but where is he?'

'He's gone to Scabinory with our cousins.'

'Your *cousins*? My little brother has children and they're here too?'

'All the way from Australia,' he said and laughed at the absurdity of that statement.

His mother laughed with him and the sound, one he'd never expected to hear, warmed his heart like nothing ever had.

'Mum, we must hurry. Struan is waiting for me to bring my part of the Sacred Heart to him. Crane stole her after he murdered my father.'

'The Heart of Midlothian? That stone is the Heart of Midlothian?'

Ruairidh nodded.

'Give it to me.'

He placed the stone carefully in the palm of her hand and she
closed her filthy fingers around it. Almost immediately her hand
began to glow, until stronger and stronger beams of white and
amethyst light shot through her fingers. When she opened her
hand again the little precious stone sparkled and glowed with life.

'You've done it,' Ruairidh gasped, taking the stone from her.

A rumble of voices came from the forest behind them accompanied by the crunch of branches smashing under foot. The daiglin
hogneys had lost interest in the search and were returning to camp.

'I've got to get you out of here Mum!'

Ruairidh hit his shoulder against the cave wall then kicked it
repeatedly while Ted scraped madly at the mortar with his claws. It
flaked in places but would not give. He looked frantically around
for a stick heavy enough to make some impression, thinking with
regret about the large clubs the daiglin hogneys carried. Finding
a branch, he hit the wall with all his might. A shout rang out in
the forest as the daiglin hogneys heard the noise and crashed towards the camp, but Ruairidh paid no heed to the sound or to his
mother's pleas for him to forget about her and run. He smashed
the branch repeatedly against the wall until she reached through
the hole, catching his face firmly in her hand.

'Stop sweetheart, please. You have to go now, while you still can.'

'I won't leave you here. Not when I've just found you.'

'Darling, you must. I'll be here still when you've returned the

Sacred Heart to Scabinory. The daiglin hogneys won't hurt me. They value me far too much. I was a gift from their Ma.'

The daiglin hogneys were almost at the clearing. Ted stalked towards the sound, growling loudly. Reluctantly, Ruairidh called him.

'Here darling, take this with you,' said his mother, passing a leather bag through the hole. 'There's a flask inside. It contains my healing water.'

He placed the amethyst inside the little bag and hung it round his neck, then lifted Hammy from his jerkin pocket and handed her to his mother, covering both the little hamster and her hand with his.

'Keep her safe until I come back. And I will come back for you, Mum, don't ever doubt it. I *will* come back for you!' Then, pausing only to retrieve his father's sword from where the giants had left it leaning against the hut, he ran into the forest with Ted.

The daiglin hogneys gave chase but their big feet and heavy bodies weren't made for running. They much preferred setting traps to the effort of a hunt and, puffing and groaning with the effort, they soon gave up. When at last the forest fell completely silent, Ruairidh sat down on a log to catch his breath. Ted circled, sniffing for clues to their direction before coming to rest beside him.

'Yes, I know, we're lost, boy.'

Ted whined and Ruairidh scratched his head. 'No, it's not your fault. The forest is so thick and dark – I can't even see the stars in this wretchedly cloudy sky.'

In the distance a wolf howled, rending the silence, and another answered until their plaintive calls eerily filled the night air.

Ruairidh jumped to his feet. 'Wolves, Ted, they helped us before. Can you call them, boy?'

Ted stood stock still, pointing in the direction of the sound, his whole body trembling as he sniffed the air. He whined and licked Ruairidh's hand.

'You're right. We don't really know if the wolves meant to rescue us from the slaugh or were just attacking a common enemy, and we might bring the hounds down on us again, but we've got to try. We've got nothing else. Go on boy, I have a good feeling about this.'

Ted lifted his head skywards and let out a haunting howl. The night air came alive with answering calls and soon, silver, black and white flashes streaked from the forest coming to stand around them. Ted stood in front of Ruairidh, his hackles raised and teeth bared, making himself seem as big and intimidating as possible. A wolf pushed through the pack, larger and more magnificent than the others, coming to stand before Ted. He stood as tall as the dog but wider in the chest and more muscular. His long, black, silver-tipped coat was in top condition and across his huge head was a striking white mask that emphasised eyes as pale as the moonlight.

'I am Wolftrax, Lord of all wolves,' he growled. 'I have answered your call, brother wolf, at the bidding of Maeve, now ferrishyn queen, once Lady of the Wolves, and, my sister. Ted lowered his head and Ruairidh joined him, sinking to his knees before the magnificent Lord of the Wolves.

'You need safe passage to Scabinory,' Wolftrax said, before Ruairidh gathered himself to speak. 'Come, Prince of Alba, I will take you.' And with that the wolf turned, running in to the forest, leaving no time for hesitation on Ruairidh's part. He and Ted fell in with the pack, racing after Wolftrax, dodging trees and leaping over fallen branches. Time lost all meaning as he ran, aware only of the scent of wolves on the night air, the wind in his hair and the sound of his heart pounding in his chest. He felt stronger than he'd ever felt before and his breathing came steady and deep as he bounded on, matching the wolves stride for stride.

As though he were one with the pack, and then he knew that he was. His body had changed, taking on their wolfish energy and form. He felt wild and exhilarated as he ran with them, covering ground quickly, strong and vibrant and free.

25

BROTHERS IN ARMS

Struan led the others on through Goyle-Na-Garg, running until Rossi could go no further. She stopped, leaning against a tree to catch her breath.

'I don't understand, Struan,' she gasped. 'How could you just let him go? You heard the slaugh hounds. They're bound to pick up his scent. He and Ted don't stand a chance alone.'

Struan stood nearby, resting his hands on his knees and breathing deeply. He didn't answer.

Furious, she grabbed his arm, forcing him to face her. 'For God's sake Struan, he's your brother!'

Struan's eyes flashed angrily. 'He is first and foremost a prince o' Alba, as am I, and he at least understands duty and honour if you do not.'

'Then explain it to me.'

'The stone I carry is *spirit*, as you know, but the ferrishyn queen made a second stone. It is *spirit's* chance tae live life, as the girl Morag, if it pleases her. He wanted tae give her that chance and so he has gone on a fool's errand tae find the witch Buitseach, for if she lives, she is the only one who can bring Morag back.'

'Then we should have gone with him. We should have stuck together.'

'I offered tae go with him,' Struan said angrily, 'but he said Alba couldn't afford for all o' us tae get caught by the slaugh. He understood this and so should you, and if what you're really angry about is that he didn't include you in his plans, then don't take it out on me!'

Rossi began to protest again then stopped, realising Struan wasn't any happier with Ruairidh's decision than she was. Suddenly she understood that although Ruairidh and Struan had not yet fully accepted each other as brothers, they were now brothers in arms. She wondered when the change in Ruairidh had come about. When he'd become not one of four ordinary children from a different time, but a prince of Alba, son of a great warrior and brother of a future king.

'He told us to go, Rossco,' Drew said, putting his arm around her. 'He's got Ted with him; he'll be all right.' In truth he felt anything but confident about it.

Rossi remembered the look on Ruairidh's face when he went. He'd told them to go because he didn't want them to face the risks he'd chosen for himself. Tears ran down her cheeks and she reached for Sean and Drew.

Struan softened. 'The best thing we can do for yer cousin now is get tae Scabinory, and that will be no easy task. It lies close tae Gododdin and will be heavily defended, but if luck is on our side, we may yet meet yer cousin there.'

'And if we don't?'

Struan's expression turned dark once more. 'Then we shall pray for him and for Morag as we cast her sacred spirit into the volcano where it will forever remain, entombed in stone.'

'Volcano?' Drew asked, 'What volcano? Nobody said anything about a volcano!'

Struan frowned. 'I thought ye said ye'd been tae Scabinory before.'

'Scabinory is a pond on a hill in the middle of a field. It's not a volcano!'

'Yer mistaken. It's the side vent o' a volcano, although it will appear small compared to its big brother.'

Rossi nodded, thinking about it. 'Remember Largo Law? Grandad said it used to be part of a range of volcanoes and that Scabinory was an old volcanic vent. He said the pond up there was bottomless.'

Sean and Drew nodded, remembering the conversation they'd had with their grandfather in the car. It seemed like a lifetime ago.

'And how in the world are we going to get into an active volcanic vent?' Drew asked.

Sean slapped him on the back. 'Well, that's what I thought we had you for, Mr x-ray vision. If there's a path in, you'll have to find it.'

'It's not x-ray vision,' Drew said, irritated, 'it's some sort of virtual tele-transportation and I can't switch it on and off like a TV set.'

'Ooh, virtual tele-transportation is it?' Sean teased, laughing.

'Come on,' Struan said, 'we still have hours o' walking ahead of us. We can't sit here waiting for the slaugh hounds tae find us –

that won't do yer cousin any good at all.'

The children walked on in silence, acutely aware of the forest
sounds, but even the brownies seemed to have lost interest in
them as they journeyed in darkness through the rest of Goyle-
Na-Garg. At last the woods thinned and they came out, to their
surprise, on the dunes of a small sandy bay just as the first signs
of dawn touched on the horizon. Mist lay thick upon the sea,
limiting their vision in that direction to a hundred metres or less,
and above them a short cliff obscured their view of whatever lay
beyond.

'Where are we now?' Drew asked, bending to wash his hands
at the water's edge.

Struan stepped up on a spur of red sandstone worn into smooth,
undulating waves by the tide and looked down to the end of
the beach. The treetops there hung thickly with mist, and high
above in the distance rose a large, smoking volcano. '*Beinn Theine
Ainteas – Mountain of Fire,*' he said, pointing.

'Largo Law!' gasped Rossi.

Drew stared up at the massive volcano. 'But Largo Law isn't
anything like as big as that.'

'It's eroded with time,' Rossi explained. 'Largo Law is really just
the plug of volcanic rock at the core of the original volcano with
grass grown over it. It would have been much, much bigger at one
time – like this.'

A distant rumble sounded far beneath the ground, growing
steadily louder until the earth shook, forcing the children down.
The great volcano growled almost like a living thing, belching great
billowing clouds of smoke from its mist-shrouded peak.

'Jeez, does it do that often?' Sean asked, relieved beyond words when the shaking stopped.

'And much worse,' Struan said, ominously. 'We have felt it shake and seen its smoke rise from across the sea.'

Goose bumps suddenly rippled across Rossi's skin as she stared out across the misty water. 'Back behind the trees, everyone, hurry!

The others followed her without question, dropping to their stomachs at the edge of the forest.

'What Rossi, what do you see?' Sean asked.

She frowned. 'Nothing yet, it's just a feeling.'

They stared silently out over the water for several minutes until at last Rossi pointed through the mist. 'There!'

'I can't see anything,' Sean said.

'Keep looking.'

Moments more passed before the mist shifted, revealing a flotilla of some twenty ships heading for a neighbouring bay.

Struan released the breath he held with a sharp hiss. 'Crane's ships – reinforcements from Alba. He's expecting us. Come on, we'll have a better view from the cliff.'

They climbed the cliff separating the beach from the neighbouring cove, using the scrub as cover. When they reached the top, the sight that met them made their blood run cold. In the valley below, stretching from the beach to Scabinory, was a vast army. They watched as the ships beached and hundreds of soldiers flowed ashore.

Struan clenched his fists, seeing many men among them. 'Slave soldiers of Alba,' he spat. 'Some press-ganged from the villages, others no doubt rebels, taken in battle. Let us hope Merlich and Turpie are not among them.'

Sean surveyed the barren land laid waste by volcanic ash that lay between the edge of the woods and Scabinory. 'So how are we going to get past all these soldiers without getting caught?'

Struan's answer held little comfort. 'We'll skirt the trees for as long as we can, but eventually we'll have tae cross in the open right through the middle o' Crane's army.'

'But there's no cover at all,' Drew said. 'We'll be seen as soon as we set foot out there.'

'It is likely,' Struan said, calmly, 'but I can see no other way, can you? We will wait here 'til nightfall,' he said when the others didn't reply. 'Our chances are better under cover o' darkness.'

More ships landed on the beach below. This time vile creatures of Gododdin disembarked en masse, some even worse than those the children had seen at Sithbruaich Gate. Ugly, little dwarf-like nyaffs herded great skulking ogres, their skin gnarled with carbuncles like the bark of a tree. Thickset, bug-eyed toadies thumped up the beach on stumpy legs. On the dunes, wild-haired banshees armed with axes and bows and pointy-chinned gargoyles so hideous and terrifying that Rossi couldn't bear to look at them gathered impatiently, awaiting orders.

Instead, she lay on her back and looked up at the sky, which was brightening from grey to blue as the sun rose fully. The sky looked so normal that she almost felt she was back lying on the lawn at the Buckie House. But there was nothing normal about the scene in the valley below, where dark creatures roamed the wasteland and the sound of sparring filled the air.

She sat up suddenly and stared down at the beach below. *The Buckie House!* Grandad said there'd been buildings where the Buckie House stood for thousands of years. He said the site held special meaning to people across all time. Was the Buckie House here now? Scanning the wasteland, she saw half a dozen rough stone buildings with black thatched roofs sitting in a cluster on the grassy dunes above the beach. *Fishermen's cottages*, most probably abandoned when Crane and the Gododdin over-ran Scabinory. She remembered the ancient cave beneath the house with the severed image of a dragon painted on the rear wall, as though the cave had extended further back at one time. What if there *was* a tunnel there in the past? Where would it go? She thought of the fork in the tunnel they'd found beneath the Witching Stone. It ran downhill and they'd thought it might lead to a second entrance at Scabinory, but common sense told her now that it might lead all the way down to the Buckie House.

'What is it, Rossi?' Drew asked, seeing the strange expression on his sister's face. 'Are you alright?'

'What? Yes, I'm fine, possibly better than fine.'

Struan frowned. 'What is it? Can you sense something?'

'No, it's not that. Struan, I don't think we should try to cross the valley. There's no cover and too many soldiers, we're bound to get caught.' She pointed to the little cluster of buildings close to the beach. 'I think we should make for those cottages.'

'You've got to be joking,' Sean said, looking down at them. 'Crane's men are bound to use those cottages. For all we know Crane might be inside one, right now. Even if we can get to them, which I doubt very much, we'll never get out again.'

There was no mistaking Rossi's excitement. 'If I'm right, we might not have to. I know it seems mad, but I have a strong feeling that one of those buildings is the Buckie House or at least an ancient version of it. Remember the day I saw the writing on the shell wall? Well afterwards, Grandad took me down to the basement, but it wasn't a basement like at home, it was a really cool cave and there were paintings on the wall, paintings of kids like us, and a dragon and other things I didn't understand. One of the paintings was cut in half as though a wall had been built right through the middle of it, but it didn't make sense because the wall was solid rock.'

'So what are you saying?'

'Remember the tunnel we passed on the way to Drachen Fels? It's just a hunch, but what if that tunnel goes all the way to the Buckie House?'

'But you said there wasn't a tunnel in the Buckie House. You said it was blocked solid.'

'But so was the back of the cave at Drachen Fels,' Drew said, catching on, 'and that tunnel was definitely there only moments before.'

'Can you check it, Drew?' Rossi asked. 'Can you find out if one of those houses is the Buckie House and what or who is inside?'

Drew turned his eyes to the little huddle of cottages below them on the opposite side of the river, a kilometre or so along the beach. He frowned, concentrating all his curiosity on his target and in the flick of a switch his mind's eye soared across the space. The first cottage was a barracks for Crane's senior commanders and the next an armoury stacked with weapons. The third and fourth were stuffed with food supplies too good for the minions who packed the shoreline. This was surely Crane's private store. He entered the fifth; it was comfortably furnished, most likely Crane's private quarters. The last cottage in the row was a simple one-roomed structure, smaller than the others, with one door, two small windows and a fireplace burning cheerfully on the back wall. He knew immediately that this was the Buckie House, even though it bore little resemblance to his grandfather's home. The feeling of familiarity and belonging was strong, just as it had been the first time he'd walked through the Buckie House's gate.

He heard voices behind him and forced his mind's eye to rotate. Crane entered, taking a seat on a large wooden chair, his small stocky frame dwarfed by Ghob and many of the other hideous creatures that followed him in. It was spooky being that close to Crane, even though the man didn't know he was there, but Drew forced himself to watch and listen. Crane was furious... shouting, he could tell, but his words were frustratingly faint and distorted. Two guards forced a figure to the floor before him. When the prisoner looked up, Drew immediately recognised it as one of the slaugh from the forest. It spoke and he caught the words 'boy' and 'stolen', but then the sound simply faded to nothing. Rising in fury, Crane raised his sword and Drew snapped back into his body. He doubled over and vomited, a combination of shock at what he was sure Crane was about to do and motion sickness, having completely lost control of his re-entry.

Rossi rubbed his back anxiously. 'Are you okay, Drew?'

He straightened unsteadily, deathly pale and green around the gills. 'The Buckie House is the last cottage in the row. Crane was there with one of the slaugh. It said something about Ruairidh being stolen from them, but I couldn't catch anything else. Crane was furious.' He swallowed hard. 'I think he killed it.'

Rossi put her arms around her youngest brother, desperately sorry that he'd witnessed such a thing.

'Stolen,' repeated Struan. 'What did he mean?'

Drew shook his head, then feeling like he was about to vomit, made a mental note not to do it again.

'He must have said something else. Come on Drew, what else did ye hear?'

'Nothing. Their words were fuzzy. I couldn't tell what they were saying.'

'Can't you tune back in?' Sean asked.

'I told you, I'm not a TV, stupid!' Drew said, wanting nothing more than to sit quietly for a few minutes.

'Who could possibly have stolen Ruairidh from the slaugh?' Sean asked, turning his attention to Struan.

He shrugged. 'Any number of strange beasts that dwell in Goyle-Na-Garg might have taken him. But there is nothing we can do about it now,' he said, anticipating Sean's next question, 'except hope that he found better luck with whatever has him.'

The others stood bleakly silent, thinking about what may have happened to Ruairidh.

'Did ye see the cave? Was there a tunnel?' Struan asked, turning back to Drew.

''Fraid not, but the floor was made of flagstones, so there might be a concealed entrance. I got such a shock when Crane looked like he was going to kill the slaugh that I flashed back before I was able to focus.'

Struan stared down at the little row of cottages, considering what Drew had said. 'I say it's madness tae even attempt tae go in there. We'll be trapped for sure, and even if the tunnel does exist, which is a big if, there's no guarantee Crane doesn't already know about it. It may be his own private entrance tae Scabinory.'

Rossi shook her head. 'I think we should give the Buckie House a chance. You have to trust me on this, Struan. Our Grandad said something to me that day in the cellar. He said, *remember you'll always be safe in the Buckie House no matter what.*'

Struan locked eyes with her, searching for uncertainty and thinking about the grandfather he'd never met. She returned his gaze steadily, pleading with him to trust her.

'We'll go then,' he said, deciding, 'as soon as night falls.'

26

CRANE'S FURY

Crane swept from the cottage, his fury little eased by killing the slaugh. Its admission that Ruairidh had slipped through his net was just one of a long list of failures and disloyalties on the part of his minions as far as he was concerned. From the shore of the Lothian Sea he'd seen the children escape the clutches of the useless murdhuacha and knew they'd likely made it to Elphame with Morag alive. He'd set the slaugh to watch for the children in Goyle-Na-Garg forest. Knowing they'd twice had them in their grasp and lost them, once to the wolves and then to creatures as stupid as the daiglin hogneys, had sent him into a murderous rage, but it was what Drew hadn't heard the slaugh tell Crane that fuelled his fury now. Kate was somewhere in Goyle-Na-Garg, despite his most trusted men swearing they'd buried her body along with that of the boy, long ago.

Crane's brow set in a deep scowl. The ferrishyn knowingly sent the boy to his mother, of that he was certain, but why? It wasn't in their interests to distract Ruairidh from returning Morag to Scabinory. There was only one plausible reason. Morag's injuries must be worse than he thought. Unable to heal her, the ferrishyn had sent her to Kate, perhaps in the form of a talisman. That boy almost certainly carried the Sacred Heart!

Crane's mouth set in a hard, thin line. The daiglin hogneys, it seemed, had two things he wanted. For almost as much as he wanted Morag, Crane still wanted Kate. He called Ghob to him.

'Ghob, my friend, go to the forest and find the boy. Bring me everything he carries with him, *everything*, no matter how small or how useless it appears to you. And Ghob, there is one there I would also have you fetch for me. Find the witch, Buitseach, and take her to Gododdin to await me there.'

27

BACK TO
THE BUCKIE HOUSE

The day passed slowly for the children, hiding and dozing amongst the trees on the cliff above Crane's army and taking turns standing watch.

'We have tae move fast and quiet as wee mice,' Struan said when night fell at last. 'You in the middle, archer,' he said to Sean, 'so you have time to fire your arrows should we be attacked from the front or rear. You with me, Rossi, so I can hear ye easily should ye get any feelings o' foreboding like, and this time, Drew, you've got our backs.'

Drew's chest puffed with pride at Struan's faith in him, but as he followed him out of the forest, the other boy turned to him again.

'Yer spear, man,' he whispered, nodding to where Drew had left it leaning against a tree. 'Ye'll no be much good tae us without it.'

Drew fetched it red-faced, for once glad of the dark.

They stole towards the camp, using every rock and gully on the landscape to shelter them from enemy eyes, glad of the cloaks that covered them from head to foot. They crossed the fast-flowing

River Leven without incident, Struan having scouted the safest spot. As they approached the camp, Rossi, Drew and Struan concealed their swords beneath their cloaks to stop firelight reflecting on the blades, while Sean held his bow armed and ready. Reaching the edge of the camp, they crawled commando-style to the top of a small bluff on the landscape and looked down on the scene below.

Rossi swallowed hard. Close up, the true might of Crane's army was terrifying. Thousands of fierce creatures of Gododdin slept around campfires, while grotesque, heavily armed gargoyles patrolled the camp perimeter.

'Ready everyone?' Struan whispered. The others nodded. 'Then kill it, Sean,' he said, pointing to a gargoyle that was about to pass beneath them.

Sean hesitated.

'I said kill it! What's the matter with ye?'

'I've never killed anything in cold blood before,' Sean said. 'That slaugh I shot was sort of an accident.'

'It's a beast, not a man. It would eat ye as soon as look at ye.' Exasperated, Struan reached for his father's bow. 'I'll do it!'

'No,' Sean said, drawing the string taught.

Rossi placed a hand on his shoulder. 'For Ruairidh and Morag,' she whispered as he let the arrow fly, felling the creature before it ever knew what hit it.

'Now,' whispered Struan, not wishing to waste a second of the precious few minutes Sean had won them. They followed him past snoring beasts, their soft-soled shoes padding softly on the ground until they reached the stone cottages. Suddenly a horn bellowed through the night air, rousing the creatures from their sleep, and the camp quickly erupted into chaos. The children huddled behind a large pile of decaying lobster creels that leaned against the Buckie House wall, dangerously exposed to the beach behind them.

'They've found the guard's body,' whispered Struan. 'We have to get inside that house fast.'

A cretin marched past and entered.

'What's going on?' they heard Crane bark when the creature presented itself.

'The perimeter has been breached, Sire, and a guard shot dead,' came the whining reply. 'A've organised a search o' these houses and the surrounding dunes.'

'Fool!' bellowed Crane. 'They're heading for Scabinory, not here. The guard must have spotted them skirting around the camp. Send word to the nyaffs on the western side and up the line to the gargoyles at the palisade. They must not get anywhere near that vent. I want them taken, dead or alive!'

The cretin departed immediately, screaming Crane's orders and sending the children further behind the creels.

Crane left for Scabinory in a flurry, his commanders running to keep up and the surrounding cottages quickly emptied, none suspecting that the children were outside. When the camp lay silent at last, they slipped inside the Buckie House.

'Quick,' Struan said, 'search for any sign o' a cellar.'

They scoured the floor by the light of the fire, but the flagstones all seemed similarly worn beneath the dust and sand that had trailed in from the beach. Suddenly they heard voices outside.

'This one,' Drew whispered from the back of the room. The

others gathered around him. 'Watch.' He brushed some sand to-wards the edges of the flagstone and it quickly drained away. 'I can see a space below it.'

He ran his fingers around it looking for a place to gain some purchase, but the best he could find was a sizeable chip on one corner. He inserted two fingers and pulled but couldn't budge it. Struan fetched an iron poker from the fireplace, and pushed its hooked end into the chip. The voices were close, very close. He and Sean placed their full weight on the poker and the flagstone lifted with a soft grating sound, revealing a set of stone steps.

Rossi stared down, her heart racing. Sand lay thick and undisturbed on the steps and there was no doubt in her mind that Crane didn't know the cellar existed.

The voices were right outside the door. Rossi and Drew slipped and stumbled down the steps until only Struan and Sean remained, straining to support the great stone above their heads. They lowered it into position as best they could but it fell the last few centimetres with an unavoidably loud thud. Hardly daring to breathe, they huddled on the cellar steps in pitch darkness, listening as the cottage door opened and feet shuffled above their heads.

'I tell you I heard something,' rasped one of two short, skinny nyaffs who entered with their swords drawn.

Footsteps trod warily across the floor, searching for the source of the noise. Below ground, Drew grasped Rossi's arm and she patted it reassuringly, rolling the little faerie ring between her fingers. It glowed brilliant yellow in the darkness.

'We're safe in the Buckie House,' she whispered, certain the little ring confirmed her own intuition.

'I can't see nothing here and if we can't produce the goods, we're better keeping stump,' said the other nyaff.

'Well, I ain't telling him nothing,' said the first. 'I've seen what he does to them that brings him bad news. Mad as a cut snake, he is.'

The other nyaff's tongue darted nervously between its long, rotten teeth. 'I heard tell he killed another one,' it said, fear mixing with sadistic pleasure in its voice.

'That'd be right,' came the reply and, with that, the beaky nosed pair shuffled out the door, competing to tell the most gruesome story about Crane's history with messengers.

In the darkness beneath the floor, the children breathed easy. As soon as he heard the door close, Struan set to work ripping lengths of cloth from his cloak. Tying one around his sword, he unplugged the stopper to a skin of oil he carried at his waist and doused the cloth, then, taking some flints from another pouch, he struck until a spark caught the oil and it burst into flames. Rossi held up her sword for the same treatment and soon they descended the remaining steps to a small cavern with their makeshift torches held high. Crossing to the nearest wall, Rossi illuminated paintings more vibrantly coloured but otherwise the same as she'd last seen them what must be thousands of years in the future. Breathless, she called the others over.

'We're here all right, look, here are the paintings I told you about.' She moved further in, lighting painting after painting until she came to the largest and most impressive – a great dragon twisting around five children and surrounded by a bright light. This time the image was complete but it wasn't the painting that took her breath away. It was the passage beyond that disappeared uphill into darkness.

'It's here,' Rossi said, hardly believing that what she'd hoped was actually true.

Struan had no such difficulty. 'Let's go,' he said, pushing past her.

28

STRUAN'S BETRAYAL

They followed Struan steadily uphill, stopping to tie more rags around their swords when the makeshift torches began to fail. Some distance in, the temperature, cold at first, rose dramatically and soon, met by a wall of dry heat, they were forced to shed their long woollen cloaks. Struan wiped the sweat from his brow with his sleeve, struggling with the heat much more than his Australian cousins. He fanned his tunic away from his chest, trying to trap some cool air.

'We must be getting close tae the vent now,' he said, hopefully.

Sure enough, a soft golden glow soon appeared up ahead, deepening into red as they drew closer. A low rumbling noise came from far below, growing steadily louder, and they clutched each other in alarm as the ground began to vibrate, gradually increasing in intensity until the whole tunnel shook, loosing a hail of rock. Thick, sulphurous smoke belched down the tunnel toward them, causing them to cough violently, and they crouched against the walls, shielding their faces. When the rumbling stopped, they stood, brushing the dust and grit from their hair and clothes.

'She's just clearing her throat,' Struan said, coughing.

They soon found themselves on the edge of a wide shaft. Looking up, they glimpsed the sky far above through a column of smoke, while far below, molten lava bubbled and undulated in a fire red lake. Forced back into the tunnel by the radiant heat, they leaned against the wall fanning themselves furiously.

'It's a dead end,' Sean said, disappointed, 'and Ruairidh obviously isn't here, at least not yet.'

'We've come as far as we need tae anyway,' Struan said firmly. 'All I have to do now is throw the stone in tae the lava and we can go back the way we came.'

The others stared at him in shock and total disbelief.

29

LORD OF THE WOLVES

Ruairidh, Ted, and the wolves ran on through the Pass of Gore, skirting the border with Gododdin for many miles, resting only when Wolftrax stopped to scent the air, until at last, they came to the edge of Goyle-Na-Garg forest where it bordered Scabinory. The pack lay panting under cover of the trees while Wolftrax beckoned Ruairidh and Ted up onto a rocky outcrop overhanging the river and the valley below. Night had fallen once more, this time dark and moonless, as they crept to the edge of the cliff and looked down on the sea of campfires.

'Crane's army,' growled Wolftrax. 'The evil entrails of Gododdin await you, Prince Ruairidh.'

'Where's Scabinory from here?' he asked, deciding not to dwell on that thought.

'Over there.' The great wolf raised his nose in the direction of a small hill silhouetted against the sky, its tip glowing larger and brighter than the campfires around it.

'The stone must be cast directly into the vent itself,' Ruairidh said, surveying the mass of creatures between them and Scabinory, 'and at exactly the same time as Struan casts his, though God knows how I'm going to make it to the vent never mind find him in all this.'

'The fortifications around the vent are indeed great,' Wolftrax said. 'Crane is no fool. It is well guarded. Even as quiet and swift as a wolf you cannot hope to break through.'

'But Struan and the others will try, and so must I.'

The wolf hesitated. 'There is another way… and if we are lucky, perhaps one less fortified than the vent itself. Just a little to the north is a dungeon said to be linked to Scabinory by a tunnel.'

Ruairidh looked at Wolftrax, guessing there must be a hitch. 'But if there's another entrance, why wouldn't Crane guard it?'

'I did not say it was unguarded,' growled Wolftrax. 'Getting in may be easy enough, but getting past the dragon he holds captive there is another matter. Crane will think no one fool enough to attempt it.'

'Queen Maeve said the dragon must be freed if we're to defeat the Gododdin,' Ruairidh said uncertainly, then frowned seeing the Wolf's grave expression. 'What exactly will the dragon do if I go into that dungeon?'

Wolftrax shook his great majestic head. 'That I cannot say, for dragons are unpredictable beasts and the one held captive there suffers greatly at Crane's hands. We have heard its cries of torment from the woods. It has little reason to show mercy to your kind.'

Ruairidh exhaled deeply and set his wolf's jaw, hoping the magnificent Lord of the Wolves couldn't sense his fear. 'So how do I get into this dungeon?'

'Come, I will show you.'

Wolftrax summoned four others and together, with Ted, they skirted the army encampment, drawing well back under cover of the forest when they came level with the vent. The surrounding landscape was black with volcanic ash and so barren Ruairidh didn't recognise it, despite having spent all his life in the area, albeit thousands of years in the future.

Crane's fortifications at the vent were indeed formidable. A tall timber palisade at least three metres high circled the hill about half way up its slope and behind it, standing shoulder-to-shoulder was an entire battalion. Behind them was a deep ditch filled with sharp wooden stakes and oil that could be lit at a moment's notice, creating a ring of fire around the vent as a last means of defence.

Ruairidh, Ted and the wolves continued on, emerging from the forest about two hundred and fifty metres north of their destination. Not far from the trees, a group of eight cretin soldiers stood guard around a flat wooden disc which could easily be mistaken for the cover of a large well.

'We must take them by stealth,' growled Wolftrax, 'any noise and we will be discovered.'

Ruairidh wrinkled his sensitive wolf's nose, catching the cretins' stench as they crept towards them on their bellies, using the camp debris as cover. A few metres short of their quarry, Wolftrax stopped.

'Now,' he growled, and they sprang for their throats, bringing the cretins down almost without a sound. 'Quickly young prince,' he said, 'you must be a man once more.'

Ruairidh concentrated on what it felt like to be human and

began to change. The sensation was horrible, as though his skin were turning inside out, until at last he stood shivering in the cool night air, naked but for his mother's gift hanging around his neck and his father's sword, which had remained strapped across his back as he ran.

Ted tugged at a cretin's armour and, realising what he was about, Ruairidh helped him remove the beast's boots, leather hose, vest and breastplate, gagging as he slipped the stinking garments over his head despite his wolf's sense of smell having been replaced by his own far inferior human one. Ready, he crouched beside the wooden cover and pushed it with all his might. It was heavy and he only managed to move it over by a metre or so. Deciding it was enough, he, Ted and Wolftrax stared down into the pitch-black chasm.

'It is a bottle dungeon,' Wolftrax said.

Ruairidh nodded, having seen one on a visit to a local castle with his grandfather. Bottle dungeons, as their name suggested, had a narrow entrance through a long, well-like neck, which ballooned into a wide circular chamber below. For the hapless prisoner dropped into darkness, climbing out was impossible, assuming of course they survived the fall. He wished he could throw in a lighted torch to see how deep it was, but didn't dare in case it alerted more guards. Instead he scrambled on the ground for a rock and dropped it, listening to see how long it took to hit the bottom. A second later the faint crack of rock on rock echoed back. He looked around for something to lower himself down with, and his eyes fell on a length of chain attached to a wagon nearby. He fed it carefully through the hole, but it slipped through his fingers, swinging against the mouth of the dungeon with a loud clank and sending them all to the ground. Mercifully, the sound went unnoticed. He searched his clothing for flints and accepted an unlit torch fetched by Ted from a nearby sconce.

'This is where we say goodbye for now, my friend,' Wolftrax said when he was ready.

Ruairidh nodded, managing a small smile. 'Anything I should know about dragons?'

Wolftrax thought for a moment. 'Dragons admire courage,' he said.

Ted moved closer to Ruairidh, whimpering, and he ruffled his big curly head. 'There's no way I can take you down there with me, Ted,' he said with regret. 'You have to go with Wolftrax.'

'We'll be ready when you come out of the vent,' Wolftrax said, confidently. 'Good luck, brother wolf.'

Ruairidh tucked the unlit torch behind his breastplate and nodded. Giving Ted one last hug, he climbed over the edge of the hole and disappeared down the chain into darkness.

30

THE DUNGEON

It was pitch black and eerily silent in the dungeon once Ted and Wolftrax edged the wooden cover back into place. The air was stale and smoky, smelling pungently of salt meat, like a smoke house Ruairidh had once visited where dozens of Christmas hams hung up to cure. The smell was an unwelcome reminder that a dragon lay somewhere in the darkness below. Despite his terror at the thought, Ruairidh swung down, willed on by the gentle thud of the little stone against his chest.

Suddenly his feet hit thin air and he realised he'd reached the end of the chain with no real idea how far he was from the ground. Wrapping the chain around one foot for support, he pulled the torch from behind his breastplate and held it in his teeth while he fiddled with the flints. He hadn't quite reached the bottom of the bottle's neck, he realised, waving the flaming torch beneath him. He couldn't yet see into the recesses of the chamber itself but he could see the floor some two to three metres below. He released a long breath, relieved that the length of chain had taken him so close to the ground. Something heavy dragged across the floor beyond his view and the hair on the back of his neck stood on-end.

'Who's there?' he called, sweeping the torch beneath him, but there was no reply. Then louder, trying to sound more confident than he really felt, 'I am Prince Ruairidh of Alba. You knew my father *and* my grandfather once. I don't mean you any harm, in fact I've come to help, if you'll let me.'

His voice echoed eerily. Giving up a silent prayer, he dropped the torch, slid down the chain and jumped. He rolled to break his fall then quickly found his feet. Grasping the torch in one hand and his father's sword in the other, he jerked around and back, unsure where the threat might be. The dragging noise came again and he whipped the torch higher, his heart pounding. He circled, and as his eyes adjusted properly to the gloom he saw a large humped shape, shining dully in the torchlight like unpolished brass. Horrified, he realised that the dragon lay coiled around the dungeon's huge circumference and he was standing only metres from its head.

Lying down, the creature's shoulder brushed against the dungeon roof. Its head on the end of its long, thick neck was massive but finely sculpted, like a pedigree stallion and dull gold scales edged in muddy green covered its back except for an arc of ox-blood red that ran along its horn-tipped spine, while what he could see of the skin on its underbelly was thickly ribbed and petrol blue.

Feeling like his heart might easily burst, Ruairidh took a deep breath and stepped towards it. It watched him with long narrow eyes – eyes that circled in the torchlight through all the colours of fire: white, blue and violet, red, yellow and gold – eyes that assessed him like a cat might assess its prey.

Dragons admire courage, he reminded himself as he forced one foot in front of the other until, hardly daring to breathe, he dropped to his knees just a hair's breadth from the dragon's mouth. Two small rings of smoke exited its nose, dissipating in the air around him.

'Lord Dragon,' he said, fighting to control the trembling in his voice. 'I, Ruairidh son of Rannoch, King of Alba, come before you in friendship, to offer you my help and ask for yours in return.'

Smoke curled thickly around his head and for a long moment the dragon said nothing, as though testing his resolve.

Dragons admire courage! Ruairidh chanted the phrase inside his head, as if by doing so, he might better resist the urge to flee. When at last the dragon spoke, its deep, husky voice was laced with sarcasm.

'And so, you come to fulfil your destiny, son of Rannoch *once* King of Alba. You beg my aid, though it is your kinsman from beyond Scabinory who holds me prisoner here, the last dragon, my family taken and killed, their body parts given to Carlin Meg for her evil magic. Tell me, *Prince Ruairidh,* why should I not devour you for the tasty morsel that you are?'

Ruairidh's head snapped up. 'Carlin Meg? The Witch? What's she got to do with anything? I thought Crane put you here?'

The dragon blew more smoke and Ruairidh fought the urge to cough.

'Crane thinks himself *so* powerful,' the beast growled, 'but he is merely an unwitting chattel of the witch. Only her magic could have conjured Nyu from the stone at Scabinory. They should have killed her at the end of the Great War, when they had the chance, but the ferrishyn queen would not have it. *Mercy* stayed her hand.' The dragon hissed scornfully and its eyes flamed orange. 'Oh, Carlin Meg was powerless enough then; denied the dragon's blood she needs to fuel her evil magic. She disappeared into the bowels of Gododdin with the vilest of her creatures, waiting for her time to come again, and thanks to Crane that time is fast approaching. He trades my blood with Ghob and Ghom for Gododdin fealty and they deliver it directly to the witch. Her powers grow each day. Crane thinks to control her and for now he does, but once she is fully restored none shall be her master, for it is the throne of Alba that she wants.'

'Then we'll make sure she doesn't get any more dragon's blood,' Ruairidh said firmly, taking in just how truly torturous conditions in the dungeon were.

The great beast could neither sit nor raise its head, even if the roof of the chamber had been high enough, as its neck, tail and three of its legs were chained securely to the ground and its huge wings bound tightly to its body. The remaining rear leg was suspended behind it at an unnatural angle, and on that twisted thigh a truly horrible wound wept and oozed into a channel in the floor dug especially for the purpose.

Ruairidh gagged as the stench of putrid flesh reached him. The leg hung across the entrance to a tunnel barred by an iron gate and on the wall outside was a row of spears. He understood immediately that someone or *something* stabbed the festering sore to spill the blood that Crane needed to meet his bargain with Ghob.

The blood then ran along the channel beneath the gate where it was safely collected. The dragon was in agony, undernourished and pitifully weak from years of confinement in this dark, terrible place. Sadness at its sorry state suddenly replaced his fear.

The dragon growled low in its throat, sensing pity and infuriated by it, and the sound reverberated menacingly around the dungeon. 'So again I ask, why should I spare you? Speak or I will light you like a flaming torch and watch you burn.'

Smoke billowed from its nose and sharp, searing heat hit Ruairidh's face singeing his hair. He raised his forearms to shield himself but resisted the urge to back away. When the heat waned he locked eyes with the beast. He saw pain, sorrow and wisdom from long years of life, but no cruelty.

He drew the little pouch his mother had given him over his head. 'In this vial is healing water from my mother – Buitseach. With it I can heal your wounds and restore your strength, if you'll let me.' He prayed it was true.

The dragon's eyes glowed violet. *'Buitseach?* Queen Kate lives?' It growled deep in its throat. 'She was a friend… once.'

'She's a prisoner too, her situation little better than yours,' Ruairidh said quickly, realising he had the dragon's interest at last. 'She desperately needs your help.'

The dragon contemplated this for a moment, its eyes softening from violet through green to liquid gold. Ruairidh held his breath.

'Then do it!'

Ruairidh drizzled the water over the stinking wound, hoping it would be enough. For a second nothing happened. The great beast snorted impatiently and Ruairidh's mind raced, wondering what he was going to do next. Suddenly the wound bubbled and fizzed and a bright blaze of gold and dazzling metallic green rippled from its ragged edges down the dragon's legs and tail, up over its body and along its long sinewy neck until the dull red streak lining its back glowed scarlet, its stomach flashed azure blue and the creature shone in the torchlight like a great and colourful fish. The dragon sighed, feeling his strength return, and searing orange flames licked from his mouth.

Ruairidh examined the shackles. They were held together by a large but simple screw, impossible for the dragon to remove but reasonably easy for human or human-like hands. He fixed the edge of his father's sword to the screw head and turned. It was old and rusty but after some effort it loosened and the chain linking the shackles slipped through until only the dragon's wounded leg remained tethered to the wall. The great beast stretched, relishing the relative freedom of movement, while Ruairidh examined the remaining lock. He frowned, realising the mechanism wasn't the same. This one had been replaced quite recently and required a key – he guessed to enable Crane's men to unlock and manipulate the wounded leg at will.

Footsteps sounded in the tunnel beyond the gate and Ruairidh extinguished the torch. He crouched behind the dragon's leg as light flooded the tunnel and a short, fat cretin waddled into view, keys rattling against its thigh on a large ring attached to its belt. Its grotesque face twisted in a small mean smile as it lit the sconces closest to the gate and waved a torch over the bars.

'What is it, sweetheart?' It asked in a slimy, lisping voice.

Ruairidh and the dragon stayed absolutely still.

The creature chuckled, expecting no response. 'It's time for a little milking, me thinks,' it said, relishing the prospect.

It examined the spears as if seeking a favourite and then, satisfied, threaded one through the bars and raised its arm, ready to thrust, but Ruairidh grabbed the end of the spear, surprising the creature. It let go, falling heavily on its backside.

The dragon turned to face its tormentor for the first time in twelve years. 'Behind me,' it roared, sending Ruairidh running for shelter.

Seeing the dragon's head free of its restraints the cretin froze, confused, then, registering danger, it scrambled backwards on the ground, but too late. With another great roar, the dragon blasted it with searing flame.

Safe behind the great beast's back, Ruairidh felt little of its effects, its scales deflecting the heat away more efficiently than tiles on a space rocket. But the cretin wasn't so lucky – it fell to the ground in a pile of molten ash.

The iron gates glowed white hot and malleable and the dragon swung its powerful tail, reducing them to a twisted heap.

Ruairidh leapt to retrieve the keys. 'Come on,' he said, opening the last of the shackles, 'let's get out of here.'

The great beast turned awkwardly and followed him out into a much larger tunnel. Someway in, Ruairidh illuminated the first few metres of a second passage. 'Where does this go?'

'To the Witching Stone at the edge of the vent,' The dragon said.

Ruairidh started up it. 'Then it's possible my brother and cousins will try to enter here.'

'It is indeed *possible*,' growled the dragon, 'but unlikely, for I scent many Gododdin soldiers overhead. We will continue to the vent. If your friends aren't there we'll search for them by air.'

Ruairidh's heart skipped a beat at what that might mean, but he followed the dragon away.

Soon the air grew hotter and the tunnel widened, coming to an abrupt end where it met the vent. Ruairidh poked his head over the edge. The tunnel above and opposite was concealed from his view by overhanging rock and he couldn't see any sign of the others.

The dragon extended its wings at the edge of the vent, relishing the heat that radiated from the lava, and stretched its neck towards the small patch of blue sky just visible through the smoke.

'Climb on, young prince,' it growled.

His heart racing, Ruairidh stepped up on the dragon's foreleg and over its shoulder, arranging himself securely between two curved horns at the base of its neck.

'Hold on tight,' it commanded.

He took one last look down and then wished he hadn't as the dragon roared and took off vertically like a rocket. He held on for dear life, certain he'd fall into the boiling lava, but suddenly they were out in the cool, clear air and his fear turned to euphoria as the dragon sailed higher for a few seconds then turned, soaring down in great circles above Crane's army.

31

DRAGON RIDER

Don't we have to drop them both together? Rossi asked anxiously when Struan removed the little stone from his pocket. 'Please, Struan, Crane doesn't even know we're here – Ruairidh still has time.'

'I agree!' Sean said, angrily.

'Me too!' Drew said.

Struan shook his head. 'No. My people can't wai–'

But a terrifying roar drowned his words as a flash of red, green and gold rocketed up the vent behind him. The children ran towards it, sticking their heads out in time to see the dragon shoot into the sky with Ruairidh clinging to its back.

'Did you see that?' Rossi gasped. 'How on earth…?'

Sean grinned from ear to ear. 'I don't know. Do you think he saw us?'

'No, he was going way too fast!' Drew said, amazed.

'Then we've got to get up there quickly if Morag is to have her chance,' Rossi said, turning to her youngest brother. 'What's on the other side of this vent Drew? Can we get there?'

Drew stared at the tunnel opposite, sending his mind's eye soaring across the void. He saw the dungeon and the passage leading up to the Witching Stone, but no way of getting to it. Frustrated, he pulled back, this time looking down at the lava as he crossed the vent. To his amazement, he saw a narrow ledge which ran around the vent to some stone steps not far below where the others stood. Ecstatic, he flashed back into his body and immediately felt sick. No sign of it improving with practice, then, he thought ruefully.

'Well, what did you see?' Sean asked.

Drew caught his breath. 'There's two tunnels on the other side. One leads to a dungeon with a broken gate – I suppose that's where the dragon came from – and the other leads up to the Witching Stone.'

'That's the one we want, but we can't get there.'

Drew's eyes shone. 'That's the thing. There's some steps leading down to a ledge just below us.

The others stared down, seeing nothing but the bubbling lava.

'But there are no steps,' Struan said.

'Yes there are,' he said, lying flat and poking his head dangerously far out over the edge of the vent.

The others did the same and immediately spotted some steep precarious steps and the start of a painfully narrow ledge that was otherwise obscured by a large overhang.

Sean thumped his brother on the arm, grinning as they sat up. 'Good one Drew. Maybe you weren't born dumb after all!'

Drew punched him back, pleased with the backhanded compliment.

'Lead the way, Drew,' offered Struan.

Drew slipped over the edge, and the others held their breath as he hung for a second above the searing lava before dropping to the top of the steps. At the bottom, he hesitated for barely an instant before pressing his back to the wall and stepping out onto the ledge. Struan nodded for Sean to go next then dropped down to the steps and beckoned Rossi. 'Come on,' he said.

Rossi shook her head. 'I can't do it, Struan. I'm scared of heights and I'm especially scared of being boiled alive by lava!'

Struan held out his hand. 'Yer the bravest lassie I've ever met, Rossi,' he said warmly, 'and I'm proud to call ye cousin. Now come on!'

He caught her as she dropped down then took her hand firmly in his. At the bottom of the steps, he waited until she nodded before stepping out with her onto the ledge.

By the time they reached the halfway point their hair stuck wet and straggling to their heads. Drew and Sean were already on the other side waiting for them when the rumbling began.

'Run!' Struan yelled, pulling Rossi's hand. 'We have tae get off o' this ledge now!'

Rossi almost overbalanced but he caught her and she ran, falling against him on the other side. They made it past a bend in the tunnel a hair's breadth before boiling hot gas roared up the vent, blasting their backs with radiant heat. On they ran, desperate for cool air, but just as they reached the tunnel leading up to the Witching Stone, Struan abruptly stopped.

'Wait,' he said, panting. 'I have tae go back, I can't leave without dropping the stone.'

Rossi grabbed his arm. 'No, Struan! We've got to give Ruairidh a chance to save Morag. If he can just see us… '

'This might be my last chance tae save my people,' Struan said, breaking free. 'Tae be so close… I can't risk it.'

A tremendous roar went up overhead as the dragon streaked across the sky, scorching the earth with searing flames, and thousands of Gododdin soldiers cried out in fear.

Crane's voice screamed above the rest. 'Stand your ground, by God! You cowards! You fools! Bring those catapults forward. I want fire! I want stones! Even if that dragon burns you to a crisp, you will stand your ground!'

Struan hesitated, wrestling with the knowledge that his brother and the dragon stood alone against a vast army. 'Come on,' he said, putting the little stone back in his pocket and heading up the tunnel towards the Witching Stone.

32

THE FIERY RING

They came out at the edge of the vent amidst a cloud of billowing smoke just as the dragon swooped in, scorching the hillside. Flames engulfed the catapults and the timber palisade, sending soldiers fleeing back down the hill only to be cut down and replaced by others brutally herded from behind on Crane's orders.

'The Standing Stanes aren't here,' Rossi said with surprise when the smoke cleared, briefly revealing the crest of the hill. But her brothers had no time to acknowledge that fact as the dragon circled again, coming in low over the vent. Struan left the shelter of the smoke, unnoticed amidst the chaos, and stepped up on the Witching Stone with the little stone clenched tightly in his out stretched fist.

Spotting Struan through the smoke, Ruairidh whooped ecstatically. 'He's here! Look dragon. Hold fire, it's my brother!'

'Hold on!' the dragon growled, and with a great roar it soared over Struan's head, letting him know they'd seen him before shooting into a sharp loop that brought them full circle again.

Braced for an attack that never came, Crane looked around for an explanation and saw Struan at the vent. Before the small Gododdin force set to guard him even knew what was happening, he ran through the smoke towards the boy, bellowing with rage.

'Struan, watch out!' screamed Rossi, sensing Crane's presence before any of them saw him.

Struan spun, meeting Crane's sword with a deafening clash as he leapt onto the Witching Stone. His battle cry alerted two guards, but the first fell with an arrow to his chest and the second with a spear before they ever reached him as Sean, Drew and Rossi emerged from the smoke, forming a protective circle around the combatants. On the other side of the ditch hundreds of eyes turned towards the battle. A long-legged banshee leapt over, mindless of the razor sharp stakes that lined it, encouraging others to try with varying success. Ruairidh watched the scene from the sky, knowing that his brother and cousins would soon be overwhelmed.

'The ditch!' he yelled.

The dragon blasted the oil-soaked stakes, shielding the children inside a blazing ring of fire, but trapping at least a dozen Gododdin guards with them. They approached, snarling but wary, taking the children's measure.

Sean slung his bow over his shoulder and drew his sword. 'Ready?'

At his side, Rossi and Drew nodded.

'Then let's not keep them waiting.'

He launched himself into the pack, aware of his sister's twin swords flashing on one side and his brother's war cry on the other.

Suddenly, a dozen silver wolves led by a golden dog flew through the flaming ring, taking the Gododdin down by their throats. Rossi and her brothers whooped ecstatically, knowing they'd never be so glad to see Ted again.

Crane was a good swordsman, despite his age and bulk, but Struan had speed and agility on his side. He leapt from rock to rock, parrying each blow and goading Crane until the older man's eye fell on Drew's spear. He plucked it from a gargoyle's dead body and swung it low, knocking Struan's feet from under him. Struan fell heavily on his back, only just deflecting the downward slam of Crane's sword. Another gargoyle fell to the wolves with a hideous scream, distracting Crane for barely a moment but it was long enough for Struan. He thrust forward, slashing Crane's sword arm. Screaming with pain and fury, the man dropped his sword. Then, clutching his wound, Crane backed away into the smoke, glaring at Struan in outraged disbelief.

Struan leapt after him, but the smoke swallowed Crane up. A moment later he heard a piercing shriek and an eagle rose from the smoke, throwing him to the ground as it whipped over him, ferrying Crane into the sky and away.

Struan turned back to the others, cursing. The oil in the ditch was almost spent. The wolves paced the circle as the Gododdin army gathered on the other side, snarling through the waning flames and both Struan and Ruairidh knew their time was up. Holding the spirit stone in his outstretched hand once more, Struan stepped up on the Witching Stone amidst the billowing smoke. The eagle screeched and swooped towards Struan with

Crane on its back, his face twisted in a scream as he realised what was about to happen, but the dragon was already over the vent.

'Now!' it roared.

Ruairidh released his little stone, now glowing with health and vitality, and it fell as though in slow motion until barely a moment later Struan dropped his too, and both stones disappeared beneath the smoke.

For what felt to the children like an age but was barely a heartbeat, nothing happened. Then, as Crane's eagle smacked into the dragon with brutal force and the great beast spun, falling from the air, a boom sounded far beneath the earth and a ripple of energy rose from the vent, undulating across the battlefield. It was all Ruairidh could do to stay on the dragon's back as the two creatures hit the violently shaking ground, tumbling and sliding towards the vent, sending Struan and the others diving from their path, and coming to a screeching halt on the very edge. The dragon broke free, rocketing back into the air and the eagle leapt after it, joined by half a dozen more of its kind. The dragon returned the attack with fire but the eagles' superior numbers and greater agility served well to pull its attention away from the field of battle.

The shaking stopped as suddenly as it had begun, and free from the dragon's fiery assault, the Gododdin rallied. They quickly doused the flaming ditch and threw down great wooden planks, charging over them towards the children almost before they were properly in place.

'Back the way we came!' yelled Struan, but it was too late. Crane's soldiers streamed from the tunnel, trapping them above ground and back into battle.

A roar went up from the bottom of the hill as the Selgovae slaves charged into the Gododdin's rear ranks and Struan's heart swelled with pride knowing that his men rallied for him. Suddenly a great horn sounded in the distance and the Gododdin army turned en masse to the west, where a long black strip appeared on the horizon and a rhythmic beating reached them on the wind. A vast army flew over Goyle-Na-Garg; golden eagles, hawks, kites and buzzards, and on their backs the ferrishyn, led by Queen Maeve, mounted on a snow-white osprey, with her sword held fiercely aloft. On her right side flew Ernissyen and on her left, Morag, and beneath them Goyle-Na-Garg came alive, as the good beasts of the forest – bears, wolves and wild-boar, attacked the Gododdin's western flank.

Morag saw Ruairidh clinging to the dragon's back as it thrashed in the air unable to shake its tormentors, and she let loose her arrows, bringing down eagle after eagle. Ernissyen saw Rossi fighting at the vent and dived. She caught his arm and swung up behind him as three great buzzards swooped for Sean, Drew and Struan, lifting them high above the battlefield.

'To the shore!' Struan commanded.

He landed among his men to loud cheering, and as he dismounted, an ugly little man forced his way through the crowd. Struan started, surprised to see him, then grinned.

'It would be my honour to stand at your side, Sire,' the little man said, bowing.

'The honour is all mine,' Struan replied before launching himself at the enemy.

High on a cliff above the battlefield, Crane stood between two eagles, watching as the ferrishyn, fighting side-by-side with the Selgovae, washed over his army. Purple with rage, he threw back his head and screamed uselessly at the sky, then, totally spent, he re-mounted and flew towards Gododdin, heedless of the fate of his men. In total disarray, the Gododdin army soon fled after him with the ferrishyn and forest beasts on their heels.

As the enemy scrambled to escape the field of battle and the eagles disappeared on the horizon, a great cheer went up from the triumphant alliance.

Ruairidh and the dragon circled one last time before landing beside Queen Maeve and Ernissyen at the edge of the vent, and Morag followed closely on her osprey.

Ruairidh dismounted and ran to her. 'You're all right,' he said, checking her from head to toe before hugging her. 'I can't believe it.'

'Yes, thanks to you,' Morag said, laughing as Ted reached them, leaping to lick their faces and whipping them mercilessly with his tail.

With one hand on Ted's head and Morag's hand firmly in the other, Ruairidh bowed before the dragon.

'My friend, you have my heartfelt thanks, but I don't even know your name.'

The dragon returned the gesture, his eyes glowing green. 'I am Farclas, Lord of the Dragon Clan, but it is I who need to thank you.'

Struan landed with the odd little man tucked behind him, closely followed by Sean and Drew. Remembering his manners, Struan bowed before Queen Maeve before hugging Rossi and thumping her brothers on the back. The little man straightened and grew, changing into Turpie, and the queen joyfully embraced her old friend while the others laughed with pleasure at seeing him again.

Struan grasped him warmly by both arms. 'So you made it after all, old man?'

'Well,' Turpie said, 'after Merlich captured the castle–'

Struan punched the air and whooped at the news of his army's success.

'Crane and what remained of his army escaped to the sea with many prisoners, and I couldn't bear to miss this, of all battles, so I stowed aboard. Besides, Merlich, I think, was glad to see me go. He never did like me much.'

They all laughed at that.

Ruairidh came forward with Morag, and Struan suddenly sobered. He waited until the others had finished greeting them before extending his hand.

'Brother,' he said, his voice breaking.

Ruairidh hesitated, staring at his brother's out-stretched hand, and the others held their breath.

A smile tugged at the corner of his mouth, spreading to a grin, and he grasped it wholeheartedly, drawing Struan into a hug. His brother hugged him back and then, filled with joy at their victory and Ruairidh's warm response, Struan threw his head back and laughed. Ruairidh looked at him, bemused for a moment, then he laughed too until they both rocked on their heels and their mirth spread through the crowd around them.

'Victorious men and women of Alba and Elphame,' the queen

said, smiling at their antics, 'I give you the King of Alba.'

Those closest to the brothers sank on one knee, bowing, and those behind followed, the action rippling all the way to the shore, until only the queen, Struan and Ruairidh were left standing.

Ruairidh stepped away from his brother, making to sink down, but Struan stopped him, shaking his head. Ruairidh watched, astonished, as his brother knelt at his feet, clenching his right fist across his chest.

'You, Ruairidh, are the first-born son o' King Rannoch and Queen Kathleen o' Alba, and rightful heir tae the throne. I pledge myself tae yer service with all that I have and all that I am.'

Ruairidh looked around at the others, struggling to absorb what Struan had just said. His cousin's mouths hung open in shock and the queen, Ernissyen and Morag smiled, bowing their heads respectfully while Turpie simply nodded. Another great cheer went up from the crowd and the words *long live King Ruairidh*, sounded over and over again.

'Then I guess this means you're not coming home with us,' Rossi said, joy mixing with sadness as she hugged him.

Ruairidh looked around at his brother and at the Selgovae, their faces filled with hope for a new beginning. His eyes came to rest lastly on Morag. He grinned. 'I guess not. Please do your best to explain to Grandad and Bridie for me...'

Ernissyen stepped forward, taking Rossi's hands in his. 'And what about you Princess, do you perhaps see a home for yourself here...' he hesitated, for once unsure of himself, 'with me?'

Embarrassed and more than a little overwhelmed by the enormity of such a question, Rossi's words tumbled out in a rush. 'I

must go home with my brothers, Ernissyen,' then, seeing the dis-
appointment in his gorgeous emerald eyes, she added shyly, 'but
who knows, perhaps some day when I'm older...'

'Then I will await that day,' he said, 'and until then you have
my gift to remember me by.' And bending, he kissed her gently
on the cheek.

Well and truly flustered, Rossi turned to her brothers. 'I think
it's time to go home,' she said.

Turpie smiled fondly at the little group. 'And so your quest
comes to an end, children, and what an end.'

'Not quite at an end yet, Turpie,' Ruairidh said, grinning broadly
at his brother. 'Struan, I've found our mother. She didn't abandon
us like we both always thought. We have to rescue her, and once
I have my mother back...'

'Once *we* have *our* mother back,' corrected Struan, wide-eyed
at the thought.

Ruairidh threw his arm around his brother's shoulder. 'Once
we have *our* mother back,' he repeated, grinning like a loon, 'we'll
be a family again.'

The queen stepped forward, her expression once more grave.
'I'm afraid you're already too late. You see I knew you had found
Buitseach as soon as Morag's health was restored, and I asked
Wolftrax to retrieve her. You met him in the woods near the daiglin
hogney's camp, I think?'

Ruairidh nodded bewildered, as Wolftrax came to stand at his
sister's side.

'The beast, Ghob, got to her first,' growled Wolftrax. 'I fear your
mother is already taken to Gododdin.'

'No!' howled Ruairidh, all joy of the previous moment forgotten. But what he would have said beyond that his cousins never knew. A deep rumbling sounded below ground, louder than any they had heard before. The earth shook violently beneath their feet and a fountain of ash and volcanic rock sprayed from the volcano's summit. In the chaos that followed there was no time for discussion. Rossi knew that if the volcano erupted, the way home through the Witching Stone might be lost forever. As the others ran to their mounts and the Selgovae and ferrishyn fled towards the forest and the ships, she pulled her brothers into the tunnel and ran, mindless of the heat and belching smoke, until she came up against a timber door. Fumbling in the dark she turned the handle and dashed upstairs, bursting out into the Buckie House's bright, sunny foyer.

33

A TALE TO TELL

Well,' the professor said, hearing their tale. 'Well, I never.' The children sat curled up on the big sofa in his study, their hands wrapped around Bridie's huge steaming mugs of hot chocolate. The ring on Rossi's finger cycled contentedly through all the colours of the rainbow as she drank.

'There was a dragon, you say?' he asked, leaning towards them eagerly.

The children nodded.

'So you do believe us, Grandad?' Drew asked.

'Why of course, I've always known this old house lived and breathed the past in ways that other old buildings do not, and as to Scabinory, it seems patently obvious it was once a place of great magic, so why shouldn't it be today?'

'Don't *you* remember going to Scabinory, Grandad?' Sean asked.

The professor frowned, searching his memory. 'Yes, I believe I do, but like snippets of a dream I had a long, long time ago.' He smiled. 'I'm guessing that's where I got my passion for history and for dragons.'

'There weren't any Standing Stanes at the old Scabinory,' Rossi said. 'Why not?'

The professor shrugged. 'Perhaps they hadn't been erected yet. A lot of water will pass under the bridge between then and now.'

'What do you think Ruairidh will do?' Drew asked, although he already knew the answer.

The professor's expression turned sober. 'Well, I think it very likely he'll go to Gododdin in search of his mother.'

The children contemplated this silently for a moment and Rossi's ring turned from pink to pulsing red.

Sean released a loud breath of air. 'Then we have to go back and help him.'

Rossi looked at her brothers' sober and expectant faces and nodded. 'Yes,' she said simply, 'we must!'

Glossary of Terms

ALBA: ancient name for Scotland.

BAIRN: Scots for child.

BANSHEE: tall and witch-like, with long black hair. They carry axes and scream and lament at every opportunity.

BROWNIE: skulking ape-like creatures who inhabit trees – silent and not known for harming people.

BUCKIE: Scots for shell.

BUITSEACH (*Boot-sea-ak*): Gaelic for witch. Buitseach is Struan and Ruairidh's mother Kate, held captive by the daiglin hogneys.

CARLIN MEG: an evil witch banished by the ferrishyn at the end of a great war. She wants the throne of Alba for herself.

CRETIN: short and fat with a small head and big, wide-spaced eyes – not very bright.

DAIGLIN HOGNEY (*Daglin Hogney*): a Scottish giant.

DRACHEN FELS (*Dracken Fels*): German, meaning dragon mountain.

DYN EDYN (*Din Eadin*): name for the ancient fortifications on the site that is now Edinburgh Castle.

ELPHAME (*Elfame*): land of the Scottish faeries.

FASH (*f-a-sh*): i.e. "don't fash yourself," Scots for 'fuss' or 'trouble'.

FERRISHYN: Scottish faeries: beautiful, fierce and honourable.

GARGOYLE (*Gar-goyle*): tall and skinny with pointy ears and chins and beaky noses.

GHOB *(Gob)*: half man/half boar; one of two evil lords of Gododdin.

GHOM *(Gom)*: half man/half boar – the other lord of Gododdin.

GODODDIN (*God-odd-in*): once faerie-folk, now corrupted by Carlin Meg.

HEART OF MIDLOTHIAN; SACRED HEART; NYU; SPIRIT; MORAG: a spiritual being, sacred to the ferrishyn and important to all the peoples of this time.

GOYLE-NA-GARG: the dark woods that surround Scabinory.

HOBGOBLIN: scrawny and toad-skinned with sharp features – almost always green.

MURDHUACHA *(Moor-hoocha)*: mythical Scottish demon mermaid.

NYAFF (*N-yaff*): thin, ugly and dwarf-like.

OGRE: (*O-ger*) very large and thickset with gnarly skin and a bad disposition. It usually carries a big club.

POOKA: a tricky creature that can take any form – notoriously hard to catch.

RUAIRIDH (*Ro-ry*): Scottish Gaelic spelling of *Rory*.

SELGOVAE *(Selgo-vay)*: an ancient Scottish tribe.

SITHBRUAICH *(Sith-broo-ick)*: gateway to Elphame, kingdom of the scottish faeries.

SLAUGH *(Slough)*: evil Scottish faeries who love to hunt humans at night with their dark hounds.

STANE: Scots for 'stone'.

TAE *(tay)*: Scots for 'to'.

TOADIE: thickset, bug-eyed creature with short stumpy legs.

YE *(yi)*: Scots for 'you'.